CHAPTER ONE

TONIGHT'S ESCAPE FANTASY STARS SIX. A HORDE of Mogadorians stands between her and my cell—which isn't technically realistic. The Mogs don't usually devote any manpower whatsoever to keeping watch on me, but this is a dream, so whatever. The Mog warriors unsheathe their daggers and charge forward, howling. In response, Six tosses her hair and turns invisible. I watch from between the bars of my cell as she slices through the Mogs, blinking in and out of visibility, turning their own weapons against them. She twists her way through an ever-increasing cloud of ash, the Mogs soon completely decimated.

"That was pretty awesome," I tell her, when she reaches the door of my cell. She smiles nonchalantly.

"Ready to go?" she asks.

And that's when I wake up. Or when I snap out of the daydream. Sometimes it's tough to tell whether I'm asleep or awake; every moment tends to take on a drowsy sameness when you've been kept in isolation for weeks. At least, I think it's been weeks. Hard to keep track of time since there are no windows in my cell. The only thing I'm really certain of is that my imaginings of escape aren't real. Sometimes it's like tonight and Six has come to rescue me, other times it's John, and other times I've developed Legacies of my own and I fly out of my cell, pummeling Mogadorians as I go.

It's all fantasy. Just a way for my anxious mind to pass the time.

The sweat-soaked mattress with broken springs that dig into my back? That's real. The cramps in my legs and my backache? Those are real, too.

I reach for the bucket of water on the floor next to me. A guard brings the bucket once a day along with a cheese sandwich. It's not exactly room service, even though, as far as I can tell, I'm the only prisoner being held in this cell block—it's just rows and rows of empty cells connected by steel gangways, and me alone.

The guard always sets the bucket down right next to my cell's stainless-steel toilet, and I always drag the bucket over next to my bed, the closest thing I get to exercise. I eat the sandwich right away, of course. I don't remember what it feels like not to be starving.

Processed cheese on stale bread, a toilet without a seat, and total isolation. That's been my life.

When I first got here, I tried to keep track of how often

THE EVENTS IN THIS BOOK ARE REAL.

NAMES AND PLACES HAVE BEEN CHANGED
TO PROTECT THE LORIEN,
WHO REMAIN IN HIDING.

OTHER CIVILIZATIONS DO EXIST.

SOME OF THEM SEEK TO DESTROY YOU.

THE LORIEN ⊏⊐ LEGACIES

BY PITTACUS LORE

Novels

I AM NUMBER FOUR

THE POWER OF SIX

THE RISE OF NINE

THE FALL OF FIVE

THE REVENGE OF SEVEN

Novellas

I AM NUMBER FOUR: THE LOST FILES #1: SIX'S LEGACY

I AM NUMBER FOUR: THE LOST FILES #2: NINE'S LEGACY

I AM NUMBER FOUR: THE LOST FILES #3: THE FALLEN LEGACIES

I AM NUMBER FOUR: THE LOST FILES #4: THE SEARCH FOR SAM

I AM NUMBER FOUR: THE LOST FILES #5: THE LAST DAYS OF LORIEN

I AM NUMBER FOUR: THE LOST FILES #6: THE FORGOTTEN ONES

I AM NUMBER FOUR: THE LOST FILES #7: FIVE'S LEGACY

I AM NUMBER FOUR: THE LOST FILES #8: RETURN TO PARADISE

I AM NUMBER FOUR: THE LOST FILES #9: FIVE'S BETRAYAL

Novella Collections

I AM NUMBER FOUR: THE LOST FILES: THE LEGACIES

(Contains novellas #1–#3)

I AM NUMBER FOUR: THE LOST FILES: SECRET HISTORIES

(Contains novellas #4–#6)

I AM NUMBER FOUR: THE LOST FILES: HIDDEN ENEMY

(Contains novellas #7–#9)

THE FALL OF FIVE

BOOK FOUR OF THE LORIEN LEGACIES

PITTACUS LORE

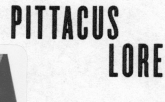

YOUNG ADULT

HARPER

An Imprint of HarperCollinsPublishers

The Fall of Five

Copyright © 2013 by Pittacus Lore

All rights reserved. Printed in the United States of America.
No part of this book may be used or reproduced in any manner
whatsoever without written permission except in the case
of brief quotations embodied in critical articles and reviews.
For information address HarperCollins Children's Books,
a division of HarperCollins Publishers, 195 Broadway,
New York, NY 10007.
www.epicreads.com

Library of Congress Control Number: 2013938121
ISBN 978-0-06-197463-2 (pbk.)

Typography by Ray Shappell
19 20   CG/LSCC   20 19 18 17 16 15 14 13
❖
First paperback edition, 2014

the guard came so that I could keep count of the days, but sometimes I think they forget about me. Or ignore me on purpose. My greatest fear is that they'll just leave me in here to waste away, that I'll just pass out from dehydration, not even realizing that I'm living my last moment. I'd much rather die free, fighting the Mogadorians.

Or, better yet, not die at all.

I take a deep swig of the warm, rust-flavored water. It's disgusting, but I'm able to work some moisture back into my mouth. I stretch my arms above my head, my joints popping in protest. A jolt of pain comes from my wrists, my stretch pulling at the still-fresh scar tissue there. And that's when my mind starts wandering again—this time not into fantasy, but memory.

I think about West Virginia every day. I relive it.

I remember darting through those tunnels, clutching that red stone Nine had loaned me, shining its alien light on dozens of cell doors. In each one I hoped to find my father, and each time I was disappointed.

Then the Mogs came, cutting me off from John and Nine. I remember the fear that came from being separated from the others—maybe they could fight off that many Mogs and Piken with their Legacies. Unfortunately, all I had was a stolen Mog blaster.

I did the best I could, shooting any Mog that got too close, all the while trying to find a way back to John and Nine.

I could hear John shouting my name above all the

fighting. He was close, if only we weren't separated by a horde of alien beasts.

A monster's tail lashed across my legs. My feet went out from under me. I lost my grip on Nine's stone and went tumbling to the ground. I hit face first, opening up a gash above my eyebrow. Blood immediately started trickling into my eyes. Half blinded, I crawled for cover.

Of course, considering the lucky streak I'd been on since arriving in West Virginia, it wasn't that surprising that I ended up right at the feet of a Mogadorian warrior. He aimed his blaster at me, could've killed me right then, but reconsidered before pulling the trigger. Instead of gunning me down, he clipped me on the temple with the butt of the gun.

Everything went black.

I woke up suspended from the ceiling by thick chains. Still in the cave, yet somehow I could tell they'd taken me deeper, to a more secure area. My stomach sank when I realized the cave was still standing at all, that I was being held prisoner—what did that mean about John and Nine? Had they gotten out?

I didn't have much strength in my limbs, but I tried pulling against the chains anyway. There was no give. I felt desperate and claustrophobic. I was about to cry out when a huge Mogadorian strode into the room. The biggest one I'd ever seen, with an ugly purple scar on his neck and a strange-looking golden cane clutched in one of his massive hands. He was absolutely hideous, like a nightmare, but I couldn't look away. Somehow, his empty black eyes held my gaze.

"Hello, Samuel," he said as he stalked towards me. "Do you know who I am?"

I shook my head, my mouth suddenly beyond dry.

"I am Setrákus Ra. Supreme commander of the Mogadorian Empire, engineer of the Great Expansion, beloved leader." He bared his teeth in what I realized was supposed to be a smile. "Et cetera."

The ringmaster of a planetary genocide and the mastermind behind an upcoming invasion of Earth had just addressed me by name. I tried to think of what John would do in a situation like this—he'd never flinch in the face of his greatest enemy. I, on the other hand, started to shake, the chains that bound my wrists clanking together.

I could tell Setrákus appreciated my fear. "This can be painless, Samuel. You've chosen the wrong side, but I am nothing if not forgiving. Tell me what I want to know and I'll set you free."

"Never," I stammered, shaking even harder as I anticipated what would come next.

I heard a hissing noise from above and looked up to see viscous black goo dribbling down the chain. It was acrid and chemical, like burning plastic. I could swear the sludge was leaving rust marks on the chain as it dribbled down towards me, and soon it was coating my wrists. I was screaming. The pain was excruciating and the goo had a stickiness to it that made it even worse, as if my wrists were covered in scalding tree sap.

I was about to pass out from the pain when Setrákus touched his staff to my neck, lifting my chin with it. An icy numbness flowed through my body and the pain on my wrists was momentarily eased. It was a twisted kind of relief; a deathly numbness radiated from Setrákus's staff, like my limbs had been drained of blood.

"Just answer my questions," snarled Setrákus, "and this can be over."

His first questions were about John and Nine—where they would go, what they would do next. I felt relieved knowing that they'd escaped, and even more relieved that I hadn't a clue where they'd be hiding. I had been the one holding on to Six's instructions, which had meant John and Nine would need to figure out a new plan, one that I couldn't possibly give away while being tortured. The paper was now missing, so it seemed like a safe bet that the Mogs had searched me while I was unconscious and confiscated the address. Hopefully Six would approach with caution.

"Wherever they end up, it won't be long until they're back here kicking your ass," I told Setrákus. And that was my one badass, heroic moment, because the Mogadorian leader snorted and immediately pulled his staff away from me. The pain in my wrists returned—it was as if the Mogadorian goop was eating right down to my bones.

I was panting and crying the next time Setrákus touched his staff to me, giving me a reprieve. The fight, what little there'd been to begin with, had completely gone out of me.

"What about Spain?" he asked. "What can you tell me about that?"

"Six . . . ," I mumbled, and regretted it. I needed to keep my mouth shut.

The questions kept coming. After Spain it was India, and then questions about the locations of Loralite stones, which I'd never even heard of. Eventually, he asked me about "the tenth," something that Setrákus seemed particularly invested in. I remembered Henri writing about a tenth in his letter to John and how that last Garde didn't make it off Lorien. When I told Setrákus that—information I hoped wouldn't somehow hurt the remaining Garde—he was infuriated.

"You're lying to me, Samuel. I know she's here. Tell me where."

"I don't know," I kept repeating, my voice shaking more and more. With every answer, or lack thereof, Setrákus pulled back his staff and let me feel the searing pain again.

Eventually, Setrákus gave up and just stared at me, disgusted. I was delirious at this point. As if with a mind of its own, the dark ooze slowly crawled back up the chain, disappearing into the dark recess it'd come from.

"You're useless, Samuel," he'd said, dismissively. "It appears the Loric only value you as a sacrificial lamb, a diversion to be left behind when they're in need of a hasty escape."

Setrákus swept out of the room and later, after I'd hung there for a while slipping in and out of consciousness, some of his soldiers came to retrieve me. They dumped me in a dark cell where I was sure they'd leave me to die.

Days later the Mogadorians dragged me out of my cell and handed me over to a pair of guys with buzz cuts and dark suits, and guns holstered beneath their coats. Humans. They looked like FBI or CIA or something. I don't know why any human would want to work with the Mogs. It makes my blood boil just to think about it, these agents selling out humanity. Even so, the agents were gentler than the Mogadorians, one of them even mumbling an apology as he clasped a pair of manacles over my burned wrists. Then, they pulled a hood over my head, and that was the last I saw of them.

I was driven nonstop for at least two days, chained in the back of a van. After that, I was shoved into another cell—this cell, my new home—an entire block in some big base where I was the only prisoner.

I shudder when I think about Setrákus Ra, something I can't help but do every time I catch a glimpse of the lingering blisters and scars on my wrists. I've tried to put that horrifying encounter out of my head, telling myself that what he'd said wasn't true. I know John didn't use me to cover his escape, and I know that I'm not useless. I can help

John and the other Garde, just like my father was doing before he disappeared. I know I have some part to play, even if it isn't clear exactly what that's going to be.

When I get out of here—if I ever get out of here—my new goal in life is to prove Setrákus Ra wrong.

I'm so frustrated that I pound the mattress in front of me. As soon as I do, a layer of dust shakes loose from the ceiling, and a faint rumbling passes through the floor. It's almost as if my punch sent a shockwave through the entire cell.

I look down at my hand in awe. Maybe those daydreams about developing my own Legacies weren't so farfetched. I try to remember back to John's backyard in Paradise, when Henri would lecture him about focusing his power. I squint hard and ball my fist up tight.

Even though it feels nuts and a little embarrassing, I punch the mattress again, just to see what happens.

Nothing. Just a soreness in my arms from not using those muscles in days. I'm not developing Legacies. That's impossible for a human being and I know that. I'm just getting desperate. And maybe a little crazy.

"Okay, Sam," I say to myself, my voice hoarse. "Keep it together."

As soon as I lie back down, resigned to another endless stretch alone with my thoughts, a second jolt ripples through the floor. This one is much bigger than the first; I can feel it in my very bones. More plaster drifts down from the ceiling. It coats my face and gets in my mouth, bitter and chalky tasting. Moments later, I hear the muffled drumbeat of gunfire.

This isn't a dream at all. I can distantly hear the sounds of a fight from somewhere deep within the base. The floor shakes again—another explosion. As long as I've been here, they've never done any kind of training or drills. Hell, I never hear anything except the echoing footsteps of the guard bringing me my food. And now this sudden action? What could be happening?

For the first time in—days? weeks?—I allow myself to hope. It's the Garde. It has to be. They've come to rescue me.

"This is it, Sam," I tell myself, willing myself to move.

I stand up and move shakily to the door of my cell. My legs feel like jelly. I haven't had much reason to use them since they brought me here. Even crossing the short distance of my cell to the door is enough to make my head swim. I press my forehead to the cool metal of the bars, waiting for the dizziness to pass. I can feel reverberations of the fight below passing through the metal, growing stronger and more intense.

"John!" I shout, my voice hoarse. "Six! Anyone! I'm here! I'm in here!"

Part of me thinks it's silly to cry out, as if the Garde could hear my cries over the massive battle it sounds like they're fighting. It's that same part of me that's wanted to give up, to just curl up in my cell and wait out my ultimate fate. It's the same part of me that thinks the Garde would be stupid to try to rescue me.

It's the part of me that believed Setrákus Ra. I can't give in to that feeling of despair. I have to prove him wrong.

I need to make some noise.

"John!" I scream again. "I'm in here, John!"

Weak as I feel, I pound my fists against the steel bars as hard as I can. The sound echoes throughout the empty block, but there's no way the Garde could hear it above the muffled gunfire coming through the walls. It's hard to tell over the increasing sounds of battle, but I think I hear footsteps rattling across the steel gangway that connects the cells. Too bad I can't see anything beyond the few feet in front of my cell. If there is someone in here with me, I've got to get their attention and just hope it isn't a Mog guard.

I grab my water bucket and dump out what's left of my day's supply. My plan—the best one I've got—is to bang it against the bars of my cell.

When I turn back around, there's a guy standing outside my door.

CHAPTER TWO

HE'S TALL AND GAUNT, MAYBE A FEW YEARS older than me, with a shock of black hair that hangs in front of his face. It looks like he's just been in a fight, dirt and sweat smudged across his pale face. I stare at him, wide-eyed—it's been so long since I've seen another person. He looks almost equally surprised to see me.

There's something off about him. Something not quite right.

The slightly too pale skin. The darkness around the edges of his eyes. He's one of them.

I back up farther into my cell, hiding the empty water bucket behind my back. If he comes in here, I'm going to clock him with all the strength I have left.

"Who are you?" I ask, trying to keep my voice steady.

"We're here to help," the guy replies. He sounds uncomfortable, like he doesn't know what to say.

Before I can ask who he means by "we," a man shoves

him aside. There are deep lines on his face, which is covered by a scruffy growth of beard. My mouth hangs open in disbelief and I take another step back into my cell, startled again, but this time for a different reason. I don't know why I expected him to look like the pictures hanging in our family room, but it's just the way I always imagined this moment. Years have passed, yet underneath the deep crevices I still recognize this man, especially when he smiles at me.

"Dad?"

"I'm here, Sam. I'm back."

My face hurts and it takes me a moment to realize why. I'm smiling. Grinning, in fact. It's the first time I've used those muscles in weeks.

We hug through the bars, the metal pressed uncomfortably into my ribs, but I don't care. He's here. He's really here. I'd fantasized about the Garde coming to rescue me. Never in my wildest dreams did I think my father would be the one saving me from this place. I guess I always thought that I'd be the one rescuing him.

"I—I've been looking for you," I tell him. I wipe my forearm across my eyes; that strange Mogadorian is still hovering nearby and I don't want him to see me cry.

My dad squeezes me through the bars. "You've grown up so much," he says, a note of sadness in his voice.

"Guys," the Mog interrupts, "we have company."

I can hear them coming. Soldiers pouring into the cell

block from below, their boots rattling the gangway as they run up the metal stairs towards us. Finally, I've found my dad, he's right here in front of me, and it's all about to be ripped away.

The Mogadorian pulls my dad away from my cell door. He turns to me, his voice commanding.

"Stand in the center of your cell and cover your head."

My instinct is not to trust him. He's one of them. Except why would one of the Mogadorians bring my father here? Why would he try to help us? There's no time to think about that now, not with other Mogadorians—ones I can guarantee aren't here to help—closing in.

I do as he ordered.

The Mogadorian reaches his hands through the bars of my cell, focusing on the wall behind me. Maybe it's because I was just thinking about them, but for some reason, I'm reminded of those early days when we tested John's Legacies in the backyard. It's something about the way this Mogadorian focuses—the determination in his eyes undermined by shaking hands, like he doesn't quite know what he's doing.

I feel something pass through the floor beneath me, like a ripple of energy. Then, with a piercing crack, the wall behind me crumbles. A piece of the ceiling shakes loose, smashing my toilet. The floor shifts and moves beneath my feet, and I'm thrown to the ground. It's like the entire block of cells has been hit by a tiny earthquake. Everything is tilted. My stomach turns over, and it's not entirely due to the shaky floor. It's fear. Somehow, that Mogadorian just knocked down a wall with his mind. It was almost as if he was using a Legacy.

But that's impossible, right?

Outside my cell, my dad and the Mogadorian have been knocked backwards against the gangway's railing. The door of my cell is cockeyed now, the metal warped and bent. There's enough space for them to squeeze through.

As the Mogadorian pushes my dad towards the door of my cell, he points to the opening in the wall behind me.

"Go!" he shouts. "Run!"

I hesitate for a moment, glancing at my dad. He's already squeezing through the bars. I reassure myself that he'll be right behind me.

I cough as some of the dust from the destroyed wall enters my lungs. Through the opening in the wall I can see the inner workings of the base; pipes and ventilation shafts, clumps of wiring and insulation.

Wrapping my legs around one of the larger pipes, I start shimmying down. Pins and needles shoot through my weakened legs and for a moment I'm worried that I'll lose my grip and slip. But then the adrenaline kicks in and my grip tightens. Escape is so close, I have to push myself.

I see my dad's shadow in the opening above me. He's hesitating.

"What're you doing?!" my dad shouts at the Mog. "Adam?"

I hear the Mogadorian—Adam—reply, his voice resolute. "Go with your son. Now."

My dad starts climbing down after me, but I've stopped. I'm thinking about what it was like to be left behind in one of these places. Mogadorian or not, this Adam guy just broke me out of jail and reunited me with my father. He shouldn't have to face down those soldiers alone.

I call up to my dad. "We're just going to leave him?"

"Adam knows what he's doing," my dad answers, but his voice sounds unsure. "Keep moving, Sam!"

Another vibration strikes, nearly shaking me loose from the pipe. I look up to check on my dad, just as another shock wave jostles loose the gun he's been carrying in the back of his pants. I'm clinging too tightly to the pipe to catch it and the weapon goes plummeting into the darkness below.

"Damn it," he grunts.

The Mogs must have closed in on Adam and he's fighting back. Shortly after the shock wave comes a metallic rending sound, a sound that can only be the gangway coming apart—I can picture it tearing loose from outside the cells, the whole structure crumbling with it. A couple loose bricks tumble down from above, and Dad and I both duck until it's safe again.

At least Adam's giving them a fight back there. But we need to move fast before he brings the place down on top of us.

I keep shimmying down. The space inside the walls is tight, a claustrophobic's worst nightmare, with screws and loose wires ripping at my clothes.

"Sam, up here. Help me with this."

My dad stopped in front of a ventilation shaft that I hadn't noticed. I slip a little when I climb back up, but he reaches down to steady me. Together, we hook our fingers through the metal grate and yank it loose.

"This should lead us outside."

No sooner are we army-crawling through the shaft than a massive explosion rocks us. We stop moving as the metal duct creaks and whines, both of us braced for the whole thing to collapse, but it holds.

We can hear screaming and sirens through the walls of the base. The fighting that I heard before has only intensified.

"Sounds like a war out there," my dad says, crawling forward again.

"Did you bring the Garde?" I ask him, hopefully.

"No, Sam, it was just Adam and me."

"Pretty amazing timing, Dad. You and the Garde all manage to show up at the exact same time?"

"I think this family was due for some good luck," my dad replies. "Let's just be thankful for the distraction and get the hell out of here."

"It's them fighting out there. I know it. They're the only ones bold enough to attack a Mogadorian base." I pause, forgetting about the danger for a moment, a giddy smile exploding onto my face as I realize my father just broke into a Mog base. "Dad," I say, "I'm so glad to see you and everything, but you have so much explaining to do."

CHAPTER
THREE

AN ACRID CLOUD OF BLACK SMOKE BILLOWS OUT from the base. Sirens blare above the crackling of fire. I can hear footsteps beating across the pavement nearby, humans and Mogadorians shouting emergency orders. It's chaos. And from the sound of explosions off in the distance, I could tell it wasn't just confined to our section of the base either. Something big was going down around here—and that could only mean one thing.

That's perfect. They're too distracted to search for us right now.

"Where the hell are we?" I whisper.

"Dulce Base," my dad answers. "Top-secret government base in New Mexico, co-opted by the Mogadorians."

"How did you find me?"

"It's a long story, Sam. I'll tell you when we're clear of this place."

Slowly we inch our way along a back wall, trying to

stay away from the commotion. We stick to the shadows, just in case any guards should peel away from the madness inside. My dad leads the way, clutching the bent steel grate from the ventilation shaft we climbed out of. It's not much as far as weapons go, but it could do some damage. Still, it's better if we avoid a fight. I'm not sure how much energy I have left after what we just went through.

My dad points into the darkness, beyond the collapsed wreckage of what used to be a watchtower, into the desert.

"Our ride is parked out there," he says.

"Who knocked down that watchtower?"

"We did," my dad answers. "Well, Adam did."

"How—how is that possible? They aren't supposed to have powers like that."

"I don't know how it's possible, Sam. But I do know he's different from the others." My dad reaches out, squeezing my arm. "He helped me find you. And, well . . . I'll tell you the rest once we're out of here."

I rub my face; my eyes hurt from the smoke. Also, I still can't believe this is happening. My father and I skulking around a government base, escaping from hostile aliens. Weirdly, it's sort of like a dream come true. We keep inching along, angling our way to a patch of shadows where it'll be a straight sprint towards the fence and into the desert.

"I can't figure out how you and the Garde both managed to get here at the same time."

"We don't know for sure it's the Garde."

"Come on, Dad," I say, jerking my thumb at the flames rising from the base. "You said this is a Mog place and that the government's in cahoots with the Mogs, so we know it's not the army. What the hell else could cause all this?"

My dad stares at me, seeming a little amazed. "You know them. I can't believe you know them," he whispers, shaking his head guiltily. "I never meant to get you into this mess."

"You didn't, Dad. It's not your fault my best friend turned out to be an alien. Anyway, I'm in it now and we have to help them."

It's hard to tell in the darkness and smoke, but it's almost as if my dad is seeing me for the first time. During our hurried reunion inside the base, he was probably seeing that little kid I was when he first disappeared. But I'm not a child anymore. From the look on his face—a mixture of sadness and pride—I think he realizes that.

"You've turned into a brave young man," he says, "but you know we can't go back in there, right? Even if the Garde are here, I won't risk it—won't risk you."

He starts moving again and I follow, our backs to the wall as we approach a corner of the base's exterior wall. My feet move sluggishly, but it's not from my exhaustion. My heart knows we shouldn't be running and my body is joining in the protest. The chaos around the base reminds me of the cave in West Virginia and of what happened afterwards— the chains, the torture—that could happen to Adam if we leave him behind, or the Garde if they're in there fighting. I want to do something besides running away.

"We can help them," I blurt out. "We have to!"

My dad nods. "And we will. But we won't help anyone by getting killed while blindly racing back into a heavily fortified military base that also happens to be on fire."

That speech sounds familiar. It takes me a second to realize it's exactly the kind of advice I used to give to John, right before he'd rush off to do something brave and stupid.

As I'm struggling to come up with a sound argument for reentering the base, my dad peeks around the corner and rapidly jerks back. A second later, I can hear two sets of running footsteps approaching.

"Mogs," he hisses, hunkering down. "Two of them. They're probably setting up a perimeter."

As the first Mogadorian guard comes sprinting around the corner, my dad swings the steel grate low, crunching right into the Mog's shins. He tumbles to the ground, landing hard on his ugly face.

The second guard tries to get his weapon up, but my dad is on him. They start wrestling over the blaster; my dad has the advantage of surprise and adrenaline. The Mogadorian is stronger, though, and slams my dad against the wall, the weapon still pinned between them. I hear a rush of breath escape my father.

I dash to the first guard before he can collect himself. I kick him hard in the side of the head, so hard that I can feel my toes immediately swelling up inside my worn-out sneakers. I grab his blaster, spin around, and fire.

The shot sizzles into the wall next to my dad's head. I correct my aim and shoot again.

My dad spits out black ash as the Mogadorian disintegrates in front of him. Not wanting to take any chances, I shoot the Mogadorian lying at my feet. I watch his body explode in a puff of soot that spreads across the pavement. It's a pretty satisfying sight.

When I look up, my dad is staring at me with a mix of wonderment and pride.

"Nice shooting," he says. He picks up the second Mog blaster and peers around the corner again. "Coast is clear, but more will be coming. We need to get moving."

I look back at the base, wondering if my friends are still fighting for their lives inside. Sensing my hesitation, my dad gently grabs on to my shoulder.

"Sam, I know it might not count for much right now, but you have my word that we're going to do everything we can for the Garde. Saving them, protecting Earth . . . it's my life's work."

"Mine too," I reply, realizing as I say them that the words are true.

He pokes his head around the corner again and then motions for me. We sprint into the open, heading towards the fallen watchtower where my dad says there will be a way through Dulce's fence. I half expect blaster fire to erupt behind us at anytime, but it never comes. I glance over my shoulder at the smoke curling upwards from the base. I hope the Garde and Adam made it out alive.

My dad's old Chevy Rambler is parked right where he said it'd be. We drive east through the desert until we cross into Texas. We don't hit any roadblocks and we aren't chased by any dark government patrol cars; the roads are dark and empty until we get closer to Odessa.

"So," Dad begins casually, like he's asking me how my day was at school. "How'd you end up being best friends with one of the Garde?"

"His name's John," I reply. "His Cêpan actually came to Paradise looking for you. We just met at school and had, uh, some mutual friends."

I look out the window, watching Texas fly by. It's been awhile since I thought of high school, of Mark James, of the manure in my locker and that psychotic hayride. It's hard to believe I once considered Mark and his crew the most dangerous people in my world. I laugh softly and dad glances over at me.

"Tell me everything, Sam. I feel like I've missed so much."

So I do. I begin with meeting John at school, jump to the battle on the football field, and finish with our time on the run and my capture. I have tons of questions for my dad, but it actually feels really good to talk. It's not just that I spent weeks alone in that cell; I've missed confiding to my father.

It's late when we pull up to a motel on the outskirts of town. Even though Dad and I are both filthy—we look like we just tunneled out of prison, which we pretty much did—the tired old man renting rooms doesn't ask us any questions.

Our room is on the second floor with a view of the neglected motel pool, filled with equal parts murky brown water, dead leaves and fast food wrappers. Before heading up, we stop back at the car to grab some gear. My dad pulls a backpack out of the trunk and hands it to me.

"This was Adam's stuff," he begins awkwardly. "There should be some clean clothes in there."

"Thanks," I reply, studying my father. There's a worried look on his face. "I'll keep it safe for him."

My dad nods, but I can tell that he's thinking the worst. He's worried about this Mogadorian guy and, suddenly, I'm wondering if he worried this much about me when he was away all those years.

With a grunt, I shoulder Adam's pack and head towards the motel room. Apparently, there was a bond between my father and Adam that I can't really understand, and part of me starts to feel a little jealous. But then my dad puts his hand on my shoulder as we walk and I'm reminded just how long I've been searching for him, how he saved me and how he left Adam behind to do it. He abandoned the

Mogadorian who has somehow developed a Legacy to save me. I put aside my petty thoughts and try to think rationally about what it all means.

"How did you meet Adam?" I ask as he unlocks our door.

"He rescued me. The Mogadorians were holding me prisoner. Experimenting on me."

The motel room is small and about as grungy as I expected. A cockroach skitters out of sight beneath the bed when we turn on the light. The place smells like mildew. There's a small bathroom and, even though the tub is dotted by islands of mold, I'm looking forward to taking a shower. Compared to washing myself with ice-cold water from a metal bucket, this place is paradise.

"What kind of experiments?"

My dad sits down on the foot of the bed. I sit next to him and together we stare at our reflections in the smudged hotel mirror. We make quite the pair—both of us filthy and gaunt from our recent imprisonments. Father and son.

"They were trying to get into my mind. To tear out anything useful I might know about the Garde."

"Because you were one of the ones who met the Garde when they came to Earth, right? We found your bunker in the backyard. I pieced some stuff together."

"Greeters," my dad says sadly. "We met the Loric when they landed, helped them to get on their feet and on the run. Those nine children, all of them so frightened. And yet, that ship landing, it was one of the most amazing things I'd ever seen."

I smile, thinking back to the first time I saw John use his Legacies. It was like a curtain being pulled back revealing a universe of possibility. All the nerdy alien books I'd read, that I'd so badly wanted to be true—suddenly, they were.

"We proved easier to hunt than the Garde, I suppose. We had families. Lives that couldn't just be uprooted. The Mogadorians found us."

"What happened to the others?"

My dad's hands shake a bit. He sighs. "They were all killed, Sam. I'm the last one."

I stare in the mirror at the haunted look on his face. Imprisoned by the Mogs for all these years; I feel bad asking him to go back to what must be horrible memories.

"I'm sorry," I say. "We don't have to talk about it."

"No," he replies, resolute, "you deserve to know why I wasn't—why I wasn't in your life as much as I should've been."

My dad's face is scrunched up like he's trying to remember something. I let him take his time, leaning down to unlace my shoes. My toes are swollen from where I kicked that Mog in the face. I start rubbing them gently, making sure there aren't any bones broken.

"They were trying to rip things out of our memories. Anything that might help them hunt the Garde." He pushes a hand through his hair, rubbing his scalp. "What they did to me . . . it left gaps. There are things I don't remember. There are important things—things that I know I should remember, but can't."

I pat him on the back. "We'll find the Garde and maybe they'll, I don't know, have some way to reverse what the Mogs did to you."

"Optimism," my dad says, smiling at me. "It's been so long since I remember feeling that."

My dad stands up and grabs his backpack. He pulls out one of those cheap-looking plastic cell phones they sell over the counter at gas stations and looks forlornly down at the screen.

"Adam has this number," my dad says. "He should've called by now to check in."

"It was crazy back there. Maybe he lost his phone."

My dad's already punching in a number. He holds the phone up to his ear, listening. After a few seconds of silence, he hangs up.

"Nothing," he says, sitting back down. "I think I got that boy killed tonight, Sam."

CHAPTER FOUR

I TAKE WHAT HAS TO BE THE GREATEST SHOWER of my life in that grungy motel bathroom. Even the dark mold that spreads from the drain to the curled edges of the rubber bath mat can't dampen the experience. The hot water feels amazing, washing away weeks of Mogadorian captivity.

After wiping fog off the cracked bathroom mirror, I take a long look at my reflection. My ribs show, my stomach muscles pronounced enough to give me a starving person's six pack. I have dark circles under my eyes and my hair is grown out more than it's ever been.

So, this is what a human freedom fighter looks like.

I pull on a T-shirt and jeans that I found in Adam's backpack; I have to use the very last notch on the belt to secure the jeans and they still hang loose around my hips. My stomach growls and I pause to wonder what kind of room service a sleazy motel like this might have. I bet the old man behind the front desk would be happy to send over a grilled-cheese-and-cigarette-butt sandwich.

Back in the room, my dad has set up some of his equipment. There's a laptop open on the bed, a program scanning news headlines running. He's already trying to figure out our next move. It's late, well past midnight, and I haven't slept. Still, badly as I want to hook up with the Garde, I was hoping our next move could be a stack of pancakes at the nearest diner.

"Anything?" I ask, squinting at the laptop.

My dad isn't paying the program any attention. He's sitting against the wall, still clutching that cheap cell phone, looking indecisive. He glances listlessly over at the laptop. "Not yet."

"He probably won't call until he's someplace safe," I say. I reach down to ease the phone out of his hand, but he pulls it away.

"It's not that," he says. "There's another phone call we need to make. I've been thinking about what to say the entire time you were in the shower, and I still don't know."

His thumb traces out a familiar pattern on the phone's keypad, like he's working himself up to actually dialing. I'm so locked into this idea of finding the Garde and fighting the Mogadorians that, at first, I'm not even sure who he's talking about. When it dawns on me, I thump down on the bed, feeling as speechless as my father.

"We have to call your mother, Sam."

I nod, agreeing, but not really knowing what I'd say to Mom at this point. The last time she saw me, I'd just been in a fight with Mogadorians in Paradise and run off into the night with John and Six. I think I yelled that I loved her over my shoulder. Not my most sensitive exit, but I really did think I'd be back soon. I never dreamed I'd be taken prisoner by a race of hostile aliens.

"She's going to be pretty mad, huh?"

"She's mad at me," my dad says. "Not you. She'll just be happy to hear your voice and know you're safe."

"Wait—you saw her?"

"We stopped in Paradise before heading to New Mexico. It's how I found out you were missing."

"And she's all right? The Mogs didn't go after her?"

"Apparently not, but that doesn't mean she's all right. It's been hard for her with you gone. She blamed me and she's not entirely wrong about that. She wouldn't let me in the house, understandably, so we had to sleep in my bunker."

"With the skeleton?"

"Yes. Another one of my memory gaps—I've got no idea who those bones belong to." My dad narrows his eyes at me. "Don't change the subject."

A part of me is worried that Mom will ground me over the phone, and part of me is worried that the sound of her voice will make me want to forget about this whole war and rush home immediately. I swallow hard.

"It's the middle of the night. Maybe we should wait until tomorrow?"

My dad shakes his head. "No. We can't put this off, Sam. Who knows what might happen to us tomorrow?"

With that, suddenly resolute, my dad dials the number to our house. He holds the phone to his ear nervously, waiting. I have memories of my mom and dad together—old memories from before he disappeared. They were happy together. I wonder what must be going through my father's head right now, having to break the news that we're still not coming home. He's probably feeling the same guilt I am.

"Answering machine," my dad says after a moment. He looks almost relieved. Then, he covers the phone with his hand. "Should I . . . ?"

He trails off as the tinny beep of the answering machine sounds in his ear. His mouth works soundlessly as he tries to figure out what to say.

"Beth, this is—," he stammers, running his free hand through his hair. "It's Malcolm. I don't know where to begin—this answering machine may not be the best place—but, I'm alive. I'm alive and I'm sorry and I miss you terribly."

My dad looks up at me, his eyes watery. "Our son is with me. He—I promise to keep him safe. One day, if you'll let me, I'll explain everything to you. I love you."

He holds the phone out to me with a shaky hand. I take it.

"Mom?" I begin, trying not to overthink what I'm about to say, just letting it go. "I—I finally found Dad. Or he found me. We're doing something amazing, Mom. Something to keep the world safe that, uh, isn't dangerous at all, I promise. I love you. We'll be home soon."

I hang up the phone, staring down at it for a moment before looking up at my father. His eyes are still shining as he reaches out and pats me on the knee.

"That was good," he says.

"I hope it was all true," I reply.

"Me too."

CHAPTER FIVE

THE NEW DAY'S FIRST RAYS OF LIGHT SLIP between the buildings, beating back the cool night air, turning Chicago's sky first purple and then pink. From the roof of the John Hancock Center, I watch the sun slowly rise over Lake Michigan.

It's the third night in a row I've come up here, unable to sleep.

We made it back to Chicago a few days ago, the first half of the journey in a stolen government van, the second onboard a freight train. It's pretty easy to sneak across the country when one of your companions can turn invisible and another can teleport.

I walk across the rooftop, peering over its edge as Chicago starts coming to life. The streets, the arteries of the city, are soon pumped full of bumper-to-bumper traffic and commuters hustling across the sidewalks. I shake my head as I look down at them.

"They've got no idea what's coming."

Bernie Kosar ambles over to me in beagle form. He stretches, yawns and then nuzzles my hand.

I should feel happy to be alive. We battled Setrákus Ra in New Mexico and didn't suffer any casualties. What's left of the Garde—with the exception of the still missing Number Five—are all downstairs, safe and sound, mostly recovered from their injuries. And Sarah, she's down there, too. I saved her.

I look down at my hands. Back in New Mexico, they were covered with blood. Ella's blood and Sarah's blood.

"They're so close to their world ending and they don't even know it."

Bernie Kosar transforms into a sparrow, flies out over the gap between the John Hancock Center and the nearest building, and finally lands on my shoulder.

I'm looking at the humans down below, but really I'm thinking about the Garde. Everyone's just been chilling out since we came to Nine's tricked-out penthouse. A little rest and recuperation was definitely in order; I just hope they haven't forgotten how close to ultimate defeat we came back in New Mexico, because it's all I can think about.

If Ella hadn't somehow wounded Setrákus and that explosion in another part of the base hadn't driven off the rest of the Mogs, I'm not sure we would've made it out. If I hadn't developed a healing Legacy, Sarah and Ella would have died for sure. I can't get the image of their burned faces out of my mind.

We'll never get that lucky again. If we go in unprepared the next time we face Setrákus Ra, we won't all survive.

By the time I come down from the roof, most of the others have woken up.

Marina's in the kitchen, using her telekinesis to whisk a bowl of eggs and milk while simultaneously wiping some smudges from what used to be a spotless tile countertop. Since the seven of us (and BK) moved in, we haven't exactly taken the best care of Nine's fancy apartment.

Marina waves when she sees me. "Good morning. Eggs?"

"Morning. Didn't you cook last night? Someone else should take a turn."

"I really don't mind," Marina says. She cheerfully pulls a smoothie blender down from a shelf. "I still can't believe this place. I'm kinda jealous Nine got to live here for so long. It's so different from what I'm used to. Is it weird that I just want to try everything out?"

"That's not weird at all." I help her finish wiping down the counter. "As long as we're staying here, we should at least start taking turns cooking and cleaning."

"Yeah." Marina nods, glancing at me sideways. "We should figure that out."

"What's with the look?"

"It's nothing, dividing up chores is a good idea," Marina says, then nervously looks away. She definitely has something else on her mind.

"Come on, Marina. What's up?"

"I just—" She picks up a dishtowel, wringing it while she speaks. "For so long, I was living without direction, not really knowing what a Garde should be like. Then, Six came to find me in Spain and showed me. And then we met up with you and Nine, right before you led us into battle against the most evil Mogadorian in existence. It was like—wow, these three really know what they're doing. They can handle themselves."

"Uh, thanks."

"But now it's been days since we got back, and I'm starting to get that feeling again. Like we don't know what we're doing. So I guess, what I'm wondering, is if there's a plan beyond chore duties?"

"Working on that," I mumble.

I don't want to tell Marina that our next move— or lack thereof—is what's been keeping me up at night. We have no idea where Setrákus Ra might be holed up after the fight in New Mexico and, even if we did, I still don't feel like we're ready to take the fight to him. We could go looking for Number Five; the locater tablet we found in Malcolm Goode's underground bunker showed us a dot off the coast of Florida that pretty much has to be him. And then there's Sam. Sarah swore that she saw him in New Mexico, but we never came across him at Dulce. With Setrákus Ra apparently able to take on other people's forms, I'm starting to believe that's who she saw, and that Sam's being held somewhere else. Assuming he's still alive.

So many decisions to make, not to mention the training we should be doing. Yet I've been dragging my feet these last few days, too stuck on our near defeat in New Mexico to focus on making a plan. Maybe it's the comfort of Nine's penthouse after a near-death experience, not to mention years on the run for all of us, but it seems like the entire group needs a breather. If any of them have been beating themselves up over not having a proper plan, they haven't shown it.

Oh, and there's something else distracting me too. I guess it's sort of like Marina wanting to try out all the appliances in Nine's fancy kitchen; I want to spend some time just being with Sarah. I wonder what Henri would think of that. He'd be disappointed in my lack of focus, I know that, but I can't help myself.

As if on cue, Sarah wraps her arms around my waist from behind, nuzzling her face into the back of my neck. I was so wrapped up in my own thoughts that I didn't even hear her pad into the kitchen.

"Good morning, handsome," Sarah says. I turn around and give her a slow, sweet kiss.

Stressed out as I've been, I'm sort of getting used to mornings like this. Mornings where I get to wake up and kiss Sarah, then have a normal day with her, and go to bed knowing she'll be there when I wake up.

Sarah puts her face close to mine, whispering. "You were up early again."

I grimace; I thought I'd been quiet sneaking out of bed in the morning to go think things through on the roof.

"Is everything all right?" Sarah asks.

"Yeah, of course," I say, trying to distract her with another kiss. "You're here. How could it not be?"

Marina clears her throat, probably worried we're going to start making out right in the kitchen. Sarah winks at me and turns away, plucking Marina's floating whisk out of the air and taking over on the eggs.

"Oh," Sarah says, looking back at me. "Nine's looking for you."

"Great," I reply. "What's he want?"

Sarah shrugs. "I didn't ask. Maybe he wants to share some fashion tips." She touches a finger to her lips thoughtfully, studying me. "Actually, that probably wouldn't be so bad."

"What do you mean?"

Sarah winks at me. "He lost his shirt. Again."

I groan, heading out of the kitchen to go find Nine.

I realize the penthouse is his home and he has a right to make himself comfortable, but he's been strutting around shirtless almost every opportunity he gets. I'm not sure if he expects the girls to suddenly start fawning over him, or if he's just doing the whole gun-show thing to annoy me. Probably both.

I find Six sitting in the penthouse's spacious living room. Her legs are tucked underneath her on a plush white couch, a cup of coffee cradled in her hands. We haven't talked much since coming back from New Mexico. I'm still not totally comfortable being around her and Sarah at the same time. I think Six might feel the same, because I definitely get the sense that she's avoiding me. Six looks up when I enter, her eyes half opened and drowsy. She looks as tired as I feel.

"Hey," I say. "How was she last night?"

Six shakes her head. "She was up all night. She's just now getting some good rest."

Add Ella's nightmares to the list of problems we need to deal with. They've been a nightly thing ever since we left New Mexico, so bad that Six and Marina have been alternating sleeping in her room, trying to make sure she doesn't get too freaked out.

I lower my voice. "Does she tell you what she sees?"

"Bits and pieces," Six says. "She hasn't been real talkative, you know?"

"Before New Mexico, Nine and I had visions that seemed a lot like nightmares," I say, trying to think this through.

"Eight mentioned something similar."

"At first we thought they were Setrákus Ra taunting us somehow, but they also seemed like some kind of warning. At least, that's how I thought of them. Maybe we should try figuring out what Ella's mean."

"Sure, I guess they could be some coded message," Six says dryly, "but have you considered there's a simpler explanation?"

"Like what?"

Six rolls her eyes. "Like she's a kid, John. Her Cêpan just died, she was almost killed herself just a couple days ago, and who knows what's in store for her next? Hell, I'm surprised we don't all have nightmares every freaking night."

"There's a comforting thought."

"These aren't real comforting times."

Before I can reply, Eight appears on the couch next to Six. She jumps, nearly spilling her coffee and immediately fixes Eight with a steely glare. Eight puts his hands up defensively.

"Whoa, sorry," he says. "Don't kill me."

"You have got to stop doing that," Six replies, setting down her coffee.

Eight is dressed in workout clothes, his curly hair shoved underneath a fuzzy sweatband. He nods to me, then aims his most disarming smile at Six.

"Come on," Eight says, "you can take it out on me in the Lecture Hall."

Six stands up, pleased by the idea. "I'm going to pummel you."

"What're you guys working on?" I ask.

"Hand to hand," answers Eight. "I figured since Six pretty much murdered me back in New Mexico—"

"For the last time, that was not me," Six interrupts, annoyed.

"—the least she could do is show me some new moves so I can defend myself the next time she attacks."

Six tries to punch Eight in the arm, but he quickly teleports behind the couch.

"See?" Eight grins. "I'm already too quick for you!"

Six bounds over the couch after him and Eight sprints off towards the Lecture Hall. Before giving chase, Six looks back at me.

"Maybe you should try talking to Ella," Six says.

"Me?"

"Yeah," she replies. "Maybe you can decide if her visions mean something or if she's just traumatized."

As soon as Six leaves the room, there's a heavy thud on the floor behind me. I turn around to find Nine grinning at me, shirtless just like Sarah said he'd be, gripping a sketchpad in his meaty hands. I glance up at the ceiling.

"How long were you standing up there?"

Nine shrugs. "I do my best thinking upside down, dude."

"I didn't realize you did any thinking."

"Okay, fair point, you usually do enough thinking for all of us." He thrusts the sketchpad at me. "But check this out."

I take the sketchpad and start thumbing through the pages. They're covered with floor plans drawn in Nine's precise hand. It's like the architecture of some military base, yet it looks strangely familiar.

"Is this—?"

"West Virginia," Nine declares, proudly. "Every detail I could remember. This should come in handy when we make our assault on the place. I'm sure it's where that fat jerk-off Setrákus is hiding out."

I sit down on the couch, tossing the sketchpad on the cushion next to me. "When I wanted to attack the cave, you were totally against it."

"That was after you'd run into a force field like a dummy," he replies. "I said we needed numbers. We've got numbers."

"Speaking of which, did you check the tablet this morning?"

Nine nods. "Five's staying put for now." We've been keeping an eye on our locater tablet since returning to Chicago. Five—the one Garde we haven't made contact with—has been on an island off the coast of Florida for the last few days. Before we left for New Mexico, he was in Jamaica. His moving around is standard Loric on-the-run protocol. Finding him, even with the tablet to point us in the right direction, might not be easy.

"Now that we've had a chance to rest up, I think we should make it a priority. The more of us the better, right?"

"And maybe while we're searching for Five, Setrákus Ra mounts a full-scale invasion of Earth." Nine slaps the front of his sketchpad for emphasis. "We've got him on the run. We should finish it off now."

"On the run?" I ask, staring at Nine. "That's not exactly how I remember it."

"What? He did retreat, didn't he?"

I shake my head. "You think you're ready for a rematch?"

"You tell me." Nine curls one of his arms behind him and juts the other out overhead, a bodybuilder pose. I can't help but laugh.

"I'm sure he'll be intimidated by flexing."

"It's more intimidating than sitting around, any-way," counters Nine as he flops down on the couch next to me.

"You really think we should go storming West Virginia? After the beating we took at Dulce?"

Nine looks down at his fists, clenching and unclenching them, probably remembering how close he came to being finished off by Setrákus. How close we all came.

"I don't know," he says after a pause. "I just wanted to give this to you so you know it's an option, all right? You might not think I'm, like, capable of learning my limitations and shit like that—but, back in New Mexico? I was maybe, just slightly, over my head trying to fight Setrákus alone. Six went off on her own too, Eight got wrecked, and everyone else was getting shot up. But you kept it together, man. You kept us together. Everyone knows it. I still don't buy your bullshit about being Pittacus reincarnated or whatever, but you've got that team-captain vibe. So you do the leading and I'll do the ass kicking. It's what we're best at."

"Best? I don't know—Six is pretty good at ass kicking, too."

Nine snorts. "Yeah, she was super-badass in her freaking ceiling cocoon. That's not the point, Johnny. The point is, I need you to tell me what to punch. And I need you to tell me soon or I'm gonna go stir crazy up in here."

I take another look at Nine's sketchpad. From the look of it, he probably got right to work on these drawings as soon as we returned from New Mexico. For all his bluster, at least he's been trying his best to come up with a way to take the fight to the Mogadorians. Meanwhile, I've been stuck in this rut, unable to sleep, thinking myself in circles alone on the rooftop.

"I wish Henri was here," I say, "or Sandor. Any of the Cêpans, really. Someone that could tell us what to do next."

"Yeah, well, they're dead," replies Nine, bluntly. "It's up to us now, and you're always the one with the ideas. Hell, the last time I wouldn't go along with your plan, I almost had to throw you off a roof."

"I'm not a Cêpan."

"No, but you're a freaking know-it-all." Nine pats me hard on the back, which I've come to realize is as close as he gets to real affection. "Quit whining, cut down on the snuggling with your little human girlfriend, and come up with some brilliant plan."

A week ago I would've bristled at Nine calling me a whiner and needling me about Sarah. Now, I know he's just trying to motivate me. This is his version of a pep talk and, embarrassing as it is, I sort of need to hear it.

"What if I just don't have a plan?" I ask quietly.

"That, John-boy, is simply not an option."

CHAPTER SIX

I'M BACK ON THE ROOF OF THE JOHN HANCOCK
Center. This time, I'm not alone.

"We don't have to talk about it, if you aren't ready,"
I say gently, looking at the huddled form sitting Indian
style on the roof next to me.

Ella has a blanket wrapped around her shoulders
even though it isn't that cold on the roof. Somehow
she looks smaller than usual, and I wonder if stress is
causing her to revert back to a younger age. Beneath the
blanket she's wearing one of Nine's old flannel shirts.
It comes all the way down to her knees. Lately, it seems
like the only time she's able to sleep peacefully is in
the afternoons. She probably wouldn't have even gotten
out of bed at all today if Marina hadn't gently prodded
her to come up here and talk with me.

"I'll try," she says, her voice hard to hear above the
wind. "Marina said you might be able to help."

Thanks, Marina, I think. I've barely spoken to Ella one-on-one since we first met in New Mexico. I guess this is a good opportunity to get to know her better, although I wish it was under better circumstances. I badly want to help her; I'm just not sure I know how— I'm hardly an expert on these visions, or a psychiatrist, if that's what she needs. This is the kind of talk that would normally be left to a Cêpan, but like Nine reminded me earlier, we're all out of those.

I try to sound confident. "Marina's right. I've had dreams before."

"Dreams about him?" Ella asks, and by the way her voice drops there can be no doubt who she's talking about.

"Yeah," I reply. "That ugly freak has spent so much time in my head, I should be charging him rent."

Ella smiles a little. She stands up, kicking some loose gravel across the roof. Tentatively, I put my hand on her shoulder. She sighs, almost like it's a relief.

"It always starts the same way," Ella begins. "We're back at that base, fighting Setrákus and his minions. We're, you know, losing."

I nod. "Yeah, I remember that part."

"I pick up a piece of metal from the floor. I dunno what it is exactly, a broken piece of a sword maybe. When I touch it, it starts glowing in my hand."

"Wait," I say, trying to piece this part together. "Is that what happened or is this just in the dream?"

"That's what happened," she says. "I was scared and just grabbed the first thing I could. My big plan was to just chuck stuff at him until he stopped hitting Nine."

"From where I was standing, it looked like some kind of dart," I say, remembering the fight, all the smoke and chaos. "A glowing dart. I thought it was something you got from your Chest."

"I never had a Chest," Ella replies sullenly. "I guess they forgot to pack me one."

"Ella, do you know what I think?" I'm trying to be comforting, but the excitement is hard to keep out of my voice. "I think you developed a new Legacy back there and we were all too panicked to realize it."

Ella looks down at her hands. "I don't get it."

I pick up a handful of the loose stones from the roof and hold them out to her. "I think you did something to that broken piece of sword. And when you hit Setrákus Ra with it, you hurt him."

"Oh," she replies, not sounding at all thrilled.

"Do you think you could do it again?" I hold the stones out towards her.

"I don't want to," she answers sharply. "It felt . . . wrong, somehow."

"You were just scared . . . ," I start, trying to encourage her, but when she takes a step away from me, I realize I've made a mistake. She's still shaken up by the fight, these dreams, her Legacies. I let the stones drop back to the roof. "We all were. It's okay. We can worry about that later. Finish telling me about the dreams."

She's quiet for a moment, and I think maybe she's withdrawing completely. But, after a moment, she starts again.

"I throw the piece of metal at him," she says, "and it sticks inside him. Just like at the base. Except, in my dream, instead of retreating, Setrákus turns to face me. Everyone else—all of you guys—disappear, and it's just me and him alone in that smoky room."

Ella wraps her arms around herself, shivering. "He pulls the dart out and he smiles at me. Smiles at me with those horrible teeth. I'm stuck standing there like an idiot while he walks over and touches my face. Like, caresses it with the back of his hand. His touch is ice cold. And then he talks to me."

I feel like shivering too, actually. The thought of Setrákus Ra strolling up to Ella and putting his disgusting hand on her, it turns my stomach.

"What does he say?" I ask.

"Um," she pauses, lowering her voice. "He says, 'there you are' and then, 'I've been looking for you.'"

"And then what happens?"

"He—he gets down on his knees." Her voice drops to a chilled whisper. "He holds one of my hands in both of his, and he asks me if I've read the letter."

"What letter? Do you know what he's talking about?"

Ella hunches the blanket tighter around her shoulders, not looking at me. "No."

I can tell by the way she answers that Ella isn't being totally honest. There's something about this letter—whatever it might be—that's shaken her up almost as much as these visions of Setrákus Ra. From her description, I don't know if these dreams are like the ones I've had, like the one where Setrákus showed me Sam being tortured to try baiting me into fighting him, or if it's like Six suggested and these nightmares are simply a result of all the really awful things Ella's been through lately. I don't want to press her any further; she already seems close to tears.

"I wish I could tell you I could make the dreams go away," I begin, finding myself doing my best Henri impression, "but I can't. I don't know what causes them. I only know how painful they can be."

Ella nods, looking disappointed. "Okay."

"If you see him in a dream again, just remember he can't hurt you. And when he tries to hold your hand, you punch him right in his ugly face."

Ella cracks a smile. "I'll try."

I'm not sure if anything I said really helped Ella, but one detail from our conversation sticks with me. Whatever she hit Setrákus Ra with, I'm sure that it was the result of her developing a new Legacy. She charged up that projectile and, somehow, it hurt him, or at least distracted him enough that we were able to get our Legacies back. Now I just need to convince her to try doing it again, and hopefully figure out exactly what this new Legacy can do. If it worked once, maybe it will work again. If I'm going to put together a plan to finally kill Setrákus Ra, I'm going to need every weapon we have at my disposal.

I head down to the Lecture Hall, hoping to find something in my Chest or in Nine's arsenal that might help draw out Ella's Legacy. I remember when Henri used the warming stone on me to help me first gain control of my Lumen. I wonder if something like that would help Ella.

I'm deep in thought when I hear the muffled sound of gunshots.

I flinch automatically, hunching down, my hands growing hot as my Lumen switches on. It's instinct. I know the difference between Mog blasters and Nine's gun collection, which some of the others have taken to practicing with. I also know we're safe here, at least for now; if the Mogs knew where we were, all of us together, their assault would be a hell of a lot noisier than one gun going off. Even considering all that, my heart is still pounding and I feel ready for a fight. I guess Ella isn't the only one jumpy from the battle in New Mexico.

I push my way through the heavy double doors of the Lecture Hall, my hands glowing dimly because I'm still a little on edge. I'm expecting to find Nine twirling a gun outlaw style into its holster, killing time by shooting up paper targets.

Instead, I find Sarah squeezing off the last round from a small handgun. The bullet tears through the shoulder of a paper Mogadorian hanging at the far end of the room.

"Not bad," says Six as she pulls off a pair of noise-canceling headphones. She's standing next to Sarah, watching over her shoulder. Six uses her telekinesis to pull the paper Mog closer. Most of Sarah's shots ripped through around the edges, or caught the Mog in the arms and legs. One, however, tore through right between his eyes. Sarah pokes her finger through that hole.

"I can do better than this," she says.

"It's not as easy as cheerleading, huh?" Six asks good-naturedly.

Sarah unloads her spent cartridge and jams home a fresh one. "You've obviously never tried a full layout twist."

"I don't even know what that is."

Watching this scene play out, I feel suddenly and inexplicably nervous. Admittedly, there's something about her waving a gun around that makes Sarah hot in a dangerous way that I'd never really considered. But it also makes me feel guilty, like I'm the reason she's stuck here taking target practice instead of being back in Paradise, living a normal life. Plus, there's the fact that I haven't mentioned kissing Six to Sarah, or even talked about it with Six, and now here the two of them are, hanging out. I know I should come clean about that to Sarah. Eventually. When she's not carrying a loaded weapon, maybe.

I clear my throat, trying to sound casual. "Hey, what's going on?"

Both girls turn around to look at me. Sarah smiles big and waves with the hand not holding the gun.

"Hey, babe," she says. "Six was just helping me learn to shoot."

"Yeah, cool. I didn't realize that's something you wanted to do."

Six gives me a strange look, like *who wouldn't want to learn to shoot?* An awkward moment passes between us, where I'm feeling almost mad at her for giving Sarah this lesson without my permission. Not that Sarah needs my permission to do anything. The whole situation has me feeling flustered, and I must look it, because Six eases the gun out of Sarah's hand. She clicks the safety on and holsters it.

"I think that's good for now," Six says. "Let's do some more tomorrow."

"Oh," replies Sarah, sounding disappointed. "All right."

Six pats Sarah on the arm. "Good shooting." Then, she fixes me with a tight smile that I'm not at all sure what to make of. "Later, guys," she says, and breezes past me out the door.

Sarah and I stand in silence for a moment, the lights of the Lecture Hall buzzing overhead.

"So," I begin, awkwardly.

"You're being weird," she says, eyeing me, her head tilted to the side.

I pick up the paper Mogadorian, examining Sarah's handiwork while I figure out what to say. "I know. Sorry. I just never took you for the armed and dangerous type."

Sarah frowns at me. "If I'm going to be with you, I don't want to be a damsel in distress."

"You're not."

"Come on," she snorts. "Who knows how long I would've rotted in New Mexico if you hadn't shown up? And then, I mean, John, you pretty much brought me back to life."

I slide my arm around her, not wanting to think about Sarah at my feet, nearly dead. "I'd never let anything happen to you."

She shrugs me off. "You can't say that for sure. You can't do everything, John."

"Yeah," I say, "I'm starting to realize that."

Sarah looks up at me. "You know, I thought about calling my parents today. It's been weeks. I wanted to tell them I'm all right."

"That's not really a good idea. The Mogadorians or the government could be monitoring your house for phone calls. They could be tracking us."

The words sound so cold and I regret them almost right away, how quickly I'm slipping into paranoid-and-practical-leader mode. But Sarah doesn't seem offended. In fact, it looks like it's exactly what she expected me to say.

"I know," she says, nodding. "That's exactly what I thought, and it's why I didn't actually go through with it. I don't want to go home. I want to stay here with you guys and fight. But I don't have any Loric superpowers. I'm just dead weight. I want to practice shooting so I can be more than that."

I grab Sarah's hand. "You are more than that. I need you here with me. You're pretty much the only thing keeping me from completely melting down."

"I get it," she says. "You're going to save the freaking world and I'm going to help you. That whole saying about behind every great man there is a great woman? I can be that for you. I just want to be a great woman with excellent aim."

I can't help but laugh, the tension between us

breaking. I lift Sarah's hand and kiss it. She wraps her arms around my waist and we hug. I don't know what I was so tied up in knots about; having Sarah here just makes everything seem easier. Coming up with a battle plan to take down the Mogadorians? No problem. And as for that one kiss with Six, it just doesn't seem to matter anymore.

Eight teleports into the room with a puff of displaced air. He's wide-eyed and excited, but turns sheepish when he sees us.

"Whoa," Eight says. "Sorry, I didn't expect canoodling."

Sarah snickers, and I glare jokingly at Eight. "This better be good."

"You should go to the workshop and see for yourself. I've gotta go get the others."

With that cryptic message, Eight teleports away. Sarah and I exchange a look, then rush out of the Lecture Hall and into Sandor's old workshop.

Nine is already there, his arms crossed as he watches the bank of television screens on the wall. They're all tuned to the same image, a newscast from some local station in South Carolina. Nine pauses the broadcast when we enter, freezing a still image of the gray-haired anchor.

"I turned on some of Sandor's old programs the other day," Nine explains. "They scan news feeds for weird shit that might be Loric related."

"Yeah, Henri had the same thing set up."

"Uh-huh, typical boring Cêpan stuff, right? Except this popped up tonight."

Nine restarts the broadcast, the anchor resuming his teleprompter reading.

"Authorities are at a loss to explain the vandalism of a local farmer's crops early yesterday morning. The prevailing theory is high-school prank, but others have suggested . . ."

I tune out the anchor's theories as the image switches to an overhead shot of a twisting, mazelike emblem burned into the cornfield. It might look like a juvenile prank to the newscaster, but we recognize it immediately. Burned into those crops with jagged precision is the Loric symbol for Five.

CHAPTER
SEVEN

"IF FIVE'S TRYING TO FIND US, THIS IS ABOUT
the dumbest damn way possible," Nine says.

"She could be scared and alone," counters Marina,
softly. "On the run."

"No Cêpan in their right mind would go burning up
crops, so they must be alone. Still . . ." Nine trails off,
his brow furrowing. "Wait—what do you mean 'she'?
Five's a chick?"

Marina rolls her eyes at *chick*, then shakes her head.
"I don't know. Just a guess."

"Setting a field on fire seems like a guy thing," Six
puts in.

"I remember Henri reading a story about a girl lifting a car off someone in Argentina," I say. "We always
thought that could be Five."

"Sounds like a tabloid story to me," Six counters.

"Guy or girl doesn't matter," interrupts Nine, waving

at the computer screens. "Scared doesn't haven't to mean stupid."

I find myself agreeing with Nine. Assuming this message is actually from Five and not some elaborate Mogadorian trap, it's a really bad way to get our attention. Because if we noticed it, then the Mogadorians definitely did too.

We've all crowded into Sandor's workshop. Nine has paused the newscast on the overhead shot of the Loric symbol while we figure out what to do next. I have the macrocosm from my Chest open, the holographic Loric solar system floating peacefully in the space over the table.

"He must not have his Chest open," I say. "This would change into the globe if he did."

Eight stands next to me, clutching a red communication crystal he pulled from his chest. It's the same one we found in Nine's and used to try sending Six a message when she was in India.

"Are you out there, Five?" Eight speaks into the crystal. "If you are, you should probably stop setting things on fire."

"I think he can only hear you if his Chest is open," I explain. "In which case, he'd show up on the macrocosm."

"Ah," says Eight, lowering the crystal. "They couldn't have packed us cell phones?"

Meanwhile, Nine has plugged our locater tablet into one of Sandor's computers. The newscast blips out of existence, replaced by a map of Earth. There's a cluster of pulsing blue dots in Chicago—that's us. Further south, there's another dot, moving extremely fast from the Carolinas towards the middle of the country. Nine looks over at me.

"He's made a lot of miles since I checked on him this morning. First time he's come in from the islands, too."

Six points at the screen, tracing a line back to where the crops were burned. "It makes sense. Whoever it is, they're on the run."

"They're moving really fast, though," puts in Sarah. "Could they be taking a plane somewhere?"

The dot on the screen suddenly takes an abrupt northward turn, crossing through Tennessee.

"I don't think planes move like that," says Six, her brow furrowing.

"Super speed?" Eights asks.

We watch as the blue dot crosses right through Nashville, never slowing down or changing directions.

"There's no way they just zipped through a city at that speed on a straight line," Six says.

"Son of a bitch," growls Nine. "I think this idiot can fly."

"We'll have to wait until they stop moving," I say. "Maybe then they'll open their Chest and we can send a message. We'll watch in shifts. We need to get to Five before the Mogs do."

Marina volunteers to take the first shift. I linger in the workshop after the others have gone. Even with all this excitement about Five, I haven't forgotten about our other problems, specifically Ella and her nightmares.

"I talked to Ella today," I begin. "In her nightmares, Setrákus Ra asks her if she's opened some letter. Any idea what that could mean?"

Marina looks away from where Five's pulsing beacon cruises across Oklahoma. "Crayton's letter, maybe?"

"Her Cêpan?"

"Back in India, right before he died, Crayton gave her a letter." Marina frowns. "With everything that's happened, I almost forgot about it."

"She hasn't read it?" I ask, feeling a little exasperated. "We're fighting a war here; it could be important."

"I don't think it's that easy for her, John," Marina says, levelly. "Those are Crayton's last words. Reading it would be like admitting that he's really gone and not coming back."

"But he is gone," I reply quickly. Too quickly. I pause, thinking back to when Henri was killed. He'd been like a father to me and, even more than that, he was the only constant in a life spent constantly on the run. For me,

the idea of Henri was almost like the idea of home—
wherever he was, that's where he was safe. Losing him
was like having the world ripped out from under me.
I was older than Ella when it happened, too. I shouldn't
expect her to be able to just brush it off.

I sit down next to Marina, sighing. "Henri—my
Cêpan—he left me a letter too. He gave it to me when he
was dying. We were on the road for days before I could
bring myself to read it."

"See? It's not so easy. Plus, if Setrákus Ra showed
up in my dreams and told me to do something, I'd definitely do the opposite."

I nod. "I get it. I do. She needs to grieve. I don't mean
to sound heartless. When all this is over, when we win,
we'll have time to mourn the people we've lost. But
until then, we need to gather all the information we can
and find anything that might work to our advantage."
I wave my hand at the screen with Five's location. "We
have to stop just waiting around for the next crisis and
start acting."

Marina thinks about what I've said, gazing at the
holographic macrocosm of Earth we've left open just
in case Five should open his or her Chest. This is probably what she was expecting to hear from me this
morning when she gently asked if I had a plan for us.
I didn't then—and I don't exactly now—but the first

step definitely has to be figuring out what we have to work with, and Ella is key to that.

"I'll talk to Ella," she says. "But I won't force her to do anything."

I hold up my hands. "I'm not asking you to. You guys are close. Maybe you could nudge her along?"

"I'll try," she says, at last.

Eight appears in the doorway of the workshop, holding two cups of tea. Marina's face lights up when she sees him, although she quickly looks away, suddenly acting really interested in the macrocosm. I notice a blush creeping up her cheeks.

"Hey," Eight says, setting down the tea. "Sorry. I, uh, only made the two cups."

"It's cool," I reply, catching a meaningful look from Eight that suddenly makes me feel like a third wheel. "I was just leaving."

I stand up and Eight takes my seat in front of the macrocosm. Before I'm even out the door, Eight whispers some joke to Marina that immediately gets her giggling. I've been so focused on Sarah and my agonizing battle planning that I hadn't put much thought into how much time Marina and Eight have been spending together. That's good. All of us deserve a little happiness, considering what we're facing.

It's almost dawn when Eight comes to our room, waking me and Sarah. The others are already gathered in the workshop. Six sits in front of the computers, Marina next to her.

"Another brain-dead maneuver from our missing compadre," Nine says by way of greeting. He's standing on the wall using his antigravity legacy. Ella is sitting Indian style on his back, wrapped up in a blanket. I arch an eyebrow at her.

"Did you sleep at all?"

"Don't want to," Ella says.

"She's been helping me with my strength training," announces Nine. He hunches his shoulders, jostling Ella. She almost falls off his back, but laughs—a rare laugh—and hangs on. She slaps his back in annoyance. "Didn't even feel that."

Ignoring the others, Six turns to me. "Five stopped moving about an hour ago. Then started up again."

I glance at the tablet's screen. Five's beacon has cruised along west since the last time I looked in. It now hovers around the eastern border of Arkansas.

"The genius stopped just long enough to send us another message," grouses Nine.

Marina narrows her eyes at Nine. "Do we really need to be critiquing what Five does? He or she is probably alone and scared."

"Honey, I spent months in a Mogadorian jail cell for my stupidity. I've earned my right to color commentate—ow."

Ella slaps Nine on the back again and he shuts up. I stay focused on Six and the computer screen.

"Just tell me what happened."

"One hour ago, this was posted in the comment section of a news story about the crops burning," says Six, thankfully keeping it matter-of-fact. She opens up a window and drags it over to where we can all see it on the big screen.

> **Anonymous writes: Five seeking 5. Are you out there? Need to meet. Will be with the monsters in Arkansas. Find me.**

"What does it mean?" asks Sarah. "It's like a riddle."

Six clicks open a web browser, bringing up the cheesy-looking website of something called the Boggy Creek Monster. "We found this on Google. It's a dumb little tourist attraction in Arkansas called the Monster Mart."

"You think Five is headed there?"

"We won't know for sure until he stops moving," Six answers, gesturing at the blue dot on the tablet. "But I'd bet yes."

"Does he think the Mogadorians don't have Google?" Nine spits.

"Speaking from experience," Six says, "the Mogadorians monitor the internet like hawks. If we're seeing this, then you can bet they've seen it too and are trying to figure it out. They'll likely trace his IP address first and waste some time looking for his location, which is good because we can tell from this that he's moved on from wherever he sent the message. Even so, they'll figure it out eventually."

"Then we better move fast," I say.

"Hell yeah," Nine says, hopping down from the wall and catching Ella as she tumbles after him. He sets her down and cracks his knuckles. "Finally, some freaking action."

It's like something in me clicks and, after days of overthinking our position, a plan just comes spilling out of me. "Our advantage here is that we know Five's exact location. Hopefully, that gives us a head start on the Mogs. We need to be fast and we need to be sneaky. Six and I will go to Arkansas. With her invisibility, we should be able to sneak Five out without tipping off the Mogadorians. We'll bring Bernie Kosar, too."

"Oh, the dog gets to go?" Nine says flatly.

"His shape shifting will make it easy for us to scout ahead," I counter. "And he can make it back to you guys if something goes wrong. If we're captured, Eight, I expect to see you teleporting our violent friend Nine here into my cell within twenty-four hours. And, if the unthinkable happens—"

"It won't," Six interrupts. "We've got this."

I look around the room. "Does everyone agree?"

Eight and Marina nod, their faces grim but confident. Ella gives me a small smile from her spot next to Marina. Nine doesn't look too thrilled about being left out of the mission, but he grunts his approval. Sarah says nothing, looking away.

"Good," I say. "We should be back in two days max. Six, get whatever you need and let's head out."

It's taken a few days, but for the first time, I actually feel like a leader.

Of course, that leadership feeling doesn't last all that long. I'm back in my room, stuffing a backpack with a change of clothes and some things from my Chest: my dagger, my bracelet, a healing stone. Sarah comes in carrying a holstered pistol from Nine's armory and wordlessly stuffs it in a backpack of her own, covering it with a change of clothes.

"What're you doing?" I ask.

"I'm coming with you," she says, and gives me a defiant look like she's expecting an argument. I shake my head in disbelief.

"That wasn't the plan."

Sarah shrugs her backpack on and faces me, her hands on her hips. "Yeah, well, it wasn't my plan to fall in love with an alien either, but sometimes plans change."

"This could be dangerous," I tell her. "We're trying to beat the Mogadorians to Five's location, but we don't know that we will for sure. We're going to have to use stealth and Six can only turn two people invisible at once."

She shrugs. "Six says we can just bring the Xithi-whatever. That stone. She can use it to copy her powers."

My eyebrows shoot up. It's a good idea. But I'm more interested in something else she said. "You already talked to Six?"

"Yeah, she's cool with it," Sarah replies. "She understands. There's nothing about this life that isn't dangerous anymore. I'm getting used to the idea of my boyfriend fighting an intergalactic war, but I'll never get used to just watching from the sidelines and hoping everything turns out okay."

"But it's safe on the sidelines," I answer weakly, even though I already know this is a losing argument.

"I'd feel safer being with you. After all that's happened, I don't want to be apart anymore, John. Whatever dangers you have to face, I want to be by your side."

"I don't want to be apart either, but—" Before I can mount any further protest, Sarah steps forward and shuts me up with a quick kiss. It's really not fair that she can do that during an argument.

"Just stop there," she says, smiling at me. "You've done the whole chivalrous routine, okay? It's cute, I like it, but it's not changing my mind."

I sigh. I suppose part of being a good leader is knowing when to accept defeat. I guess I should grab the Xitharis stone out of my Chest too.

Nine rides the elevator down with us to the parking garage. I can tell he's still fuming, even more so now that he realizes Sarah is coming along for the mission.

"We're leaving the tablet here in case something goes wrong and you end up needing to track us," I tell Nine. "Hopefully, Five stays put for a while. If we can't find him once we're in Arkansas, we'll be in touch for an update."

"Yeah, yeah," Nine replies, shooting a sidelong look at Sarah. "This is starting to look less like a rescue mission and more like you going on a leisurely road trip with two hot chicks," Nine grumbles.

Sarah rolls her eyes. I glare at Nine. "It's not like that. You know we need you here, in case something happens."

"Yeah, I'm backup," he snorts. "Johnny, do I have to start dating you to get some action around here?"

Sarah winks at him. "It might help."

Nine looks me over. "Ugh. Not worth it."

Six and Bernie Kosar are already waiting for us downstairs. Nine shows us to the row reserved for Sandor's extensive car collection, eventually pulling the tarp off a silver Honda Civic. It's the least flashy vehicle left in Sandor's collection; we don't want to be attracting any unnecessary attention while we're on the road. BK immediately bounds into the passenger seat, excited to get going.

"It's fast," Nine explains. "Sandor outfitted all of these in case we needed to move ass in a hurry."

"Does it have nitrous?" Sarah asks.

"What do you know about nitrous, sweetheart?" Nine replies.

Sarah shrugs. "I've seen *Fast and Furious*. Show me how it works. I've always wanted to drive something really fast."

"Well, all right," says Nine, grinning at me. "Maybe your girl does have some uses, John-boy."

While Nine shows Sarah the controls inside the Civic, I join Six at the trunk, where we load our gear. I'm still feeling blindsided that Sarah's coming along with us, and apparently I've got Six to blame for that.

"You're mad at me," she says, before I can even start in.

"I'd appreciate a heads up the next time you invite my girlfriend along on a dangerous mission."

Six groans, slamming the trunk closed and rounding

on me. "Oh please, John. She wanted to come along. She can think for herself."

"I know she can," I whisper back, not wanting Sarah to overhear. "Nine wanted to come along too. We have to consider what's best for the group."

"You don't want her feeling like dead weight, do you? This is a good way to show her that she's not."

"Wait. Dead weight?" I think back to my conversation with Sarah in the Lecture Hall. Those were the exact words she used. "Were you eavesdropping on us?"

Six looks a little guilty at being busted, but more than anything she looks increasingly angry with me, her eyes flashing. "So what? I thought you might finally grow a pair and tell her that we kissed."

"Why would I do that?" I snap, struggling to keep my voice low.

"Because the longer you put it off the more awkward it gets, and I'm getting sick of it? Because she deserves—"

Before Six can finish, the Civic roars to life, Sarah revving the engine. Nine steps back from the driver-side window, looking pleased with the way Sarah's gunning it. Sarah leans out the window, peering back at Six and me.

"You two coming or what?"

CHAPTER
EIGHT

THE PENTHOUSE FEELS EVEN LARGER AS SOON AS John, Six and Sarah are gone. I'm still not over the size of this place; it's almost big enough to contain the entire monastery of Santa Teresa. I know it's silly, but I find myself tiptoeing through it, feeling like I'm constantly disturbing these riches Nine and his Cêpan amassed.

The tiles in Nine's bathroom are heated—they actually warm and dry your feet when you get out of the shower. I think of all the times I sat on my mattress, picking splinters out of my feet after crossing the uneven wood floors of Santa Teresa. I wonder what Hectór would think of this place, and I smile. Then, I wonder what kind of person I would be if my Cêpan had been Sandor instead of Adelina; a showy but dedicated guardian, frivolous in his purchases but not one to abandon his duties. It's pointless to think such thoughts, yet I can't help it.

But if I hadn't been stuck so long in Santa Teresa,

I never would have crossed paths with Ella. I never would have journeyed to the mountains with Six and met Eight.

All the hardship, in the end, was worth it.

I stifle a yawn with the back of my hand. None of us got much sleep last night, not with the excitement of finding Number Five. It was supposed to be my night sleeping in Ella's room, shaking her awake when the nightmares got too bad. Actually, I don't think Ella slept a wink in between the meeting and tagging along with Nine during his shift watching Five's beacon. Apparently, to her, spending time with Nine is better than getting some rest. I wish I knew how to help, but my healing Legacy doesn't extend to the dream world.

I find Ella curled up in a chair in the penthouse living room. Nine is stretched out on the nearest couch, snoring loudly, his hands curled around the contracted metal tube that turns into the staff I've seen him use with such deadly efficiency. He must have gotten it from his Chest when he still thought there was a chance John would bring him along on the mission. Nine clutches the weapon like a teddy bear, probably dreaming of killing Mogadorians.

"You should get some sleep too," I whisper.

Ella looks from me to the sleeping Nine. "He said he was just going to rest his eyes and then he'd show me some ass-kicking techniques."

I giggle. There's something hilarious about Ella

parroting Nine's language.

"Come on, there will be time for training later."

Nine grumbles something in his sleep and rolls over, burying his face in the couch cushions. Ella stands up slowly and we tiptoe out of the room.

"I like Nine," she announces as we walk down the hall. "He doesn't care about stuff."

My brow furrows. "What do you mean?"

"He never asks me how I'm doing or, like, worries about me. He just makes gross jokes and lets me walk on his shoulders across the ceiling."

I laugh, but I feel a bit wounded. All of us have been so worried about Ella, always trying to get her to open up about Crayton—I'm still supposed to do what John asked and get to the bottom of that letter—and along comes Nine, taking her mind off her troubles with bluster.

"We're just worried about you," I say.

"I know," Ella replies. "It just feels better not to think about it sometimes."

Maybe this is a good time to give Ella that gentle nudge John was talking about. "My Cêpan, Adelina, she spent a long time trying not to think about her destiny—about our destiny. But eventually she didn't have a choice. She had to face it."

Ella doesn't say anything, but I can tell by the way her face is scrunched up that she's thinking about my words.

I find myself detouring away from the bedrooms and instead heading back into Sandor's workshop. I stand over the plugged-in tablet, watching the dots that represent Four and Six crawl slowly towards Five's stationary dot in Arkansas.

"Are you worried about them?" Ella asks.

"A little," I reply, although I know the others will be fine. Even after meeting Nine, Six is still the toughest and bravest person I've ever met. And Four is everything Six said he would be—a good guy, the leader we need, even if sometimes I can tell he feels like he's in over his head.

"I hope Five is a boy," announces Ella. "There aren't enough boys for all of us."

My mouth hangs open for a moment, and then I start to laugh. "Are you matching us up already, Ella?"

She nods, looking at me mischievously. "There's John and Sarah, of course. And you and Eight."

"Wait a second," I say. "Nothing's happening with me and Eight."

"Psshh," interrupts Ella, continuing on, "and if I grow up to marry Nine, who does that leave for Six?"

"Who's getting married now?"

Eight's standing in the doorway behind us, that charming smirk of his lighting up his face. How long has he been standing there? Ella and I exchange a surprised look and start laughing.

"Fine," says Eight, sidling over to gaze at the tablet. "Don't tell me."

Our shoulders brush when he gets close and I don't move away. I still think about that desperate kiss we shared in New Mexico. It was probably the boldest move of my entire life. Much as I'd like to, we haven't kissed again since. We've talked a lot, sharing stories about our years on the run, comparing the fragments of our memories of Lorien. The time just hasn't felt right for anything more.

"They're really taking their time, huh?" Eight says, watching Four and Six move south.

"It's a long drive," I reply.

"Good," he says, grinning. "That should give us some time."

Eight's wearing a red and black T-shirt for something called the Chicago Bulls and a pair of blue jeans. He steps back and gestures at his wardrobe, like he's asking Ella and me for our approval.

"Do I look American enough in this?"

◻

"Are you sure we should be doing this?"

I'm feeling nervous as the elevator glides down from the penthouse to the lobby. Eight stands next to me, practically bouncing with excitement.

"We've been here for days and still haven't actually seen

the city," he says. "I'd like to see more of America than military bases and apartments."

"But what if something happens while we're away?"

"We'll be back before they even make it to Arkansas. Nothing's going to happen on the drive down there. If it does, Ella can use her whole telepathy thing and call us back."

I think about Nine, who was still sound asleep on the couch when Eight and I crept past him. Ella watched us go, smiling conspiratorially at me, while she curled back up in her chair next to Nine.

"Won't Nine be mad if he wakes up and we're not there?"

"What is he? Our babysitter?" Eight cracks merrily, reaching out to shake me gently by the shoulders. "Loosen up. Let's be tourists for a couple hours."

Gazing down from the windows of Nine's penthouse never gave me a real sense of how truly busy the streets of downtown Chicago are. We exit into the midday sun and are immediately hit with a wall of noise, people talking, car horns blaring. It reminds me of the marketplace back in Spain, except times a thousand. Eight and I both find ourselves craning our necks upwards, trying to take in the buildings that tower above us. We're walking slow, people shooting us annoyed looks as they're forced to cut around us.

It's a little intense for me out here. All these people,

the noise, it's way more than I'm used to. I find myself slipping my hand into the crook of Eight's elbow, just to make sure we aren't accidentally separated and lost in the crowd. He smiles at me.

"Where to?" he asks.

"That way," I point, picking a direction at random.

We end up on the waterfront. It's much more peaceful here. The humans wandering around the shore of Lake Michigan are like us—not in a rush to get anywhere. Some of them sit down on benches, eating their lunches, while others jog and bike by us, exercising. I feel suddenly sad for these people. So much hangs in the balance and they have no idea.

Eight touches my arm gently. "You're frowning."

"Sorry," I reply, forcing a smile. "Just thinking."

"Less of that," he says with mock sternness. "We're just out for a walk. No big deal."

I try to put the doom and gloom out of my mind and act the part of a tourist like Eight said. The lake is crystalline and beautiful, a few boats lazily cutting across its surface. We amble by sculptures and outdoor cafés, Eight taking an interest in everything, trying to consume as much of the local culture as possible, and cheerily trying to get me interested.

We stand before a large silver sculpture that looks like a cross between a satellite dish and a half-peeled potato. "I believe this human work was secretly influenced by the great Loric artist Hugo Von Lore," Eight says, stroking his chin thoughtfully.

"You're making that up."

Eight shrugs. "I'm just trying to be a better tour guide."

His easygoing enthusiasm is infectious, and soon I'm wrapped up in this game of making up silly stories for the various landmarks we pass. When I finally realize that we've spent more than an hour on the waterfront, I feel guilty.

"Maybe we should get back," I tell Eight, feeling like we're shirking our responsibilities, even though I know there's nothing for us to do but wait.

"Hold on," he says, pointing. "Look at that."

From the hushed way Eight speaks, I expect to see a Mogadorian scout on our trail. Instead, following his gaze, I see a chubby older man behind a food cart selling what's advertised as a "Chicago-Style Hot Dog." He hands one off to a customer; the hot dog is covered in pickle and tomato slices and chopped-up onions, barely contained in a bun.

"That's the most monstrous thing I've ever seen," Eight says.

I chuckle, and when my stomach suddenly growls, that chuckle turns into a full-on guffaw. "I think it looks sort of good," I manage.

"Have I mentioned that I'm a vegetarian?" Eight asks, staring at me with mock revulsion. "But if it's the frightening mess of a Chicago-style hot dog you desire, then so it shall be. I've never thanked you properly."

Eight starts towards the vendor, but I grab him by the arm and drag him back. He grins at me.

"Change your mind?"

"What do you mean, you never thanked me properly?" I ask. "Thanked me for what?"

"For saving my life in New Mexico. You broke the prophecy, Marina. Setrákus Ra put his sword right through me and you—you brought me back to life."

I can't help blushing and looking down at my feet. "It was nothing."

"It was literally everything to me."

I look up, putting on my best version of Eight's teasing smile. "In that case, I think I deserve more than a gross hot dog."

Eight clasps his hands across his chest like I've wounded him. "You're right! I'm a fool to think my life could be traded for a hot dog." He grabs my hand and gets down on one knee, pressing his forehead to the back of my hand. "My savior, what can I ever do to repay you?"

I'm embarrassed, but can't help laughing. I shoot apologetic looks to the people around us, most of them staring at Eight's display with curious smiles. We must look like just two normal teenagers to them, goofing around and flirting.

I pull Eight back to his feet and, still holding his hand,

continue on down the lakefront. The sun winks across the surface of the lake. It's not quite the sea I was named for, but it's beautiful all the same.

"You can promise me more days like these," I tell Eight.

He squeezes my hand tightly. "Consider it done."

Eight and I finally come back to the penthouse, our bellies full of greasy Chicago pizza. We've still got hours before Four and Six arrive in Arkansas, and Ella never sent up any telepathic alarm. Everything is just as we left it.

Except Nine is awake and standing so close to the elevator door that we almost crash into him when we enter.

Nine doesn't move when we come in, he just stands there with his arms crossed over his chest and glares at us. "Where have you two been?"

"Geez," says Eight, inching around Nine's bulk. "How long have you been standing here waiting for us? Aren't your feet tired?"

"We just went out for a bit," I explain, feeling more than a little timid around Nine. It reminds me of getting caught sneaking back into the orphanage after curfew, and I briefly picture Nine trying to take a ruler to my knuckles. "Is everything all right?"

"Everything's fine," snaps Nine, focusing more on Eight than me. "You can't just go gallivanting around the city without telling me."

"Why not?" counters Eight.

"Because it's bullshit," growls Nine. I can see his mind working, like he's trying to think of something else to say. "It's irresponsible and careless. It's stupid."

"It was a couple hours," complains Eight, rolling his eyes. "Spare me the Cêpan lecture."

It is kind of funny to see Nine so enraged about us acting out of line, especially considering the stories I've heard Four tell about their time together on the road. Strangely, it's also endearing. He puts on this big show of being this tough-as-nails loose cannon, but when he woke up to find us gone, he was actually concerned about us.

I touch Nine on the arm, trying to defuse the situation. "I'm sorry we worried you."

"Whatever, I wasn't worried," Nine snarls, jerking his arm away from me and rounding on Eight again. "You think that was a lecture? Maybe I should show you the kind of lectures I used to get, back when I was a cocky little dumbass."

Eight wiggles his fingers at Nine, just egging him on further. Most of the time his joking around is charming, but this is one of those times when I wish he'd just cut it out. Nine steps right up to Eight; they'd be nose to nose if Eight was a few inches taller. Eight doesn't back down, still smiling, like it's all just a goof.

"Come on," says Nine, his voice low. "I've seen you in the Lecture Hall playing patty-cake with Six. You ain't trained with me yet."

Eight glances down at an imaginary watch. "Sure, dude. I've got some time to kill."

Nine smiles. He looks over his shoulder at me. "You too, Nurse Marina. Your boyfriend's gonna need you."

CHAPTER
NINE

"I'M GOING TO WHIP YOU INTO SHAPE," DECLARES Nine. "That way, the next time there's a mission, we won't be the ones left sitting on our asses."

Eight and I stand in the Lecture Hall side by side, watching as Nine circles around us, sizing us up like some kind of army drill instructor. I feel like rolling my eyes, and I can tell Eight is barely suppressing a fit of laughter. Still, I do feel sort of guilty about basically sneaking out with Eight, and I'm sure a little training couldn't hurt. Plus, I think Nine is still bummed about being left out of Four's rescue mission, and he seems really into this whole training thing. I decide to humor him.

"Unless you'd rather just be benchwarmers? You want to hang out and go eat pizza while the rest of us kill Setrákus Ra?" Nine snarls as he stops in front of us, staring us down.

"No, sir," I say, trying to be serious. Eight immediately bursts out laughing.

Nine ignores Eight for now, focusing instead on me. "Healing and night vision. That's about it, huh?"

"I can breathe under water," I add helpfully.

"All right," says Nine, considering my Legacies, "maybe you'll develop a good fighting Legacy one day. Maybe you won't. We'd still all be dead if it wasn't for you, I guess. I know Johnny's supposed to have the healing thing now, too, but I think he only heals girls he's dating, so the rest of us still need you. Anyway, we'll need to practice your speed and agility, so that when one of us goes down, you'll be able to get to us. And maybe your healing will, like, evolve into something else if we practice with it enough."

To my surprise, most of what Nine says actually makes sense. Except one thing nags at me. "How are we going to practice my healing?"

Nine's smile is sinister, something I'd be really afraid to see from across the battlefield. "Oh, you'll see. As for you," he continues, turning to Eight, "I thought you were pretty badass when we first met, and then you took a sword to the chest first chance you got. Nice job."

Eight's expression darkens as he's reminded of his run-in with Setrákus Ra. "He tricked me."

"Uh-huh," says Nine. "Way I remember it, you were so focused with copping a feel—er, hugging—fake Six that you got stabbed. You give a lot of hugs in the middle of a battle, bro? Use your head."

"It seems like you could use a hug right now," says Eight, grinning mischievously.

Before Nine knows what's happening, Eight shape shifts into his four-armed Vishnu form, leaps forward, and wraps Nine up in a tight embrace. I can see the muscles in Nine's neck and shoulders tense as Eight squeezes him.

"Let me go," warns Nine through gritted teeth.

"You're the boss."

Eight teleports, taking Nine with him. He reappears just inches away from the ceiling and releases Nine. Disoriented, Nine doesn't have a chance to gather himself and crashes to the floor on his back. Before Nine even lands, Eight has teleported back to my side.

"Ta-da," he says, reassuming his normal form.

"You're just going to make him mad," I whisper. Eight only shrugs.

Nine hops back to his feet and rolls his head from side to side, cracking his neck. He nods, looking almost impressed.

"Pretty good move," he says.

"Maybe I should be training you," quips Eight.

"Try it again."

Shrugging, Eight shape shifts again. He wraps Nine in the same hug, this time approaching warily, as if he's expecting Nine to launch a counterattack. I'm expecting the same thing, cringing as I wait for Nine to throw an elbow into Eight's face. Surprisingly, Nine doesn't fight back at all.

Eight teleports them back to the ceiling again, but this time, when he's released from Eight's grasp, Nine quickly reaches his hand up to touch the ceiling. It makes me queasy just to watch; Nine's gravity shifting so that instead of falling to the floor, he's doing a handstand on the ceiling. It all takes no more than a second.

Eight's already teleported away, reappearing back at my side. Just like Nine was expecting. Nine launches himself from the ceiling and, as soon as Eight materializes, Nine is plummeting towards him. Eight only has a moment to notice that Nine isn't lying on the floor where he expected him to be. The next thing he knows, Nine's foot is connecting with his sternum, sending him flying to the ground.

Eight picks himself up onto his elbows, wheezing, the wind knocked out of him. Nine stands over him, his hands on his hips.

"Predictable," Nine says. "Why would you teleport back to the same place?"

In answer, Eight coughs, rubbing his chest. Nine reaches down and helps him to his feet.

"It's all about surprise with you, man," Nine explains. "You gotta keep 'em guessing."

Eight lifts up his shirt. There's a foot-shaped bruise already forming over his ribs. "Damn. That was like getting hit with a sledgehammer."

"Thanks," says Nine, and looks at me. "Here's some practice for you."

I place my hands gently on Eight's chest. The icy feeling of my Legacy tingles in my fingertips, passing through me and into Eight. It's only a bruise so it's easy; I don't even have to concentrate. Which is good, because it's not that easy for me to concentrate while touching Eight's chest. If this is what training is going to be like, I could get used to it.

"Thanks," says Eight, when I step back.

On the other side of the room, Nine has grabbed one of the stuffed Mogadorian training dummies and dumped it on the ground. He stands over it, looking at us.

"Okay, here's the game. We're going to pretend this dummy is—I don't know—Number Four. He gets hurt all the time, right? So, he's wounded and, Marina, you need to get to him and work your magic. Eight, you're going to help her."

"And what are you going to be doing?" I ask.

"I'm going to be the surprisingly good-looking Mogadorian that's standing in your way."

Eight and I exchange a look. "Two on one?" he says. "Sounds easy."

"Cool," says Nine, extending his pipe staff and twirling it menacingly over his head. "Let's see what you got."

Eight puts his arm around me, pulling me into a quick huddle. "He expects us to go right at him," he whispers.

I nod, catching on to the plan quickly. "You should just teleport the body back to me."

Eight holds his hand up to me for a quick high five, then spins back to face Nine. "Ready?"

"Bring it on."

Eight starts forward and Nine stalks out to meet him in the center of the room. As soon as he's drawn Nine a few yards away from the dummy, Eight disappears, reappearing over the dummy. It's not that Nine doesn't notice what Eight's up to—he just doesn't care. He bounds a few steps forward, coming straight for me. Caught off guard and more than a little nervous with Nine charging me, I backpedal. Nine is far too quick for me.

When Eight reappears with the dummy, Nine is standing with the tip of his staff pressed against the side of my neck.

"Good job," he says to Eight. "Now you've got a wounded friend and a dead healer."

I've never trained like this before, so Nine coming right at me felt really intimidating. I have to get over that feeling. I know Six wouldn't have just let Nine put that staff up to her throat. I need to prove to these boys that even though I don't have the offensive firepower they do, I can still fight back.

With Nine distracted by Eight, I slap the point of his staff away from my neck.

"Not dead yet," I say, as I lunge forward and punch him in the mouth. Immediately, a flare of pain courses through my hand and wrist.

Nine staggers back a step as Eight whoops with happy surprise. Nine whips his head back around to look at me, blood lining his teeth as he grins.

"Good!" he shouts, delighted. "You're getting it!"

"I think I broke my thumb," I reply, looking down at my swollen knuckles.

"Next time, keep your thumb outside your fingers when you punch," Eight says, balling up his fist to demonstrate.

I nod, feeling sort of dumb that I'd make such a basic mistake, but also a little thrilled that I just socked Nine right in the face. He seems to have appreciated it too, looking at me with a newfound respect as he wipes the blood off his face. I touch my hand, again feeling the icy sensation of my Legacy, intensified this time as it passes into my own hand.

Nine has picked up the dummy and dumped it back on the other side of the room. "Ready to try again?"

Eight and I huddle up for a second time. "Maybe I should introduce him to our old friend Narasimha?"

"Which one is that?"

"Lots of arms, lots of claws."

"Sounds perfect," I say. "Keep him busy and I'll flank him."

We break our huddle and Eight immediately transforms into one of his massive avatars. His handsome features melt away, replaced by the snarling face and golden mane of a lion. He grows to about twelve feet, ten arms sprouting out of his sides, each of them tipped with razor-sharp claws. Nine whistles through his teeth.

"Now we're talking," Nine says. "One of your parents must've been a Chimæra. Probably your mom."

"Funny," replies Eight, his voice a gravelly roar while in this shape.

I stay behind Eight as he stalks towards Nine, waiting for an opening to make a break for the dummy. Eight lunges forward, slashing at Nine with all his arms, forcing Nine to duck and weave away, parrying some of the blows with his staff. Nine prods at Eight with his staff, trying to keep him at bay, looking for an opening of his own.

As Nine twirls his staff for a counterattack, focused on Eight, I see a chance to make a difference. I reach out with my telekinesis and yank Nine's staff out of his hands. He's not expecting it, so the force sends him off balance, right into the waiting claws of Eight. Nine is slashed across the chest, his shirt torn to ribbons, the skin beneath cut open in gashes wide enough to need stitches. Both Eight and I hesitate at the sight of those wounds.

"I didn't mean to get you that bad," says Eight, the sympathy not really coming through his lion-head rumble.

Nine's eyes have lit up, though. "It's nothing!" he

shouts. "Keep going!"

I've never seen anyone so excited by the sight of his own blood.

Just like that, Nine is on the run. Eight gives chase, but he's lumbering in this form and Nine is freakishly quick with his super-speed Legacy. Nine races up the nearest wall and flips over the charging Eight. He manages to land right on Eight's back, with one of his arms hooked around his neck. Being so large, it's nearly impossible for Eight to reach around and get at Nine, which must've been exactly what Nine had planned. With his free hand, Nine starts punching Eight, aiming for the pointy ears that poke through the tufts of his mane.

Eight roars in pain and then reverts to his normal shape. He crumples beneath Nine's weight.

Meanwhile, with Nine distracted, I make a run for the dummy.

"Watch out, Marina!" Eight shouts.

I hear Nine's pounding footsteps behind me. Behind me and above me. I roll to the side just as Nine dives off the ceiling, trying that same jump-kick move he used to surprise Eight. Missing me, Nine rolls, putting himself between me and the dummy.

Nine's staff is just a few feet away. As he starts advancing towards me, I grab it with my telekinesis and send it flying at his head.

The blow smacks Nine in the back of the head, making

him stagger, and giving me an opening to sprint past him. He shakes it off quickly, though, and is right back on my tail.

Out of the corner of my eye, I see Eight has gotten unsteadily back to his feet.

"Slide!" he shouts.

Not thinking, just acting, I do as Eight says. I slide to the ground like a baseball player would. I see Eight start to throw a punch at thin air, but in the middle of the motion he teleports. He reappears right in front of me. I go sliding between his legs and his punch goes sailing over my head, right into Nine's jaw. Running full speed and suddenly stopped by a right cross, Nine is flipped head over heels.

I scramble to my feet and reach the dummy. I place my hands over an imaginary wound and shout, "Healed!"

There's a moment where the room is totally silent except for the three of us breathing heavily. Eight sits down hard, gently rubbing the side of his face. I notice that his ear is swollen closed and his neck is puffy with fresh abrasions from where Nine was punching him, so the damage he endures in his other forms must be carried over to his regular one.

Nine lies on his back, groaning. His chest is shredded from where Eight slashed him, he's got a fresh black eye, and I think I notice a trickle of blood from where I struck him with his staff. Suddenly, his groans turn to laughter.

"That was awesome!" Nine hollers.

Psychotic as his love of violence might seem, I find myself smiling and agreeing with Nine. That was actually a really good workout. It felt amazing to be able to push myself like that in an environment that wasn't life or death.

"Man," says Nine, picking himself up from the ground. "I had no way to dodge that last punch. Good move, dude."

Eight turns his bruised face up towards Nine. "Yeah. I owed you one. Or, like, ten."

I kneel down next to Eight and start healing his injuries. The icy feeling isn't so startling anymore; in fact, it's starting to feel more and more natural.

"Why'd you shape shift back?" Nine asks, picking at the gashes on his chest. "That lion dude bullshit was giving me fits."

"I have to really concentrate to keep the form," explains Eight. "Getting my head bashed in was definitely not helping my focus."

"Okay," says Nine, thinking this over. "Sandor's got some nonlethal weaponry stashed somewhere. You should let me shoot stuff at you, and we'll work on keeping your concentration."

"Yeah," Eight says dryly, "sounds like a blast."

With Eight's face returned to its far more appealing not-bruised state, I start to work on Nine's wounds. "You know," I tell him, "you're actually really good at this."

"Fighting? Uh, yeah, I know."

"Not just fighting. I guess, um, thinking about fighting."

"Strategizing," puts in Eight. "She's right. I don't think I would've come up with that teleport punch if you hadn't pushed me. And awful as getting shot at sounds, I actually think that practicing might be a good idea."

Nine puffs up, even more than usual. "Well, you're welcome."

"Don't let it go to your head," I say, watching the last cut on his chest slowly knit closed beneath my fingertips.

I glance up at Nine to find him looking past me, towards the doorway of the Lecture Hall. "Hey Ella," he says, "did we wake you up?"

I turn around to see Ella standing in the doorway. She's dressed in street clothes, the first time I've seen her out of pajamas or one of Nine's baggy flannels in days. I'd think her getting dressed was progress, except her eyes are red-rimmed from crying. Ella doesn't look at any of us, her eyes pinned to the floor.

"What's wrong, Ella?" I ask, taking a few steps towards her.

"I—I just wanted to say good-bye," Ella replies. "I'm leaving."

"Like hell," says Nine. "No more field trips today."

Ella shakes her head, her hair whipping around her face. "No. I have to. And I'm not coming back."

"What's gotten into you?" I ask. And that's when I notice it. Clutched tightly in Ella's hands, practically crumpled from the way she keeps wringing it, is a piece of paper. Crayton's letter.

"I'm not one of you," Ella whispers, fresh tears streaking down her cheeks.

CHAPTER
TEN

My dearest Ella,

If you are reading this, then I dread the worst has already happened. Please know that I loved you as if you were my own daughter. I was never meant to be your Cêpan. The role was thrust upon me the night our planet fell, and it was not something I was prepared or trained for. All the same, I would not trade away these years with you for anything on Lorien or Earth. I hope I have done enough for you. I know you are destined for great things.

I hope that one day you can understand the things that I've done, the lies that I've told you, and find it within your heart to forgive me.

When you were small, I told you a lie. Soon, that one lie became many lies, and those lies became our life. I am sorry, Ella. I am a coward.

You are ten, in that only ten Garde survived the attack on Lorien, but you are not the Tenth. You were not a part of the

Elders' plan to preserve the Loric race, which is why you were not sent to Earth with the others. This is why you do not bear the same scars as Marina and Six. You were never under the protection of the Loric Charm.

The Elders did not select you. Your father did.

You hail from one of Lorien's oldest and proudest families. Your great-grandfather was one of the ten Elders that used to govern our world. This was in the time before our home planet reached its full potential, before our people unlocked the power of Lorien and, by living in harmony with the planet, were gifted with Legacies. Our young planet was at a crossroads, caught between a desire for rapid development and a need to protect what is natural and life-sustaining.

It was a time of death, a time still shrouded in mystery even to our greatest historians. During these dark ages, war raged amongst our people. Many perished in needless conflict, but eventually the forces of peace prevailed. A new age dawned on Lorien—the golden time that you were born into, and that the Mogadorians so brutally ended.

Your great-grandfather was one of the casualties of the Secret Wars, the conflict between the Mogadorians and the Loric that was covered up by our government to preserve the illusions of a Lorien utopia.

As a young man, your father, Raylan, became obsessed with this war. You see, after the war, when the surviving Elders reconvened, they limited their number to nine rather than the original ten. Your father believed that the vacant place amongst the Elders belonged to your family. Our Elders had never been chosen by ancestry or heredity, yet your father still believed that your family's house had somehow been wronged by history.

These obsessions made him into a bitter and distrustful man and Raylan became something of a recluse. He made a home for himself deep in the mountains—more a fortress than a home. For companions he kept a menagerie of Chimæra.

I was hired to tend your father's beasts. He cared for little except his secret histories and his animals.

Until he met your mother.

Erina was Garde, assigned by the Elders to keep an eye on your father. Some believed that he was a danger to our people. Erina saw something else in him. She saw a man who could be rescued from himself.

Your mother was beautiful. You remind me of her more and more every day. She had Legacies of flight and Elecomun, the power to manipulate currents of electricity. So she would fly above your father's home and create these brilliant displays, like fireworks made from lightning.

Your father distrusted Erina and openly challenged her reasons for coming to the mountains. Yet, night after night, he would come to the courtyard to watch your mother fly with the Chimæra.

One of your father's Legacies allowed him to manipulate the spectrum of light. It seems a silly thing—like your Aeturnus—but it has many uses. He could darken the world

around an enemy, making it hard for them to see. Or, in the
case of his courtship of your mother, he could change the colors
of her lightning strikes. Bright pinks and oranges ripped across
the sky at night. Your father, for the first time in many years,
was enjoying himself.

They fell in love and soon were married. And then, you came.

Erina had made many friends serving with the Garde and
they would come to visit, welcomed by your parents. They are
gone now.

The Mogadorians came. Our planet burned.

During his days as a recluse, your father had amassed a
sizable collection of relics that once belonged to your family.
He had even spent a large sum of money restoring an old
fuel-powered spaceship that he believed was used by your
great-grandfather in the last Loric war. When Erina moved
in, she convinced your father to donate many of these items to
a museum, the ship included. When the Mogadorians came,
they first destroyed our ports, cutting off any conventional
means of escape. Your father immediately thought of the old
ship waiting dormant in the museum.

While others on our planet fought against the invasion,
your father planned to escape. Somehow, he knew our people
were doomed.

Your mother would not flee. She insisted that they go and
join the fight. They argued, their most ferocious fight ever.

You were the compromise. Raylan promised to stay only if
you were allowed to escape. I can still remember your mother's

tear-streaked face as she kissed you good-bye. Your father pressed you into my arms and I was ordered to make a run for the museum. Raylan's menagerie of Chimæra joined us, acting as our bodyguards, many of them dying on the way.

This is how I became your Cêpan.

I watched our planet die through the portholes of a departing spaceship. I felt like a coward. The only time I ever stop feeling ashamed is when I look at you, Ella, and see what that cowardice saved.

What is done is done. You were not part of the Elders' plan. That does not make you any less Loric, or any less a Garde. Numbers do not matter. You are capable of greatness, Ella. You are a survivor. One day, I know, you will make our people proud.

I love you.

Forever, your faithful servant,

Crayton

I stop reading aloud and lower Crayton's letter with shaky hands. There are tears in my eyes. I can't imagine what it would feel like to have such a huge part of my identity just ripped away from me. Everyone is silent, even Nine. Ella makes a small snuffling sound, her arms wrapped tightly around herself.

"You're still one of us," I whisper to her. "You're Loric."

Ella starts to sob, choked words escaping her in a torrent. "I'm—I'm a fraud. I'm not like you. I'm just some rich guy's daughter who got launched off the planet because her dad was a creep."

"That's not true," says Eight, putting his arm around Ella.

"I wasn't chosen," Ella cries. "I'm not—it was all just lies."

Nine takes the letter out of my hands, glancing it over. "So what?" he says dismissively.

Ella looks at him, her eyes widening. "So what?"

"The charm is broken," Nine continues. "The numbers don't mean shit. You can be Ten, you can be Fifty-Four, it doesn't mean anything. Who cares?"

Nine sounds so callous, just brushing off what is such a major blow for Ella. She looks stunned. I'm not sure that she's even hearing Nine.

"What Nine is so indelicately trying to say," interjects Eight, "is that it doesn't matter how you got here. Just because we flew in on different ships doesn't mean we're not the same."

"Shit," grumbles Nine, "I wish there'd been more self-ish dudes like your pops. We could have a whole army."

I shoot Nine a look and he puts his hands up, making a zippering motion across his mouth. Even with Nine's total lack of tact, between the three of us, it seems like we've managed to calm Ella down. Her crying is slowing and, after a moment, she drops her hastily packed bag to the floor.

"I just feel so lost without Crayton," she whispers to me, her voice husky. "He died thinking he was a coward because he never told me the truth and—and he wasn't. He was good. I just wish I could tell him so."

She trails off, a fresh batch of tears wetting my neck as she cries. So that's what this is really about; it's not so much what Ella learned about herself, although I'm sure that was shocking, but what she learned about Crayton. I stroke her hair, just letting her cry.

"I wish every day I could have just one more conversation with my Cêpan," Eight says quietly.

"Me too," Nine agrees.

"It never gets easier," Eight continues. "We just have to keep going. To live up to what they expected us to be. Crayton was right, Ella. One day, you will make our people proud."

Ella pulls me and Eight into a hug. We stay like that for a while, until Nine steps forward to awkwardly pat Ella on the back. She looks up at him.

"Is that the best you can do?"

Nine sighs dramatically. "Fine."

He wraps his arms around the three of us and squeezes, practically lifting us off the floor. Eight groans and Ella lets out something that's part laugh and part wheeze. I'm getting crushed too, but I can't help smiling. I lock eyes with Ella and I can tell, right then, that there's no place else she'd rather be.

CHAPTER
ELEVEN

BY THE MIDDLE OF THE DAY WE'RE CRUISING
through Missouri, just a few hours away from Arkansas. It took us longer than expected to get out of Chicago,
Nine's tricked-out ride not having a super-spy special
feature to evaporate gridlock. At first I'm a little nervous with Sarah behind the wheel, the way she weaves
between lanes and seems to tailgate every chance she
gets, until I realize that all the other drivers are doing it
too. I guess that's just part of big-city driving.

With Chicago behind us, the highway opens up.
There's nothing but grain fields on either side of us. We
zip past semitrucks as they rumble along, making good
time now, not even having to use the nitrous Sandor
installed. The last thing in the world we need is to be
pulled over. I bet I'm still red flagged in most government databases, not that any of us even has a license for
a highway patrolman to run, which is another potential

problem in and of itself. When we make it back to Chicago, I need to see if Sandor left any forgery material around. We need some new fake IDs.

"You ever try turning a whole car invisible?" Sarah asks Six, who hasn't said much since we set out. She lounges in the backseat with Bernie Kosar in her lap. "I mean, you are touching it."

"Huh," Six replies, sitting up. "Never tried it."

"Don't," I say, maybe a bit too sharply. "Someone could crash right into us."

"Thanks, John. If you hadn't said anything, I probably would've just turned us invisible here in public, while we're flying along at like seventy miles per hour. Good thing you're here to keep me in check and Sarah from driving too fast."

I open my mouth for a comeback, something about how Six is a bit of a loose cannon and I can't predict what she might do next—like invite my girlfriend along on a dangerous mission—but think better of it when I notice Sarah looking at me. Her eyebrow is raised, like she's confused by Six's tone. She's probably been picking up on the bad vibes between Six and me since we left Chicago. It's definitely not something I want to try explaining, so I just shrug, brushing the whole thing off.

Six is right that I've been obsessively checking our speed. Every time Sarah's foot gets heavy on the gas, I tap her gently on the leg. She slows down and looks at me apologetically, like it's not her fault, the car just begs to be driven fast. Maybe I shouldn't be so anal and just let her race down the highway, consequences be damned. That's probably what Six or Nine would do.

Every moment, I'm dreading the feeling of a new scar burning itself into the flesh of my leg. What if the Mogadorians get to Five before we do, all because I wouldn't let Sarah floor it?

These are the kinds of thoughts that I've been losing sleep over the last few nights—not specifically about Five, but on leading our group in general. There's just no way to plan for every eventuality, no matter how hard I think things over. It'd be so much easier if I had an attitude like Nine's where I could just go out and hit things.

And to top it off, there's suddenly this drama with Six. All because of one stupid kiss.

Basically, there's no aspect of my life right now where I don't feel in over my head.

We end up stopping at a gas station in Missouri. Six busies herself pumping the gas. Bernie Kosar ambles around the parking lot, sniffing the pavement and stretching his legs. Sarah and I head towards the store to pick up some bottles of water and pay for the gas. About halfway across the parking lot, she stops abruptly.

"So," she says, "maybe you should go talk with Six."

I blink at her, taken aback. I glance behind us at Six. If it was possible for someone to pump gas angrily, she'd be doing it. The way she jams the nozzle into the gas tank, it's like she's stabbing a Mogadorian. "Why?"

"You two are obviously mad at each other about something," Sarah says. "Go work it out."

I don't know what to say, so I just stand there awkwardly. I can't tell Sarah what Six and I are arguing about because, first of all, I'm not even entirely sure and, second of all, it sort of involves our relationship. I really don't want to get into all this right now; especially not when we have more important things we should be worried about.

Sarah is unmoved by my silent protest, smiling slightly as she shoos me back towards Six. "Come on, you two need to be able to work together."

She's right, of course. We can't have whatever weirdness that exists between me and Six bog down this mission.

Six watches me approach through narrowed eyes. She jams the fuel pump back into its home with way more force than necessary. We stand looking at each other from opposite sides of the car.

"We should talk," I say.

"Sarah made you come over here, didn't she?"

"Look, I know you don't really like her—"

"That's just it, John," she interrupts. "I do like Sarah.

And she loves you."

I stare at Six, trying to sort this out. "All right, I get that you're mad at me because we haven't really talked about everything since going to Chicago. With Sarah around it just seemed . . . weird."

"John, I'm not mad at you because we kissed and now you're back with your girlfriend. I thought I liked you, John. You know, as more than a friend. But then I got dumped in that cell with Sarah and saw the way she talked about you. And now every day I see the two of you together. Whatever was between us back when we were on the run, it's not like what you and Sarah have. Watching the two of you is almost enough to make me believe Henri's crap about Loric only falling in love once."

I nod, agreeing with Six. What she's saying is definitely true, but how am I supposed to respond? *Yeah, you're right, I totally like Sarah better than you*? It's probably better if I just keep my mouth shut.

"I guess," Six continues, "I feel shitty for kissing you while you were supposed to be with Sarah."

"In our defense," I say, "we did think she'd sold us out to the government."

"It was also our first time meeting other Garde. Once that excitement was over, you were always waiting to go back to Sarah, huh?"

"It wasn't like that at all, Six. I wasn't thinking

ahead, or biding my time, or whatever." My mind drifts back to that moonlit walk Six and I took, holding hands so we could be invisible. "When we were together, I'm not sure I'd ever felt so comfortable with another person before. Like I could just be myself."

For a moment, Six's hard voice turns almost wistful. "Yeah, me too."

"But it's different with Sarah," I say, gently. "I love her. I'm more sure of that now than ever before."

Six claps her hands as if the matter is settled. "Good. So, let's forget about it. You and I are just friends, and you and Sarah are the happy couple. I'm cool with that. All this love triangle crap makes me want to barf."

"Six . . . ," I start, not really sure what to say. It almost feels like she's letting me off the hook here, or trying to push me away.

"No, listen," Six says, cutting me off. "I'm sorry I got into your business with Sarah. Whether or not you want to tell her about us kissing is your thing. I don't care. I just . . ." She glances over to the gas station, where Sarah is finally emerging. "When I got tossed in that cell with her, the way she talked about you—she's given up so much to be with you, John. She's basically betting her life on you. Maybe I'm being nosy and it isn't my place, but I just want to make sure you're up for that."

"I'm trying to be," I say to Six, and turn to watch

Sarah approach. What Six said rings true. I know Sarah has given up a normal life to be here with me, facing danger. I love her, but I haven't figured out how to strike the right balance between keeping her safe and letting her be involved in my chaotic life. I might never figure that out. Right now, it's enough that she's here with me.

Six calls for Bernie Kosar and they get back into the car. Sarah stops in front of me, her eyebrows raised.

"Everything cool?"

I have the sudden urge to wrap her in a hug, so I do. She makes a surprised little noise and I kiss her on the cheek. She squeezes me back.

"Everything's cool," I say.

I take over driving when we leave the gas station. BK crawls into Sarah's lap and paws at the window until she rolls it down. The car floods with cool spring air. BK hangs his head out the window, his beagle tongue lolling out of his mouth. I guess Chimæra or dog, it still feels good to have the wind hitting your face as you cruise down a highway.

The fresh air feels pretty good to me too. I don't know if everything will ever be squared away between Six and me, but I feel better after our talk. At least I know where I stand now. The mood in the car has changed; there's not as much tension hanging between the three of us. I relax a little, leaning back in my seat, watching the mile markers skip by.

Sarah gently taps my leg. "Too fast."

I smile guiltily and slow down. Sarah has her arm out the window, her hand flat as she lets it surf across the currents of wind. Her blond hair is blown about her face wildly. She looks beautiful. For a moment, I pretend that it's just the two of us and we're on a road trip to someplace fun and normal. I still believe that could happen for us one day. If I didn't, there'd be no reason to keep fighting.

Sarah meets my eyes and I swear she must read my mind. She rests her hand on my leg.

"I know we're on a serious mission here," Sarah says, "but what if we were just taking a regular road trip, like normal people? Where would you go?"

"Hmm," I reply, thinking it over. My fantasy with Sarah and myself didn't really have a destination. It was enough just to be in a car with her. "So many options . . ."

Before I can decide, Six leans forward from the backseat. "I didn't really get to see much of it when we were there because of all the running and fighting, but Spain looked pretty interesting."

Sarah grins. "I've always wanted to go to Europe. My parents backpacked there after college. It's how they met."

"So Europe is your answer too?" I ask Sarah.

"Yeah," she replies. "There are still places I'd like to

see in America, I guess. Getting locked up by the government has kinda soured me, though."

"That is a drawback," I agree, chuckling.

Sarah turns around in her seat to look at Six. "We could go to Europe together. Um, if you're not too busy restoring your planet and all."

Sarah's so enthusiastic that Six can't help but smile back. "That could be fun."

"That's where I'd like to go," I tell Sarah, putting my hand over hers.

"Europe?"

"Lorien."

"Oh," Sarah replies, a note of sadness in her voice surprising me. I try to explain.

"I'd like to show you Lorien the way I've seen it in my visions, the way Henri used to describe it to me."

I catch Six rolling her eyes at me in the rearview mirror. "That's not really the game," she says. "Pick someplace that you could actually get to without building a spaceship."

I think it over for a moment. "I don't know. Disney World?"

Six and Sarah both exchange a look and then start laughing.

"Disney World?" exclaims Six. "You're so cheesy, John."

"No, it's sweet," says Sarah, patting my hand. "It's

THE FALL OF FIVE

the most magical place on Earth."

"You know, I've never actually been on a roller coaster. Henri wasn't down with the whole amusement-park thing. I used to see the commercials and I always wanted to go."

"That's so sad!" exclaims Sarah. "We're definitely going to get you to Disney World. Or at least on a roller coaster. They're amazing."

Six snaps her fingers. "What's that one ride? It's supposed to be like a rocket ship?"

"Space Mountain," answers Sarah.

"Yeah," replies Six, and then hesitates as if she's worried she's about to divulge too much. "I actually remember looking that up online when I was little. I insisted to Katarina that it had something to do with us."

The thought of a young Six investigating Disney World is priceless. The three of us share a laugh.

"Aliens," mutters Sarah jokingly. "You need to get out more."

CHAPTER TWELVE

NIGHT HAS FALLEN BY THE TIME WE CROSS THE Arkansas state line. Luckily, we know exactly where we're going. The billboards started popping up about twenty miles back, the huge and hairy face of the Boggy Creek Monster inviting us to visit Fouke's one-and-only Monster Mart. We're close now, and the tree-lined highway is pretty desolate, so I break my own rule and really start gunning it.

Sarah peers out her window, craning her neck at one of the faded Monster Mart signs.

"Just a couple more miles," she says quietly.

"Are you ready?" I ask, sensing some apprehension in her voice.

"I hope so," she says.

I pull the car over just before the exit for Fouke. This isn't exactly a thriving tourist destination. More like the kind of dinky small-town thing that bored traveling families will stop off at to snap a few pictures and get a bathroom break.

"Probably a good idea to go on foot from here," I say, glancing at Six. "We'll want to be invisible."

Six nods. "Agreed."

We pile out of the car and into the dark woods that separate the highway from the town. Bernie Kosar briefly stretches his legs before taking on the form of a sparrow. He lands on my shoulder, awaiting instructions.

"Scout ahead, BK," I say. "See what's up there."

As BK soars off into the night, the three of us ready ourselves. I snap my bracelet onto my wrist; I certainly haven't missed the painful tingling feeling I get whenever I wear it, but I'll definitely feel safer with it on. I tuck my dagger into the back of my pants. Watching me, Sarah takes her gun out of her backpack and shoves it into the waistband of her jeans as well. All those road-trip fantasies of a couple hours ago are gone. It's time for action. We start into the woods, the dim lights of Fouke about a mile away through the trees. Sarah grabs hold of my arm.

"Do you think we'll see the Boggy Creek Monster?" she asks, widening her eyes in mock terror. "From the pictures, it looks a lot like Bigfoot. Maybe we can make friends."

Six warily scans the woods around us. "Some dumb

folk legend isn't the monster I'm worried about running into."

"Besides," I add, trying to keep things light for Sarah's benefit, "who needs a sasquatch when we've got Nine waiting for us back in Chicago?"

Like Six, I'm also searching the woods for any sign of Mogadorian ambush. It's eerily quiet out here, the dead branches that crunch beneath our feet sounding like fireworks. I hope that we've beaten the Mogs to Five's location, that they weren't as quick to figure out his weird riddle as we were. The fact that there isn't a new scar on my ankle and that the small town up ahead doesn't appear to be engulfed by flames from a recent battle are both really good signs. Still, we have to stay on our guard. There's no telling what might be waiting for us up ahead.

As we get closer, Six reaches her hands out to us. Sarah has to let go of my arm to take hold of Six. I wish there was time for one last hug, just a quick moment to reassure her. With each of us holding one of Six's hands, she turns us invisible. We walk on.

We're deep in the woods, the highway far behind us, when I notice BK gliding in circles through the trees.

Down here, I call out to him.

I let go of Six's hand so that BK can see us. He flutters down, transforming into a squirrel as soon as he hits the ground.

"BK says there's a guy up ahead," I tell them. "No sign of any trouble."

"Good. Let's move."

I take Six's hand and we pick up the pace, soon emerging from the woods and into the small town of Fouke. It really isn't much more than just a pit stop. The road that connects to the highway exit continues on to the east. I see a few small houses in that direction and what I assume is the town proper. Where we are is pretty much the beginning of the town, right where travelers would pull off from the road. There's a two-pump gas station next to us and a post office across the street. All the windows are dark, everything closed and locked up for the night.

And then, there's the Monster Mart.

The billboards on the way into town really over-sold it. The Monster Mart is really just a convenience store with Boggy Creek Monster T-shirts and hats on sale in the window. The main attraction is the twelve-foot wooden statue of the Boggy Creek Monster, a hairy beast that looks like it's part man, part bear, and part gorilla. Even at this distance, I can see the statue is pretty much covered in bird poop.

"There!" whispers Sarah excitedly.

I see him too. There's a boy up ahead, sitting cross-legged at the base of the statue. He looks bored as he unwraps a sandwich from some wax paper. A backpack rests next to him, but no sign of a Loric Chest that I can tell. I expected him to at least have that. It would've made it easy to identify him. Then again, it would've made it easier for the Mogadorians too.

I start forward, but Six stays planted, not letting go of my hand.

"What is it?" I whisper.

"I don't know," she replies quietly. "He's just out here all alone? It all seems too easy. Like a trap."

"Maybe," I say, looking around again doubtfully. There are no signs of life except for us and the boy at the statue. If the Mogadorians are lying in wait, they're doing a really good job hiding.

"Maybe he just got lucky," Sarah whispers. "I mean, he has managed to stay hidden longer than the rest of you."

"How do we know he is who he says he is?" Six continues.

"Only one way to find out," I say.

I let go of Six's hand and start across the street.

I don't try to conceal my approach. He notices me almost as soon as I step away from Six and into the yellow glow of the streetlights. He drops his sandwich and hops quickly to his feet, reaching both hands into his pockets. For a moment I think he's about to pull some kind of weapon on me and I feel my Lumen start to warm up in anticipation. Instead, he pulls two small balls from his pockets, one of them a rubber bouncy ball and the other a steel ball bearing. He rolls them deftly across his knuckles, watching anxiously as I approach. It's like some kind of nervous tic.

I stop a few yards away from him.

"Hey."

"Uh, hey," he replies.

At this distance I can finally get a good look at our would-be Five. He's about my age, shorter and stockier, not necessarily chubby but definitely built like a barrel. His hair is brown and short, a military buzz-cut style. He's wearing one of those goofy Boggy Creek Monster T-shirts and a pair of baggy jeans.

"Are you waiting for me?" I ask, not wanting to just come out and ask if he's Loric. He could be some weird country kid eating a sandwich at night all by himself, I guess.

"I don't know," he replies. "Let me see your leg."

I hesitate for a moment, then reach down and lift up the leg of my pants. He breathes a sigh of relief as he looks over my scars. Then, he lifts up his jeans and shows me his matching set. Through some deft sleight of hand, the two balls disappear back into his pocket and then Five strides forward, his now-empty hand extended.

"I'm Five," he says.

"Four," I reply. "My friends call me John."

"A human name," he says. "Man, I've had too many of those to even remember."

We shake hands. His grip is like a vise, he's so excited. For a moment, I'm worried he won't let go. I clear my throat and try to discreetly tug my hand away.

"Sorry," he says, dropping my hand awkwardly. "I'm just psyched. I've waited so long for this. I wasn't sure anyone would see my message. It's not easy making a crop circle, you know? I didn't want to do it again."

"Yeah, that wasn't such a good idea," I say. I start looking around again, still worried that Mogadorians are going to appear at any moment. Crickets chirp nearby and beyond that I hear the sound of engines from the highway. Nothing to get nervous about, but I still can't shake the feeling of being exposed.

"Not a good idea?" Five says excitedly. "But you found me! It worked. Did I do something wrong?"

Five seems so eager to please, like he's just waiting for me to congratulate him on his crop-burning stunt. It's as if he never considered it could attract unwanted attention, which strikes me as naïve. Maybe I'm judging him too harshly, but he seems soft to me. Sheltered. Or maybe I've spent too much time around hard cases like Six and Nine.

"Don't worry about it," I tell him, "it's fine. We should get going."

"Oh," he mutters, his face falling. He looks away from me, scanning the area. "Is it just you? I hoped maybe you'd gotten together with some of the others."

On cue, Six and Sarah materialize at my side. Five stumbles backwards, nearly tripping over his backpack.

Six steps forward. "I'm Six," she says, blunt as ever. "John is too nice to tell you that your crop-circle stunt probably could've gotten you killed. It was stupid. You're lucky we got here first."

Five frowns, looking from Six to me. "Wow. I'm sorry. I didn't mean to cause trouble. I just—I didn't know what else to do."

"It's okay," I say, nodding at his pack. "Grab your stuff. We can talk it out on the road."

"Where are we going?"

"We're bringing you back to the others," I say. "We're all together now. It's time to start the fight."

"You're all together?"

I nod. "You're the last one."

"Wow," Five says, looking almost embarrassed. "Sorry I'm late to the party."

"Come on," I say, waving again at his pack. "We really need to move."

Five leans down and grabs his backpack, and then looks at Sarah, who's been standing by silently. "What number are you?"

She shakes her head. "I'm just Sarah," she says, smiling.

"A human ally," breathes Five, shaking his head.

"Guys, my mind is officially blown."

Six shoots me a look of bewilderment. I've got the same feeling. Maybe we've been through too many fights and close calls, but it seems like Five is way too casual. We should already be on the move, away from this place, and he just wants to stand here and chat.

"Look," Six snaps, "we can't just stand around gabbing. They could be co—"

Six is cut off by the sudden roar of a noise overhead. It's a sound made by no earthly machinery. We all look up just as the silver Mogadorian ship throws on its floodlights, momentarily blinding us. Five, shielding his eyes, turns to look at me.

"Is that your ship?" he asks.

"Mogadorians!" I shout at him. Already, dark shapes are descending from the ship, the first wave of Mogadorian warriors on their way to attack.

"Oh," says Five, blinking confusedly at the ship. "So that's what they look like."

CHAPTER
THIRTEEN

"GET THE XITHARIS STONE OUT!" I SHOUT TO
Six. "If we all go invisible now, we can get away before
they're on us." She begins fumbling through her bag
and pulls it out, but it's too late.

Before she can do anything, the air around us crackles as the first wave of Mogadorians let loose with
blaster fire.

My bracelet expands just in time to deflect a pair of
shots that would've hit me right in the chest.

Instead, the fire hits the ground close enough to Six
to send her toppling backwards. As she's falling, she
tosses Five the Xitharis Stone, but he just stares at it,
clearly unsure of what it is. There's no time to school
him. Beyond the first group of Mogs, I can see more
of them zipping down on ropes from the belly of their
ship. We're going to be outnumbered in a bad way soon.

Sarah has already dived behind a nearby parked car.

On her side in the dirt, she squeezes off shots with her pistol. I watch the first two kick up dirt at the feet of the nearest Mogadorian, and then the third nails him right in the sternum. The Mog disintegrates and Sarah takes aim on another.

Six went invisible as soon as she hit the dirt. I'm not sure where she is now but storm clouds are suddenly roiling overhead on what moments ago was a calm and clear night. She's definitely getting ready to strike.

Five is next to me, rooted in place, still staring at the rock in his hand. My shield is taking a lot of blaster fire now. Five would probably have already been gunned down if he wasn't right next to me.

"What are you doing?" I scream at him, roughly grabbing his arm. "We have to move!"

Five's eyes are wide and unresponsive. He lets me pull him backwards. I toss him to the ground behind the statue of the Boggy Creek Monster. The wooden statue quickly explodes into a thousand charred pieces, but the concrete base holds off the rest of the blaster fire for now. I let my Lumen ignite on my unshielded hand, building up a sizable fireball. Five watches me, staring in shock at the swirling flames. I ignore him for the moment and lean out from cover, launching the fireball at the nearest group of Mogs. It engulfs three of them, turning them to ash instantly. The rest scatter.

I hear raindrops starting to fall, although none are

hitting me. In fact, the rain seems localized over by the Mogadorian ship. Thunder rumbles. Whatever Six's play is, I trust her.

"Are you all right?" I shout over to Sarah. The car she's hiding behind is only a few yards away, but it feels like the length of an entire battlefield.

"I'm fine!" she yells back. "You?"

"I'm good, but I think Five is shell shocked or something!"

I notice three Mogadorians cutting across the street, trying to flank Sarah. Before they can, I reach out with my telekinesis and yank their blasters out of their hands. Seeing them, Sarah shoots the closest one right between the eyes. Before the rest can draw their swords, a lithe shape lunges at them from the shadows.

Bernie Kosar in the form of a panther, his black fur nearly indistinguishable from the night, tears out the throat of a Mog he's pinned down, then slashes the other across the face. That group decimated, BK slinks around the side of the car, staying close to Sarah.

Keep her safe, I direct the thought at BK.

The Mogs that I scattered before are already regrouping, or maybe it's just another group descended from the ship. I sling two more fireballs in their direction. That should keep them busy for a moment.

I grab Five and shake him until he looks at me. The shoulder of his shirt is singed from where my hand was still too hot from the Lumen. He flinches, staring at me with wide eyes.

"What the hell is the matter with you?" I yell.

"I'm—I'm sorry," he stammers. "I've never seen a Mogadorian before."

I look at him in disbelief. "Are you kidding me?!"

"No! Albert, my Cêpan, he told me about them. We trained for—for fighting. I've just never actually done it."

"Great," growls Six, suddenly materializing next to us. "We've got a total rookie."

"I—I can help," Five mumbles. "I was just caught off guard."

I'm not feeling too convinced, and although we fought the first wave of Mogadorians off, I can still see their shapes moving through the darkness nearby.

"Is it over?" shouts Sarah from her position. "Because I'm almost out of bullets!"

"There are more coming," I yell back to Sarah, and then look at Six. "Can you take down their ship?"

Six concentrates for a moment. Lightning shears through the night sky, right into the side of the Mogadorian ship. It rocks back and forth, and I can see some Mog soldiers lose their grip on their ropes and plummet fifty feet to the ground. She's cooked up one serious storm and is just waiting to unleash its full fury.

"They might've flown in here," Six says, "but they sure as shit won't be flying out."

I look down at Five. His shaky hands have retrieved those two balls from his pockets once again. Not exactly confidence inspiring.

I glance over at Sarah and see her taking aim and hitting a Mogadorian that was trying to creep up on us. Not long ago, this is the kind of fight we would've run from, happy to just escape with our lives. Now, though, I feel like it's a fight we can actually win.

I lock eyes with Six. "Let's send Setrákus Ra a message. If he wants to get one of ours, he's going to need to send more than one ship."

"Hell yeah," answers Six, and raises both her hands to the sky.

The dark clouds around the Mogadorian ship begin to roil and swirl. Three bolts of lightning slice through the tumultuous sky, striking the side of the ship in rapid succession. I can see pieces of the metal hull breaking loose and careening to the ground below.

Probably realizing that they're in trouble, the Mogs try to gain some altitude and get away from the localized storm. The Mogs already on the ground redouble their efforts to get to us, blaster fire sizzling through the air. I inch closer to Six so that my shield will deflect any stray shots that come her way. Sarah stays hunkered down behind the car, firing blindly over the hood.

"You need to hurry up!" I shout at Six through gritted teeth.

"Almost there," she snaps, her face tight with concentration.

Hailstones the size of fists buffet the ship, causing it to shake erratically. Just when it seems like it might be able to pull upwards, Six twists her hands over her head. The clouds suddenly coalesce—I can feel the force of the winds from back here—a tornado gathering right beneath the ship. The ship lurches and then tips sideways, its pilots losing control.

The ship plummets to the ground, landing with a thunderous crash in the woods by the highway. Seconds later, a tower of flame shoots into the night sky, followed by a thunderous explosion. Then, everything is quiet. The storm overhead clears and the night is peaceful once again.

"Wow," murmurs Five.

"Nice work," I tell Six.

Her eyes have already moved to her next targets. We might have taken down their ship, but there are still plenty of Mogadorians approaching. A couple dozen, at least. Blasters and swords at the ready.

"Let's finish them off," Six says, turning invisible.

I'm eager to jump into the fight. First, I look down at Number Five. He's peeking at the incoming Mogadorians uncertainly.

"It's okay if you're not ready for this," I tell him. "Hang back."

Five nods mutely. I step out from behind what's left of the Boggy Creek Monster statue. Immediately, there's a Mogadorian leveling his blaster at me. Before he can shoot, something hits him in the back of the knees from behind. The sword he carries strapped across his shoulders is unsheathed by invisible hands and plunged through his spine. He disintegrates and, briefly, through the cloud of ash, I can make out Six's silhouette.

I run to where Sarah is still crouched behind a parked car. The side that faced the Mogadorians is melted in spots but Sarah appears unharmed. As soon as I slide to the ground beside her, Bernie Kosar sprouts wings and takes off, hurling himself at a pair of Mogs. The remaining Mogadorians look almost confused. Their ship destroyed, half their number already killed—I doubt they were expecting a fight like this. Good, let them be the scared ones for once.

"You okay?" I ask Sarah.

"Yeah," she replies breathlessly. She holds up her gun. "I'm out."

I reach out with my telekinesis and reel in one of the discarded Mogadorian blasters. Sarah plucks it out of the air.

"Cover me," I tell her. "We're finishing this."

I stride out from behind the car, practically daring the Mogadorians to come at me. A pair hunkered down in front of the gas station fire at me. My shield deploys immediately, absorbing their shots. I think about hurling a fireball at them, but I don't want to blow up the gas station. We've already damaged poor Fouke, Arkansas, enough.

I use my telekinesis to grab their blasters, smashing them to the ground. Then, I raise my hand to the Mogs and motion for them to come on. They grin, their tiny teeth gleaming in the moonlight, and unsheathe their swords. They sprint towards me.

As soon as they're a safe distance from the gas station, I launch a fireball that engulfs them both. Idiots.

Another group of Mogs has regrouped enough to make a focused assault. They charge me all at once, trying to surround me. Before they can close in, I feel something rubbery wrap itself tightly around my waist and I'm yanked backwards, away from the incoming Mogs. Startled, I look down. An arm is coiled around me. A really long, stretched-out arm.

As soon as I'm clear, Sarah starts lighting up the group of Mogs with blaster fire.

I look back down in time to see Five's arm coil back to its normal shape and return to his T-shirt. He looks at me sheepishly.

"Sorry if I interrupted," he says, "thought you might get pinned down."

"What did you just do?" I ask, both curious and a little grossed out.

"My Cêpan called it Externa," Five explains. He holds up the rubber ball that he's been fondling since we showed up. "It's one of my Legacies. I can take on the qualities of whatever I'm touching."

"Nice," I reply. Maybe the new guy isn't so useless after all.

One of the Mogadorians manages to skirt Sarah's blaster fire and charge us. Five steps in front of me. His skin suddenly gleams in the moonlight, shiny and silver. I remember the other ball he was carrying— a steel ball bearing. The Mog swings his sword at Five in an arc that should cleave right into his forehead, but with a resounding clang, the sword bounces off Five's head. The Mog is stunned as Five winds up, delivering a massive haymaker, his steel-coated hand crushing the Mog's skull.

Five looks back at me. "Never, uh, actually tried that before." He starts laughing, relieved.

"Seriously?" I can't help but laugh too, Five's nervous energy contagious. "What if it hadn't worked?"

Five just shrugs, rubbing the spot on his forehead where the Mog's sword made contact.

We turn to watch a pair of Mogadorians fleeing towards the woods, Bernie Kosar snarling at their heels. Before they reach the tree line, Six appears in front of them. She slashes through them both with her borrowed Mogadorian sword.

I look around. The area is clear. The Monster Mart and its surroundings are pock-marked from blaster fire, and there's still a plume of smoke curling up from the woods. Besides the dark patches on the ground where the dead Mogadorians turned to ash, there is no sign of our attackers. We wiped them out.

Sarah walks over to us, the Mog blaster propped up on her shoulder. "Is that it?"

"I think so," I say, keeping my voice level. I feel like fist-pumping and high-fiving, but want to keep it cool. "For once, I think we caught them by surprise."

"Is it always this easy?" Five asks.

"No," I tell him. "Now that we're all together, though . . ." I trail off, not wanting to jinx it. That fight couldn't have gone much better. Granted, it was only one ship worth of Mogadorians; they've got entire armies stationed in West Virginia and elsewhere, not to mention Setrákus Ra. Even so, we mowed them down in record time, and I don't think any of us suffered an injury. Yesterday, when Nine was all gung-ho for storming West Virginia and seeking out a rematch with Setrákus Ra, I'd tried to get across that I didn't think we were ready for that. Now, after this performance, maybe it's time to reconsider our odds.

"Where's Six?" I ask, glancing around. "Someone must've heard that ship crash. We need to get out of here before the cops show."

As if in answer, a low rumble comes from the tree line, from the direction where the Mogadorian ship fell. I shine my Lumen that way just in time to see Six sprinting towards us, waving her arms.

"Incoming!" she shouts.

"What's incoming?" Five asks, swallowing.

"Sounds like Piken," I reply.

There's a sharp breaking noise—the sound of a tree being uprooted and snapped. Something huge is coming this way. I put my hand on Sarah's shoulder.

"Get back," I tell her. "You need to stay behind us."

She looks at me, her grip tight on the Mogadorian blaster. For a moment, I'm worried she's going to argue, even though she knows fighting a Piken is way different than being in a firefight with Mogs. Shooting from behind cover is one thing. Going toe-to-toe with a monster that thinks blaster fire tickles—that's something else entirely. Sarah touches my hand, lets her fingers linger for just a moment, and then breaks away, running for cover near the post office.

"What the hell is that?" asks Five, still standing next to me, now pointing towards the tree line.

We both see the monster at the same time as it bursts from the trees, bearing down on Six. But I don't answer Five. I actually can't answer because, whatever this thing is, I don't have a name for it. It's like a centipede the size of a tanker truck, its wormlike body covered in cracked and leathery skin. Hundreds of tiny gnarled arms extend from its body, churning up earth as it rumbles forward with surprising quickness. At the front is a face sort of reminiscent of a pit bull—flat, with a wet snout, and a slavering mouth that opens upon rows of jagged teeth. In the center of its face is a single unblinking eye, bloodshot and full of malice. I remember the horde of creatures the Mogs had caged in West Virginia; as nasty beasts go, this guy would be at the top of my list.

Fast as Six is, she isn't faster than this thing. The centipede draws even with her and then jerks sideways. Its back half—the tail—pivots upwards, the bulk of it towering over Six for a moment before crashing down.

Six throws herself to the side just in time to avoid being crushed. Chunks of ground spray out from where the tail landed and made a huge indentation in the ground. Six is quickly back on her feet, driving her sword into the centipede's body. It hardly seems to notice, its twisting body recoiling with enough speed to jerk the sword out of Six's hands.

"How are we supposed to kill that thing?" Five asks, taking a step back.

My mind races for an answer. What advantages do we have over this one-eyed worm thing? It's fast, but bulky and confined to the ground. . . .

"You can fly, right?" I ask Five.

"How'd you know that?" he asks, his eyes locked on the beast. "Yeah, I can."

"Pick me up," I tell him. "We need to stay above this thing."

As the centipede rounds on Six again, I see Bernie Kosar leap onto its back. He's back in panther form, digging his claws deep through the monster's hide. With an annoyed squeal, the centipede rolls through the dirt, forcing BK to jump off or be crushed beneath its bulk. The distraction is enough for Six to create some distance between her and the beast. She turns invisible.

"It'll be easier if you're on my back," Five says, kneeling down in front of me.

I'd feel goofy hopping on Five's back piggyback style if it wasn't a life-or-death situation. As soon as I'm on, Five shoots into the air. It isn't like the shaky levitation we can all manage using our telekinesis; he's fast, precise, in control. Five gets us about thirty feet in the air, right above the centipede. I start bombarding the creature with fireballs, tossing them down as fast I can generate them. Charred sores open up on its back, a horrible stink rising up in the air.

"Disgusting," mutters Five.

The centipede roars in pain, coiling in on itself. Its huge eye sweeps frantically across the battlefield. Its tiny brain can't really register where the pain is coming from. I keep up the assault, hoping I can kill this thing from above before it even knows what's happening.

My next fireball flies wide of the beast as Five dips suddenly towards the ground. Jostled, I grab onto the back of his shirt until he's flying straight again. His shirt is soaked through with sweat.

"You all right?" I ask, shouting to be heard over the rushing wind and the howling centipede.

"Not easy carrying around a flamethrower," he yells back, trying to joke, but his voice sounds strained.

"Just another minute. Hang in there!"

The centipede's eye rolls back in its head and up, spotting us. It roars again, this time almost gleefully, and then its body lances upwards, all its tiny arms grasping at the air. Its hideous face shoots towards us, teeth gnashing. Five screams and we zip backwards in the air, the beast swallowing empty space where we used to be.

The sudden change in direction throws me off Five's back, my hand clutching a ripped piece of his T-shirt. I'm falling.

I'm able to push against the ground enough with my telekinesis to somewhat cushion my landing. If not for that, I probably would've broken a leg hitting the ground. Still, the wind is knocked out of me. And, to make matters worse, I hit the ground right in front of the beast.

Distantly, I can hear Six and Sarah shouting at me to run. It's too late for that. The centipede is just forty yards away, rumbling towards me. Its mouth is wide open, a foul stench emanating from the darkness of its gullet.

I brace myself and ignite my Lumen all over my body. If this thing wants to make a meal out of me, I'm going to make sure I burn going down. As long as I can jump past those rows of teeth, I can probably burn my way right through the thing. Getting swallowed by a Mogadorian centipede isn't my best plan, admittedly, but in the seconds I have before it's right on top of me, it's the best I can come up with.

As it gets closer, I see a red dot reflected in the centipede's eye, like the beam from a laser pointer. Where is that coming from?

A single gunshot explodes from somewhere behind me.

The monster's eye explodes. It's just a few yards from me, and I'm splashed with foul-smelling eye goop. It shrieks and rears up, forgetting all about me. I use the opportunity to backpedal, lobbing fireballs at the creature's underbelly as I go. The beast starts convulsing, its tail thrashing with enough force to make the ground under my feet shake. After one last, massive spasm, the centipede collapses into the dirt and begins to slowly disintegrate.

Five lands next to me, both of his hands on top of his head. "Dude, I am so sorry I dropped you."

"Don't worry about it," I reply distractedly, pushing him aside and spinning towards the Monster Mart. No one with us was packing a sniper rifle. Where did the shot come from?

Six and Sarah rush towards a tall middle-aged man with a beard as he climbs down from the top of a beat-up old car. He's holding a rifle with a laser scope. At first I think maybe he's just a Good Samaritan—who wouldn't shoot a giant worm creature if it was rampaging through their neighborhood? Then again, there's something about him that seems really familiar.

And then I notice someone else standing next to the car. He's helping the older man down from his sniper's position. When Six gets near she almost tackles him with a hug. My jaw drops and I immediately break into a run.

It's Sam.

CHAPTER FOURTEEN

SIX HUGS ME SO HARD THAT I ALMOST FALL over. Her arms are wrapped around my neck, and my hands are splayed across her back. The back of her shirt is sweaty from the battle the Garde just fought, but I don't mind that at all. I'm more focused on the way her blond hair brushes gently across my cheek. Those daydreams that I occupied myself with back when I was being held prisoner? A lot of them featured a scene just like this one.

"Sam," Six whispers, stunned, holding on to me like I might disappear, "you're here."

I squeeze her tighter in response. We hold on to each other for longer than is probably appropriate with everyone else around. Next to me, I hear my dad clear his throat.

"Hey, Six, why don't you let someone else have a turn?"

It's Sarah, sidling up next to us. Six lets me go, suddenly looking sheepish. I'm not sure I can remember seeing her tough exterior crack that much. I feel a blush creeping up my own cheeks. I'm glad it's dark out here.

"Hi, Sam," Sarah says, hugging me too.

"Hey," I reply. "Fancy meeting you here. It's a long way from Paradise."

"No kidding," Sarah replies.

Over Sarah's shoulder, I watch John jog over to us. He's joined by a stocky brown-haired guy who I assume is the Number Five who posted that message online. It's what brought Dad and me to Arkansas, his internet-scanning program having picked up the news story. We drove non-stop from Texas to make it here in time for the end of the battle.

While Five lingers at the back of the group looking nervous to be meeting so many new people, John strides right towards me. A grin splits my face—it's more than just being united with my best friend, it's the feeling that we're going to be part of something great together. We're going to save the world.

John grins back at me, clearly excited that I'm here, yet there's something in his eyes that I can't really decipher. He clasps my hand tightly.

"Just answer me one question," John says abruptly, not letting go of my hand. "Do you remember that day in your room, when you first thought I might be an alien?"

"Uh, yeah?"

"What did you do?"

I squint at John, not really sure why he's asking me this.

I glance back at my dad, who is watching this exchange curiously, waiting for me to introduce him to the Loric. "Um, I pulled a gun on you. Is that what you mean?"

"Oh, Samuel," my dad mutters reproachfully, but John grins at my response. Immediately, he pulls me into a hug.

"Sorry about that, Sam. I just had to make sure you weren't Setrákus Ra in disguise," John explains. "You have no idea how good it is to see you."

"Same here," I reply. "I've really missed having to fight giant worm creatures."

John chuckles, taking a step back from me.

Five tentatively raises his hand, stepping forward. "I'm lost. Setrákus Ra can shape shift?"

That's news to me too. I find myself subconsciously touching the burns on my wrists. I know firsthand the kind of evil Setrákus Ra is capable of. "How do you know that? Did you go up against him?"

John nods solemnly, glancing in Five's direction. "Yeah. I'd call it a draw. I'll bring you both up to speed, but first . . ." John's gaze moves to my dad. "Sam, is this who I think it is?"

My smile grows again. It feels like I've been waiting years to introduce my friends to my dad. "Guys," I say, pride in my voice, "this is my father, Malcolm. I can confirm that he's definitely not Setrákus Ra either, if you're worried about that."

My dad steps forward, shaking hands with each of the Garde and Sarah.

"Thanks for the help out there," John says, motioning to my dad's rifle. "Glad you brought some hardware."

"Looked like you had it under control," my dad tells John. "I've just wanted to shoot something Mogadorian for a very long time."

"Under control," chuckles Six, shaking her head. "Looked to me like you were about to get swallowed, John."

"So, it wasn't my best plan." John shrugs, smiling. Sarah pats him on the back encouragingly.

Five is studying my dad and me. "You're not Loric," he says matter-of-factly, like he's just put it together. "I thought for sure you must be a Cêpan, being so old and all."

My dad chuckles. "Sorry to disappoint. Just an old human, hoping to help."

Five turns to look at John, nodding. "You've got a real army here."

Six and I exchange a look. I'm not really sure if this new guy is being sarcastic or if he's really just kind of dense. Judging by her face, Six isn't sure either.

"There's the six of us here, and four waiting for us back in Chicago," John says patiently. "I don't think ten people really qualifies us for army status, but thanks."

"I guess not," mumbles Five.

"I want to hear everything about how you guys found each other," John says. He looks at my dad almost cautiously, like he just knocked on our family's door and asked if I could come out and play alien invasion. "First, Mr. Goode, I just want you to know that I never meant for Sam to get wrapped up in all this. I'm sorry I've put him in danger, but I don't think we would've made it this far without him."

"Definitely not," Six agrees, smiling at me. I look away, feeling a blush creeping up my cheeks.

My dad looks touched. "Putting ourselves in danger for the safety of Earth is a Goode family tradition. But thank you for saying that." He rests a hand on my shoulder. "I'm glad you found each other. And drop the 'mister'— Malcolm will do just fine."

There are sirens nearby, drawing closer. We might be in a rural part of Arkansas, but the local authorities would definitely notice a spaceship crashing out of the sky. They'll be here soon.

"We should get moving," Six says.

John nods, already starting to run towards the trees. "Our car is parked out by the highway."

"I'll ride with Sam and Malcolm," Six says, "and show them the way."

John, Sarah and Five head off towards the highway. Meanwhile, as flashing lights begin crawling through Fouke, my dad and I, along with Six, make for the Rambler. While my dad climbs into the driver's seat, Six touches my arm.

"I'm sorry if I, um, embarrassed you before with that hug. In front of your dad and all. I hope that wasn't weird."

"No way," I say hurriedly, wanting Six to know that hug was about the best thing that's happened to me in a long time. "That was really nice."

"Don't get used to me being all emotional," Six says, giving me a look. I think she's teasing me. "You showing up just caught me off guard."

"So you're saying I'd have to disappear again to get another hug?"

"Exactly," Six replies, and then starts to get into the backseat. She hesitates, thinking something over for a moment, and then suddenly hugs me again. "Okay. One more."

I hold Six close as my dad starts the car. His face is lit up by the car's instrument panel and even though he's pretending not to, I can tell he's watching us. If I had my way, I'd never let her go—we'd keep right on hugging until the local cops came to arrest us.

Six breaks away from me, looking into my eyes. I try to keep my expression cool and collected, but that's probably not working.

"For the record," she says, "I never thought you were Setrákus Ra. I knew you right away."

"Thanks," I reply lamely, scrambling for something better to say, like how I missed her or how amazing it is to see her now. Before I can come up with anything, Six has gotten into the backseat.

She's just buckling her seat belt when Five clears his throat. "Uh," he says. "What was that stone thing you threw at me?"

We all turn to stare at him. "The Xitharis stone, you mean?" Six asks.

"Yeah," Five says. "That. I kind of, uh, dropped it."

CHAPTER
FIFTEEN

"WOW, JOHNNY. I SEND YOU OUT FOR REIN-forcements and you come back with an old man, a nerd and this little hobbit guy. Great job."

Nine is there to sarcastically greet our group as soon as we enter the foyer of his ridiculous Chicago penthouse. So, my first impression of him during our brief meeting in West Virginia wasn't off after all. He really is a douche bag.

We're back later than anyone thought we would be. We searched for the Xitharis stone, but it was gone and we couldn't stick around any longer than necessary. And while no one seems very happy about it, it's like they're trying not to blame Five for losing it. For now, at least.

After it was clear it was gone, after Five had apologized for the hundredth time, Six just tossed her hair and shrugged. "It's a rock," she said, sounding like she was trying to convince herself. "A powerful rock, but we're pretty powerful on our own."

Still, it's clear that it hasn't endeared Five to anyone. Especially Nine.

"Be nice," Sarah warns him. Clearly the others have gotten used to his not-so-witty banter. By the way he and John slap hands in greeting, I'd say they've even become friends. Five, though, seems wounded. Next to me, he subtly tries to suck in his belly. "Hobbit guy," he repeats, under his breath.

"It's from a book," I start to explain, but he cuts me off.

"I get the reference," Five says. "It isn't very nice."

"That's Nine," says John, overhearing. "He'll grow on you. Or, well, you'll get used to him."

Five gives me a deadpan look like he doubts it and I can't help smiling in return. I think we're both feeling a bit like outsiders in this penthouse. Six tried to catch me up the best she could on the ride back, but there are a lot of new faces and stories here in Chicago, not to mention the most surreal hideout in history. I still can't believe the Garde are living in a place like this. It's the kind of lavish pad they used to tour on that MTV show, the one about rich celebrities and their jealousy-inducing lifestyles. How Nine and his Cêpan managed to put together a place like this and keep it off the Mogadorian radar to boot is pretty impressive.

John introduces everyone to Nine, who has stopped cracking lame jokes long enough to meet Five and my dad.

"And you remember Sam, right?" John finishes.

"Obviously," Nine says, striding forward to shake my hand. His grip is rough and he towers over me so that I have to crane my neck up. He lowers his voice, not wanting the others to hear. "Seriously, bro, sorry about leaving you in the cave. That was sort of my fault."

"It's cool," I reply, a bit taken aback by the apology.

Nine turns my hand over before letting me go, noticing the fresh pink scars on my wrists. "So they put you through it, huh?" he asks solemnly. By his tone it's like he's just realizing we have something in common. I guess I've joined the secret fraternity of Mogadorian torture victims.

I don't know what to say. I just nod my head.

"You made it out," Nine says, patting me hard on the shoulder. "Good for you, bro."

John starts to lead us by Nine, who's basically been standing right in our way. He sort of reminds me of one of those big dogs that jump all over visitors as soon as they come in the door. When he finally steps aside, I notice the three other Garde that Six told us about—Seven, Eight and the younger Ten. They're waiting where the living room starts, a little more patient than Nine, at least letting us get inside.

"If you're wondering what the horrible smell is, it's the vegetarian food Marina's cooking for dinner," says Nine.

"Hey," the dark-haired Seven—Marina—replies good-naturedly. "It'll be good, I promise."

"Dinner," Nine snorts, "whatever. Who cares? We've

got the whole team together! They're pudgier and dorkier than expected, but I'm cool with it. Let's go blow some shit up."

"You need to calm down, dude. We've been driving for like twelve hours," Six tells Nine, shoving a bag of equipment into his chest. "Here. Make yourself useful."

Sarah quickly follows suit, tossing her bag to Nine. Before long, he's shouldering pretty much all the stuff we carried up from the cars.

"Fine, I'll put this stuff away," Nine says as he agreeably lumbers off to put away our gear. "But then we're gonna at least talk about kicking some ass."

I notice Five staring down Nine as he leaves the room. Then, he turns to John.

"We're not really going to fight again right away, are we?"

John shakes his head. "Nine's just excited. Getting together was a huge first step. Now we need to figure out what to do next."

"I see," says Five, gazing down at his hands. "I guess I've never viewed violence as something to get excited about."

"We're not all like Nine," Marina says apologetically as she steps forward. She greets us warmly, even pulling Five into a hug, which I think both surprises him and loosens him up a bit. She definitely puts me more at ease after Nine's brusque display.

Eight introduces himself next. I get a real easygoing vibe from him, a nice change of pace from the alpha-male routine Nine pulled as soon as we showed up. Still, I can tell he's just as excited as Nine was, he's just more tactful.

"I've got so many questions for you. All of you," Eight says. "Five, I'm dying to know where you've been, to hear about everything that's happened to you."

"Uh," grunts Five. "Okay."

"I'm sure you've overcome a lot to be here," Eight continues encouragingly.

"The grunting is all John and I could get out of him in the car," Sarah whispers to me.

I can understand feeling a bit overwhelmed in this situation; you meet the last living remnants of your people for the first time and it turns out they've already been hanging out a bunch. In a way, it's nice to have Five with me, even though we're not talking much either; it's good to have someone equally awkward along in these social situations.

"You were living in Jamaica before, right?" Eight asks Five.

"That's right," Five replies. "For a little while, anyway."

Eight looks like he's expecting Five to elaborate. When he doesn't, John jumps in.

"It was a long ride back and I think everyone is a little tired. Maybe we can share stories at dinner," John suggests.

Eight nods and doesn't press Five for any more details. I get that John is trying to handle Five with kid gloves, letting him acclimate to the others at his own speed. I am a little surprised Five isn't asking more questions about the others, but part of that seems to be a reluctance to answer any questions about his own past. Judging by the fact that he showed up without a Cêpan or a Chest, I'm sure it's the kind of grim backstory all these Garde have.

With Eight done trying to wring information from Five, the last of the new Garde is able to step forward and introduce herself. Even though Six told me she'd be younger, I'm still surprised at how small Ella is in person. I can't imagine this girl stepping up to oppose Setrákus Ra, much less somehow being the key to scaring him off, but that's the way Six said it went. I'm impressed.

"I didn't know there was supposed to be a tenth Garde," says Five as he shakes Ella's hand. It's the closest thing he's had to a question about the others since we walked in.

"There wasn't. I was sort of an accident."

I notice John shoot Marina a curious look. Marina raises her eyebrows in response, mouthing, *I'll tell you later.*

Five nods at Ella's response, studying her for a moment longer before looking down at the floor.

"Huh," Five says, searching for words. "I've kinda felt that way about myself, actually. Our numbers, our Inheritances, the whole mission to Earth. I mean—how much thought did the big Elders put into this whole thing? Do you think they just, like, drew our names out of a hat?"

Everyone is silent for a moment, staring at Five. It's a pretty strange speech, especially when you consider this is the first time the remaining Garde have ever been united.

It should be a celebratory time, but Five seems intent on bringing things down.

"Um, yeah," says Eight, cheerily breaking the silence. "It is kind of funny when you put it like that."

My dad clears his throat, his voice soft. "I can assure you more thought was put into your selection than just a random drawing." He turns to Ella, giving her the same reassuring look I used to get when I'd come home from school after being bullied. "And your escape from Lorien was certainly more than an accident. More like a blessing, I'd say."

"Uh, right," says Five, still staring at the floor as he addresses my dad. "I guess the old human would be an expert on Lorien." He glances up then, forcing a smile as he notices the rest of us fixing him with weird looks. "Sorry," he adds quickly, "I'm just thinking out loud. I don't know what I'm talking about either."

"I don't consider myself an expert," my dad says diplomatically. "I'm sorry if I offended you. But I believe in the work of your Elders. If I didn't . . ." He trails off, probably thinking about the time he's spent as a Mogadorian captive.

Five looks sheepish now. "Four—uh, John—I'm pretty tired. Is there a place where I can lay down for awhile?"

"Sure, man," John replies, patting Five on the back. "Why don't I show all you guys where the rooms are?"

A few minutes ago, I empathized with Five for what an awkward situation this must be for him. But, I don't know, something about the way he talked to my dad really rubbed me the wrong way. There was almost a note of disdain in his voice, like my father couldn't possibly have any useful information about the Garde.

The whole group—minus Nine—lead us down a hallway covered in works of art that would probably fetch a small fortune at a museum auction. I still can't believe a dude like Nine lives here. I feel like I should be wearing a tuxedo just walking around. As we walk through the penthouse, Sarah and Six break off to get cleaned up from the road, and Ella excuses herself to go help Nine put away the gear. Eventually, John stops in the middle of the hallway.

"This one's free," John says, opening a door for Five. "There are some extra clothes in the drawers too, in case you feel like a change."

"Thanks," Five says, trudging into the room. He's about to slam the door, but realizes we're all lingering outside, kinda staring at him. "Uh, see you guys at dinner, I guess," he mutters, before closing the door.

"Cool dude," Eight says dryly. Marina elbows him in the ribs and shushes him. I glance towards the closed door where I bet Five is still standing, listening. I feel a little sorry for him again. It isn't easy being an outsider.

John turns to my dad and me. "Are you guys beat too? Or do you want the grand tour?"

"Nah," I say. "Lead on. This is my first penthouse."

"Mine too," my dad adds, smiling.

"Awesome," John replies, looking relieved that we aren't being as antisocial as Five. "I think you guys are really going to like the next stop."

My dad trails a few feet behind the group, admiring the artwork. Once we've continued down the hallway and put Five's room out of earshot, Eight asks the question that I think most of us are thinking.

"What's with the new guy?" He glances over at me. "Not you, Sam. You seem perfectly normal."

"Thanks."

John shakes his head, looking a little bewildered. "I don't know, honestly. He's a little strange, right? Not exactly what I was expecting."

"He's probably just nervous," Marina adds. "He'll settle in."

"Where's his Cêpan?" I ask. "What has he been doing all these years?"

"He was pretty closed off the whole car ride back," John answers. "Even Sarah couldn't get much out of him, and you know how she is."

"Yeah. She's social enough to get you secretive Loric talking about pretty much anything."

John chuckles, catching my joke right away. "Sarah is so charming she could convince an on-the-run alien to get his picture taken for the school paper."

"So charming that same alien might even throw rocks at her window in the middle of the night, even if the feds are staking out her house."

Eight and Marina exchange a look of confusion as John and I start laughing.

"You threw rocks at Sarah's window?" Marina asks John, her eyebrow cocked in amusement. "Like Romeo and Juliet?"

"Uh, allegedly, according to the FBI—oh, check it out, we're here," John says, anxious to change the subject. I smirk at Marina and nod.

At the end of the hall, John shows us into a room that looks like the Garde have been using for a base of operations. There are huge computer screens on one wall, one of them running a program similar to my dad's web crawler. The Loric Chests are stored here, along with the tablet we recovered from my dad's laboratory. The rest of the room is absolutely cluttered with various pieces of tech; some of it new and just out of the box, other pieces looking like they were recovered from a junkyard. In some places along the walls, the gadgets and spare parts are piled as high as the ceiling. My dad's face immediately lights up.

"This is quite the collection," he exclaims, his eyes scanning the room like a kid on Christmas morning.

"Nine's Cêpan, Sandor, this was his workshop," explains John. "We've put some of the stuff to use, but none of us are exactly technological whizzes." John turns to my father. "I'm hoping you could see if there's anything useful, Mr. Goode. Er, Malcolm."

My dad rubs his hands together. "With pleasure, John. It's been too long since I had a place like this at my disposal. I've got a lot of catching up to do."

"I'm also wondering if you could take a look at this," John says, motioning us through a set of double doors. "Nine calls it the Lecture Hall."

Entering a huge, high-ceilinged white room we pass by an intimidating weapons rack which makes the guns my dad acquired in Texas look like toys. The room is about the size of our high school's gym, making me marvel all over again at the overall hugeness of the penthouse. At one end of the room a large cockpit-style apparatus is built into the wall, an array of consoles set up around it. The chair looks sort of smashed, like something huge fell on top of it.

"Amazing," remarks my dad.

"We've been using this room to train. Nine says that Sandor had a bunch of traps and obstacles hooked up at one point." He taps a panel on the wall where it looks like something should shoot out, but nothing happens. "Except, Nine threw a temper tantrum and smashed the controls. Now it only sort of works."

"Sounds about right," I say. It's definitely not hard to picture Nine flying off the handle.

"That thing," he says, waving to the chair. "It's called the Lectern. If we could get it working again, I think we could really improve our training."

My dad is already kneeling down before the Lectern,

picking at frayed wires and bent steel plating. "This is very impressive work," he says.

I examine the machinery over his shoulder even though I have no idea what I'm looking at. "Can you fix it?"

"I can try," he says, turning back to John. "I'll be of service in any way possible."

"Me too," I say, giving John a quick salute. He chuckles.

"I know you just got here," John says. "I hope I'm not being pushy. Honestly, it's just really good to have you here. And, not to get all sappy, but I'm glad you guys found each other."

When John talks about me and my dad, there's a bit of longing in his voice. I wonder if he's thinking about how we could've had this conversation in Paradise, my dad and Henri dorking out about technology together, if only things had played out a little differently.

My dad shakes John's hand again, patting him on the arm as he does. "We're glad we found you, John. I know it's been hard for all of you, but you're not alone in this. Not anymore."

CHAPTER SIXTEEN

MARINA REALLY GOES OVERBOARD WITH THE DINNER spread. There are dishes heaped with rice and beans and fresh tortillas, an iced bowl of gazpacho, some kind of fried honeyed-eggplant dish, and like a dozen other Spanish dishes that I don't even know the names of. I've forgotten how good home cooking can be and I eat wolfishly, going back for seconds and then thirds.

We're all seated beneath the glittering chandelier in Nine's banquet hall of a dining room. John sits at one end, my father at the other, and the rest of us in between. I sit next to my father and Nine.

"Crazy," Nine mumbles as he scoops a tortilla into his mouth. "Never had so many people at this table."

Everyone is relaxed, just chatting and joking around. Five eats a lot, but he doesn't say much. Next to him, Ella picks at her food, looking tired yet still smiling and laughing whenever someone cracks a good joke. Six is sitting right across the table from me. I try to play it cool and not stare at her too much.

When the meal is over, John stands up and gets everyone's attention. He glances at Sarah and receives an encouraging smile. He clears his throat and I can tell he's given a lot of thought to what he's about to say.

"It's really incredible to see everyone come together like this. All of us have come so far to be here, and gone through so much. Being here—it gives me hope that we could actually win this war."

Nine lets out a high-pitched *woop woop* noise that makes everyone laugh, even cracking John's serious speech-giving face for a moment. Five looks around at everyone, a quiet smile on his face like he's finally starting to feel more comfortable.

"I know some of us have just met for the first time," John continues. "So, I thought it might be helpful if we went around the table and told our stories."

"There's a fun topic," mutters Six.

John is undeterred. "I know some of the stories—okay, probably all of them—aren't really the happiest. But I think it's important for us to remember how we got here and what we're fighting for."

Looking over at Five, I understand what John is doing. He's hoping that by telling their stories, the Garde might get their newest member to open up a little.

"Speaking as one of the new arrivals, I'd really like to

hear what you've all been through," says my dad.

"Yeah," Five chimes in, surprising everyone. "Me too."

"Okay," says John. "I can start."

John launches into a story that's more than familiar to me. He starts during his arrival to Paradise, after years on the road. He talks about meeting Sarah and me, and how it became harder and harder to keep his Legacies a secret.

John concludes his tale with the battle at our high school, Six's nick-of-time arrival and Henri's death. We're all quiet after that, none of us sure what to say.

"Oh damn," Nine says. "I almost forgot."

Nine reaches under his chair and produces a bottle of champagne chilling in a bucket of ice. I shoot a quick look at my dad, but it doesn't look like he's in the mood to play responsible adult. Instead, he holds out his glass. Quickly, Nine circles around the table, pouring for everyone. Even Ella gets a little bit.

"Where did this come from?" Eight asks.

"My secret stash. Don't worry about it." Finished pouring, Nine raises his glass. "To Henri."

Everyone raises their glasses and toasts Henri. He keeps it together well, but I can tell John is touched by the gesture. He looks down the table and gives Nine a small nod of thanks. Hell, even I'm a little surprised by Nine—between this and our little heart-to-heart in the doorway earlier, I might have to upgrade him from total douche bag to minor tool.

"Maybe you guys should recruit the entire town of Paradise to fight for us," Five says. "It sounds like a real alien-friendly place."

"We should get that on bumper stickers," I say. "'My Honor Student Fought Aliens at Paradise High School.'"

"I can go next," Six says. She keeps her story quick, starting with her capture with Katarina, moving on to their imprisonment and jumping quickly to her escape.

"To Katarina." This time, it's John leading the toast. Everyone raises their glasses again and we drink to Six's fallen Cêpan.

"And that's why you don't post shit on the internet," Nine says, referring to Six's story, but aiming a sharp look in Five's direction. Five gazes back at Nine, saying nothing.

"You were both close with your Cêpans," Marina speaks up. "My story is a little different."

Marina tells us about growing up in Spain, how her Cêpan Adelina basically neglected her, not giving her the training or knowledge that the other Garde take for granted. I'm kind of stunned that a Loric would behave that way. It's never occurred to me that they could shirk their responsibilities. It could be a really bitter story, but the way Marina describes it is sadder than anything else. Her voice gets warm when she talks about Hectór, the human who took it upon himself to protect her. In a weird way, the story almost has a happy ending, with Adelina finally accepting her duties even if it meant dying. I guess that's not super happy, actually, but the way Marina tells it makes it at least seem heroic.

Eight raises his glass. "To Hectór and Adelina," he says.

Nine goes next. Apparently, it was Nine's fault that everything fell apart in his life. He fell for a human girl who was secretly working for the Mogadorians, and she led him and his Cêpan into a trap. Nine glosses over what happened to them once they were captured. Having some firsthand experience with the horrific things that go down in West Virginia, the dark look in Nine's eyes when he finishes doesn't surprise me at all.

"To Sandor," John says.

"To Sandor and his champagne," adds Eight, which gets a smile out of Nine.

"I guess you really got lucky," Five says to John, jerking his thumb in Sarah's direction. "She could've been a Mog spy too."

"Hey," Sarah replies. "Not cool."

"They forced her," growls Nine, referring to the girl he'd fallen for. "No human in their right mind would willingly work for those sons of bitches."

"Except the government is . . . ," I say, remembering the agents that transported me from West Virginia to Dulce.

Nine turns to me. "Well, any human that'd work with those albino ash-monsters can't be in their right mind."

"Or maybe they aren't willing," John says. "I have to

believe that most humans, if they knew the truth, would be on our side."

"I used to distrust humans," says Eight. "Reynolds, my Cêpan, was betrayed by a woman he'd fallen in love with. It took me a while to get over that, but eventually I came to believe in the inherent good of humanity."

Eight goes on to tell us how he learned to control his Legacies, and that he eventually came into contact with the local villagers who believed him to be the Hindu god Vishnu reincarnated. Even though the Mogadorians knew his location, they weren't able to get to him because of a human army that protected him.

Five studies Eight, nodding, looking like something new and amazing has just occurred to him. "That's great," he says. "You tricked them into thinking you were one of their gods."

"I didn't mean to trick them, exactly," says Eight defensively. "I regret not being more honest."

"You shouldn't," continues Five. "I mean, it's great if you can, like, make friends with the humans like John and Marina did. Otherwise, better to have them fighting for you than plotting against you, right?" He glances over at Nine. "Better to be in control than blindly chasing pretty human girls around."

Nine leans forward, like he's about to get out of his seat. "What're you trying to say?"

"Mistakes have been made," John interjects carefully,

"but we need to remember that the humans are fighting the same enemy we are, even if they don't all realize it yet. We can't fight this battle alone."

"To humanity," I say jokingly, raising my glass. Everyone looks at me and I put my glass down, feeling a little light-headed.

It's tense for a moment. Nine is still staring down Five. Ella raises her hand. "I'd like to share," she says.

Her story is unlike any of the others I've heard. She wasn't sent to Earth with the other Garde. Instead, her rich weirdo father shoved her onto a spaceship along with the family's butler and a bunch of Chimæra. Looking around the table, I get the sense that not even some of the other Garde have heard this whole story. John looks particularly confused and Six listens intently.

"Wow, Ella," John says. "When did you learn all this?"

"Yesterday," she replies matter-of-factly. "It was in Crayton's letter."

Marina raises her glass. "To Crayton. A great Cêpan."

Everyone follows suit. Ella's gone quiet. I can tell this Crayton guy meant a lot to her.

"Just think," muses Five. "If our spaceship hadn't made it to Earth, you'd have to save the planet all by yourself."

Ella's eyes widen. "I hadn't thought of that."

"You could handle it," Nine says, grinning.

"So . . . ," John says, looking at Five. "We've all told you how we came to be here. Your turn—how have you managed to stay hidden for so long?"

"Yeah, dude," Eight chimes in. "Spill it."

Five slouches down in his chair. For a moment, I think he's just going to stay silent and hope that everyone forgets about him, like a kid hiding out in the back of a classroom. He's great at making pointed little comments when other people talk, but when it's time to tell his own story he's more than reluctant.

"It's not, um, exciting like your stories were," Five begins after a moment. "We didn't do anything special to stay hidden. We just got lucky, I guess. Found places where the Mogadorians weren't looking for us."

"Where was that, exactly?" John asks.

"Islands," answers Five. "Tiny islands where no one would think to look. Some that aren't even on maps. We'd go from island to island, sort of like how you guys traveled from town to town. Every few months we'd go to one of the more populated places—sometimes Jamaica, or Puerto Rico—and trade in some of our gems for supplies. Otherwise, we kept to ourselves."

"What happened to your Cêpan?" Marina gently asks.

"Uh, I guess I do have that in common with the rest of you guys. He died. His name was Albert."

"Mogadorians?" Nine asks, his voice hard.

"No, no, it wasn't like that," Five answers, hesitating. "It wasn't some big battle or brave sacrifice. He just got sick and after awhile he died. He was older, I think, than the way you guys describe your Cêpan. He could've passed for my grandfather. I don't think the voyage to Earth was good to him. He was always ill. The warm climate helped some, I guess. We were on this little island in the south Caribbean when it got really bad. I didn't know how to help him . . ."

Five trails off. We're all silent, letting him take his time.

"He—he wouldn't let me get a doctor. He was too worried that if he was examined, they'd discover something about him and we'd tip off the Mogadorians. I'd never even seen a Mogadorian. It all seemed like make-believe to me." Five laughs bitterly, almost as if he's mad at himself. "For a while, I even convinced myself he was a crazy man that'd kidnapped me. That he cut these scars into my leg while I was sleeping."

I try to imagine what life must have been like for Five, never interacting with anyone but a sickly old man. It goes a little ways to explaining why he seems so awkward around the others.

"It wasn't until my telekinesis developed that I really started to believe Albert. And that's also when he got really sick. On his deathbed, he made me promise that once my Legacies had fully developed, I'd try to find you guys. Until then, he made me promise to stay hidden."

"You did a good job of that," Six says.

"I'm sorry about Albert," adds Ella.

"Thank you," Five says. "He was a good man and I wish

that I'd listened to him more. After he was gone, it was easy for me to just go through the motions. I kept island-hopping, keeping my distance from everyone. It was—um, lonely, I guess. The days went by in a blur. Eventually, my other Legacies developed and I came to America, hoping to find you guys."

"What happened to your Chest?" John asks.

"Oh yeah, that," Five replies nervously, scratching the side of his head. "I traveled mostly by boat. Albert had taught me to find the kinds of ships that wouldn't, you know, ask too many questions. When I first landed in Florida, there were way more people than I was used to. A lone kid carrying around that damn Chest—I felt like everyone was staring at me. Like I'd just found some buried treasure on one of the islands or something. Maybe I was being paranoid, but I thought everyone was looking to steal it."

"So what did you do with it?" John presses.

"I didn't think it was smart for me to keep carrying it around. I found a secluded spot in the Everglades and I buried it there." Five looks around at the group. "Was that a bad idea?"

"I buried mine for pretty much the same reason," Six answers. "When I went back for it, someone had taken it."

"Oh," Five sputters. "Oh, crap."

"If your Chest-hiding skills are as good as your regular hiding skills, I'm sure it's still there," Eight says optimistically.

"We'll want to get that as soon as possible," John says.

Five nods eagerly. "Yeah, of course. I remember exactly where I put it."

"The Chests are imperative," my dad blurts out. He pinches the bridge of his nose, which I've noticed he's started doing whenever he's struggling to remember something. "Each of the Chests contains something—I'm not sure exactly what, or how it works—but there are items in those Chests that will help you reconnect with Lorien when the time comes."

Everyone's staring raptly at him now.

"How do you know that?" John asks.

"I—I just remembered," my dad replies.

Nine looks over at me, then back to my dad. "Uh, what?"

"I suppose it's time for my story now," he says, staring at all the expectant faces. "I should warn you that there are gaps in my memories. The Mogadorians did something to me. They tried to tear what I knew out of my brain. Things are coming back to me now, in pieces. I'll tell you what I can."

"But how did you find that out in the first place?" Eight asks. "We don't even really understand what's in our Chests."

My dad pauses, looking around at the group.

"I know because Pittacus Lore told me."

CHAPTER SEVENTEEN

YOU COULD HEAR A PIN DROP.

John is the first to speak. "How did he tell you? What do you mean?"

"He told me in person," my dad replies.

"You're telling us you met Pittacus Lore?" exclaims a skeptical Nine.

"How is that possible?" Marina asks.

"We found a skeleton in your workshop wearing a Loric pendant . . ." John swallows hard before continuing. "Was that him?"

My dad lowers his gaze. "I'm afraid so. When he arrived, his wounds were so grievous that there was nothing I could do for him."

Now the questions come on in a rush.

"What did he tell you?"

"How did he get to Earth?"

"Why did he pick you?"

"Did you know Johnny thinks he's Pittacus resurrected?"

My dad motions downward with his hands, like a conductor would when he's trying to quiet a noisy orchestra. He looks exhilarated by all the questions, and simultaneously like he's struggling to remember the answers.

"I don't know why I was chosen out of all of Earth's population," my dad explains. "I was an astronomer. My particular area of interest was in deep space, specifically with trying to make contact with alien life forms. I believed that there were signs here on Earth of visitation from aliens, which didn't exactly make me popular with some of my less imaginative colleagues."

"You were right, though," says Eight. "The Loralite is here. Those cave paintings we found in India."

"Exactly," continues my dad. "Most of my peers in the scientific community dismissed me as a madman. I suppose I must have seemed like one, ranting on about extraterrestrial visitors." He glances around. "And yet, here you are."

"Thanks for the résumé," interrupts Nine, "but can we get to the Pittacus part?"

My dad smiles. "I'd begun sending communication bursts into space from my laboratory using radio waves. I believed I was on to something. This was on my own time. I'd been—ah, dismissed, I suppose, from my position at the university."

"I kinda remember that," I say. "Mom was pissed."

"I don't know what I was expecting from my experiments.

A response, certainly. Perhaps a burst of alien music or images of a strange galaxy." My dad snorts, shaking his head at how unprepared he was. "I got more than I bargained for. One night, a man showed up at my door. He was wounded and rambling—at first I mistook him for a crackpot or a vagrant. And then, before my very eyes, he grew."

"Taller?" Six asks, an eyebrow raised.

My dad chuckles. "Indeed. It doesn't seem like much now, considering all I've seen, but it was the first time I'd seen a Legacy at work. I wish I could say that I reacted with proper scientific curiosity, but instead I think I did a fair bit of screaming."

I nod. Sounds like the Goode way.

"A Garde on Earth," breathes Marina. "Who was he?"

"He called himself Pittacus Lore."

Nine scoffs and shoots John a look. "Everyone thinks they're Pittacus!"

"You're saying you met an Elder?" John says, ignoring Nine. "Or someone claiming to be an Elder?"

"What did he look like? What did he say?" Ella asks.

"First, he told me he that his injuries were caused by a hostile alien race that would soon be coming to Earth. He told me he would not survive the night and . . . he wasn't wrong." My dad closes his eyes, willing his brain to work. "Pittacus told me much in the short time he had left, but I'm afraid the details are fuzzy. He asked me to prepare a group of humans to receive you, to help your Cêpans get on the run, to provide guidance. I was the first of the Greeters."

"What else did he tell you?" John asks, sitting forward eagerly.

"One thing I remember is about your Chests. The Inheritances. He told me they would each contain something—he called them Phoenix Stones, I think—taken from the heart of Lorien. Although he called them stones, I don't think we need to take that literally. The Phoenix Stones could come in any shape or form. And when restored to your planet, these items should jumpstart the ecosystem. I believe, right now, you are in possession of the tools to bring your home world back to life."

Marina and Eight exchange an excited look, perhaps thinking about that lush Lorien that John's always going on about.

"But what about the Chests we've already lost?" Six asks. "I thought the contents were destroyed when their Garde dies."

My dad shakes his head. "I'm sorry, I don't have an answer to that. I can only hope that what remains of your Inheritance will be enough."

"Look, restoring Lorien is cool and all," Nine says, "but I'm not hearing anything that's going to help us kill Mogadorians or protect Earth."

"My Cêpan told me each of us would inherit the Legacies of an Elder," Eight says. "I always thought I was

Pittacus, but . . ." He glances over at John, then shrugs. "Did he tell you anything about that?"

"No," my dad replies. "At least, not that I can remember right now. When your Cêpan said you'd inherit the Legacies of an Elder, he might not have been speaking literally. It could have been a metaphor for the roles you will grow up to take on in a rebuilt Lorien society. It can't be as simple as you becoming the Elders, because three of you are already lost. And Ella's presence here seems to indicate that nothing is so cut and dry."

"So we're just as in the dark as we were before," Six says curtly, then looks over at me. "Not that it isn't an interesting story."

"Hold on," says John, still mulling over what my dad said. "There's definitely information we can use. The Chests, for instance. We need to take an inventory, see if we can figure out which of our items are these Phoenix things."

"Probably anything that doesn't stab, shoot or explode," offers Nine helpfully.

"I'll try to help you there, if I can," my dad offers. "Seeing the contents of your Chests might jog something in my memory."

"What happened to the other Greeters?" Five asks. "Are they still alive?"

My dad's expression darkens. Now we're getting to the part of the story that I know something about. Pretty soon, we're going to be hitting the whole good-Mogadorian-saved-us-from-certain-death bit. My dad still hasn't given up hope for Adam; he was checking his phone right before dinner. With him not getting in touch for this long, I'm starting to think he didn't make it out. Dead or alive, I'm really not sure how Adam's existence, and our involvement with him, is going to go over with the Garde.

"I assembled the Greeters myself. They were people I could trust—like-minded scientists working on the fringes. But I can't remember their names or even their faces. The Mogadorians saw to that."

My dad picks up his glass of champagne with a shaky hand and takes a quick drink. He makes a bitter face, like it didn't help ease the pain of memory. Or lack thereof.

"We all knew the risks," my dad continues, eventually. "We took them gladly. It was a chance to be part of some-thing amazing. I still believe that," he says with a note of pride, looking around at the Garde. "Just as the Mogador-ians were searching for you, so were they searching for us. Obviously we were easier to find—we'd been living on Earth all our lives, you see. We had families. One by one they tracked us down. They hooked us up to machines, tried to rip out our memories, looking for anything that would help them in their hunt. It's why there are so many things I'm still foggy on. I don't know if the harm they did to me can ever be fixed."

Ella shoots a look at Marina, then John. "Could you guys heal him?"

"We could try," Marina replies, studying my dad. "I've never tried healing someone's mind before, though."

My dad runs a hand across his beard, frowning. "I was the only one that survived. I lost years to those bastards." He looks over at me. "I intend to pay them back."

"How did you escape them?" John asks.

"I had help. The Mogadorians had me sedated for years in a catatonic state, waking me up only when they had a new experiment to run on my mind. Eventually, though, a boy set me free."

"A boy?" Marina asks, her eyebrow raised.

"I don't get it," Eight says. "How did someone manage to get into a Mog base? Was he one of the government agents? And why did he help you?"

Before my father can answer, Five speaks up. The way he's eyeballing my dad, it's like he's already pieced together the entire story. "He wasn't human, was he?"

My dad looks first at Five, then over at John before turning his gaze on me. "He called himself Adam, but his actual name was Adamus. He was a Mogadorian."

"A Mogadorian helped you?" Marina asks quietly, as everyone else stares at my dad in stunned silence.

Nine stands up suddenly, looking over at John. "Dude, this has trap written all over it. We have to lock this place down."

John raises a hand, trying to placate Nine. None of the others stand up with Nine, which is a relief. Still, they're looking at each other anxiously and, even though I trust the Garde, I'm suddenly worried that they might not trust my dad.

"Calm down," John tells Nine. "We need the whole story here. Malcolm, what you're saying is pretty crazy."

"I know, believe me," he replies. "What I learned is that there are two kinds of Mogadorians. Some of them are grown through genetic engineering—they call them vat-born. I believe they're like the throwaway soldiers you've run into so often. The hideous ones that could never pass for human. They're bred simply for killing. And then there are others, they call themselves True-born. They are the ruling class. Adam was one of them, the son of a Mogadorian general."

"Interesting," Eight says. "I've never thought of how their society works."

"Who cares?" growls Nine. He's standing with his hands on the back of his chair, like he's ready to fling it. "Get to the part that proves this isn't some Mogadorian setup."

"They experimented on Adam with the same machines they used on my memory," my father continues, not deterred by the rising tension. "They had the body of a Garde—Number One, I believe—and they tried to download her memories into him, thinking it would help them find the rest of you."

"Her body," Marina says quietly. "That's sick."

My dad nods in agreement. "It didn't work the way the Mogadorians intended. Exposed to One's memories, I believe

Adam developed doubts about his people. He rebelled. In the process, he helped me escape and find Sam."

Nine shakes his head. "This is the kind of double-agent shit they love to pull," he insists.

"You met this Mog kid?" Six asks me.

Now everyone's looking at me with the same scrutiny they were just using on my dad. I clear my throat, feeling uncomfortable. "Yeah. He was at the Dulce Base. He held off a squadron of Mogs while my dad and I escaped."

My dad frowns, looking down at the table. "I fear he didn't survive the battle."

"Well, that's a relief," grumbles Nine, finally retaking his seat.

"There's something else . . . ," I say, glancing hesitantly at my father, wondering exactly how I should phrase this next revelation.

"What is it, Sam?" John asks.

"During the fight, he—he made the ground shake. It was like he had a Legacy."

"Bullshit on top of bullshit," snorts Nine.

"It's true," counters my dad. "I forgot about that. Something happened to him during the experiment."

Ella speaks up, a note of fear in her voice. "Is that true? They can steal our powers?"

"I don't think he stole the Legacy," my dad clarifies. "He said it was a gift from the Loric."

Eight looks around. "You guys remember giving any Mogadorians gifts?"

John folds his arms across his chest. "It doesn't seem like it should be possible."

"I'm sorry this news upsets you," my dad says, looking around. "I wanted to tell you everything, even the unpleasant details."

"Is it really that bad?" asks Marina. "I mean, if one of the Mogadorians could understand they're doing wrong, wouldn't others . . ."

"You want to count on them getting sympathetic now?" snaps Nine, and Marina stops talking.

Something occurs to me then, maybe because we'd spent so much time talking about how the Garde developed their Legacies and listening to my dad's new details on their home world. "Your Legacies come from Lorien, right?"

"That's what Henri told me," John says.

"Katarina too," adds Six.

"So, if that's the case, it doesn't seem like something that could just be ripped away by some Mog technology. I mean, if they could do that, they'd have stolen more powers from Lorien by now, right?"

"What're you saying?" John asks, his eyebrows raised.

"Well, I guess I'm saying . . . what if Adam inherited that Legacy because One wanted him to?"

On one side of me, Nine snorts derisively. On the other

side, my dad makes a thoughtful noise in his throat, stroking his chin. "Interesting theory," he says.

"Yeah, whatever," Nine says, leaning forward to peer at my dad. "You're sure this wasn't some elaborate Mog trap? You're sure they weren't tailing you?"

"I'm sure of it," my dad replies with authority.

Down the table, Five chuckles. He's been silent for most of the Adam discussion. Now, he looks around incredulously. "I'm sorry, but half the stories you guys just told me involved humans betraying you to the Mogadorians." He waves a hand at us. "These two were actually in contact with the Mogs, like, weeks ago. Hanging out. And you're just going to trust them?"

John doesn't hesitate. "Yes," he says, looking Five right in the eyes. "I trust them with my life. And if this Mogadorian defector is still alive, we're going to find him."

CHAPTER
EIGHTEEN

I CAN'T SLEEP THAT NIGHT. STRETCHED OUT ON the choicest couch in Nine's showroom of a living room, I should've slept like a baby. It was a huge upgrade over the stiff, flea-bitten motel beds my dad and I had been enduring, not to mention the wonderful accommodations of Setrákus Ra.

There is just too much to think about. Finally reunited with the Garde and my father, ready to really begin the fight against the Mogadorians, I feel uneasy. Uneasy about the future. Uneasy about fitting in with the Loric.

I wonder how my dad is sleeping. He seemed exhausted after dinner; I know answering the Garde's questions with his fractured memory put a major strain on him.

Maybe I was just feeling awkward after meeting so many new Garde. I'd had time to forge friendships with John and Six, time to get used to the whole alien thing. Being around the rest of them sort of threw me off balance.

I could handle Nine's bluster. Marina and Ella seemed normal enough. But then there was Eight, with that story about basically tricking humans into fighting for him. And Five—well, I don't think anyone really understood what his deal was yet. Sometimes he seemed like the most socially inept person in the world, and other times like he was slyly mocking everyone.

What was my role going to be here? John's buddy from high school and plucky sidekick? I want to contribute more than that. I'm just not sure how I can.

I must've slept at least a bit, tossing and turning on the couch. The ornate hands of the ridiculously expensive-looking antique grandfather clock in the corner show that it's early. I might as well get out of bed and do something. My hands are fidgeting. Maybe I can go down to the Lecture Hall, get a head start on some of the work my dad wanted to finish. I can't exactly rebuild a mainframe or anything, but I'm pretty sure I could connect some of the severed wires on my own.

The penthouse is eerily quiet as I pad through it. The floorboards creak in the hallway and almost immediately Five's door whips open, startling me. He's still fully dressed, which is odd, like he's just been crouching by his door and waiting to leap out at the first sign of trouble. One of his hands moves nervously, a pair of marble-sized balls turning over in his palm.

"Hey," I whisper. "It's just me. Sorry if I woke you."

"What're you doing up?" he whispers back suspiciously.

"I could ask you the same question," I reply.

He sighs and seems to back down a bit, like he doesn't want a confrontation. "Yeah, sorry. I can't sleep. This place weirds me out. It's too big." Five pauses, scrunching up his face like he's embarrassed. "Ever since Arkansas, I keep thinking one of those monsters is just going to show up and get me."

"Yeah, I know that feeling. It's okay. I think we're safe here." I motion down the hallway. "I'm gonna go work in the Lecture Hall. You want to come?"

Five shakes his head. "No thanks." He starts to close his door, then stops. "You know, I don't really think you and your dad are Mogadorian spies or whatever. At dinner I was just playing, uh, devil's advocate, I guess."

"Yeah. Thanks."

"I mean, if I was a Mogadorian recruiting spies I'd pick humans that seemed a little tougher, you know?"

"Uh-huh," I reply, crossing my arms. "You really don't know when to stop talking during an apology, do you?"

"Ugh, I'm sorry. That came out wrong," Five replies, knuckling his forehead. "I've got really crappy social awareness. Do you think anyone else has noticed?"

"Uh . . ."

Five smiles. "I'm joking, Sam. Of course they've noticed. I know I'm a freaking jerk. Like you said, I just can't shut up sometimes."

"If they've gotten used to Nine, they can get used to you," I offer.

"Yeah. That's, uh, heartening, I guess." Five sighs. "Good night, Sam. Don't hatch any evil plans in the Lecture Hall."

Five shuts his door. I stand in the hallway, listening to him rustling around in his room. He's a little off-putting, sure, but I can definitely understand why he'd be feeling anxious around the other Garde. I feel the same way.

I'm surprised to find the lights in the Lecture Hall already on. Sarah's there, standing in the firing-range portion. She's wearing a tank top and sweatpants. She's also holding a crossbow, which might be one of the strangest things I've ever seen. I watch her get ready to fire off an arrow.

"Can I take your picture for the yearbook?" I ask. My voice echoes in the vast space.

Sarah jumps. The arrow she was about to fire goes whizzing wide of the paper Mog hanging at the opposite end of the room. She turns around with a grin, brandishing the crossbow and gritting her teeth menacingly. I snap a picture with an imaginary camera.

"The kids in Paradise won't believe that one," I say. "But you're a shoo-in for the Most Likely to Maim award."

Sarah laughs. "God, we're a long way from yearbook meetings, aren't we?"

"Yeah, no kidding."

Sarah sets the crossbow down and surprises me with a hug.

"What was that for?"

"It looked like you could use one," she replies, shrugging. "Also, don't tell the others I said this, but it's so nice to have another human around."

I realize that Sarah is pretty much the only other teenager on Earth who knows what it's like to be friends with a bunch of aliens fighting an intergalactic war. We've never really talked about it, but we've shared a ton of the same whacked-out experiences.

"We should have like a two-person support group," I suggest.

"You know, if you'd asked me last year, I'd say the scariest thing I'd ever seen was an AP chemistry final." Sarah laughs. "And now, just yesterday, I watched my boyfriend fight a giant worm monster."

I laugh. "Life sure got crazy in a hurry."

"No wonder we're turning into insomniacs."

I wander over to the Lectern and start looking at some wires that my dad was working on before. Sarah sits down cross-legged next to me and watches.

"So you come down here and shoot a crossbow when you can't sleep?"

"It's as good as a warm glass of milk," she replies. "Actually, I've been working on learning to shoot but I didn't want to wake everyone up firing off guns."

"Yeah, probably not a good idea. Everyone's a bit on edge, huh?"

"That's an understatement."

I glance over at Sarah. It's so hard to believe this is the same girl I went to high school with. What really throws me is that we're having a conversation about artillery training.

"Been coming in here a lot, actually," she continues. "John doesn't sleep much. When he does, it's all tossing and turning. And then he slips out of bed in the morning to go brood on the roof. He thinks I don't notice, but I do."

I smirk at Sarah, arching an eyebrow. "Sharing a bed, huh?"

She kicks at me playfully. "Whatever, Sam. There are only so many bedrooms. It's not what you think, though. There's something really not romantic about hiding from murderous alien invaders, you know? Not to mention I don't like the idea of Eight just teleporting in or something." She squints at me. "Even so, don't tell my parents."

"Your secret's safe with me," I tell her. "Us humans have to stick together."

I finish reconnecting the wires and something hums to life inside the Lectern. One of the panels along the wall suddenly juts out like a piston, then retracts.

"What's that for?" Sarah asks.

"It's like combat-simulation stuff, I guess. Nine told me his Cêpan had all kind of obstacles and traps set up in here."

Sarah knocks on the floor in front of her. Something metallic rattles beneath her hand and she jerks back. "Maybe I should watch where I'm sitting."

I stop messing with the wires, wanting to wait for my dad before I go any further and also not wanting to accidentally trigger some kind of spike trap under Sarah.

Sarah gently touches my arm. "So why aren't you sleeping, Sam?"

Without realizing it, I find that I'm rubbing the scars on my wrists. "I had a lot of time to think when I was a prisoner," I tell her.

"I know what you mean."

Well, there's another thing Sarah and I have in common. "I spent a lot of time thinking about John and the others. About how I could help them."

"And?"

I open up my hands, showing Sarah what I came up with: a whole lot of nothing.

"Oh," she says. "Well, there's always the crossbow."

"I'm worried I won't be able to help. Like sooner or later I'll end up captured again, or worse, and that'll just screw things up for the others. Then I hear a story like Eight told tonight and I wonder if maybe it wouldn't have been better if John had left me in Paradise like Eight left those soldiers. Like maybe he'd be better off without having to worry about me."

"Or me," Sarah says, frowning.

"I didn't mean that," I say hurriedly.

"It's okay," Sarah says, touching my arm. "It's okay because you're wrong, Sam. John and the others do need us. And there are things we can do."

I nod, wanting to believe her, but then I look down at the scars on my wrists and remember what Setrákus Ra told me in West Virginia. I fall silent. Sarah hops to her feet, holding her hand out.

"For starters," she says, "we could go make some breakfast. They probably won't make us honorary Loriens for it, but it's a start."

I force a smile and climb to my feet. Sarah doesn't let go of my hand. She's looking at the dark purple scars on my wrists.

"Whatever happened to you, Sam," she says, holding my gaze, "it's over now. You're safe."

Before I can respond, a piercing shriek erupts from one of the bedrooms.

CHAPTER
NINETEEN

I JOLT AWAKE AS SOON AS ELLA STARTS SCREAMING. It was my night to stay with her and it had gone by peacefully. We'd stayed up late talking about the new arrivals and what Malcolm Goode had told us about Pittacus Lore and the possibility of helpful Mogadorians. Ella had finally fallen asleep and I'd hoped that maybe the nightmares plaguing her since New Mexico were finally gone for good. She hadn't had one since reading Crayton's letter. Maybe it was all stress related after all. Now that she'd gotten over the anxiety of that unopened letter, things could get back to normal.

I should've known better.

"Ella. Ella, wake up!" I shout, trying to decide if I should shake her. I'm feeling a little panicked, especially when she doesn't immediately snap awake. Ella digs at the blankets with her fingers, kicking her heels into the mattress, all while belting out steadily hoarser screams. She's moving about so much that she almost falls out of the bed. I reach out to steady her.

As soon as I touch Ella's shoulder, an image pops into my mind. I'm not sure where it comes from. It feels like when Ella talks to me telepathically, except there've never been visuals to go along with her mental voice.

What I see is horrible. It's Chicago, the same lakefront area where Eight and I wandered around just the other day. There are bodies strewn everywhere. Human bodies. The sky is filled with columns of smoke from nearby fires. The surface of the lake is covered in something viscous and black, like oil. I can hear screams. Smell the burning. Hear explosions in the distance . . .

I pull away from Ella with a gasp. Just like that, the vision is gone. I'm out of breath, shaking, my stomach feeling queasy.

Ella has stopped screaming. She's awake now, looking up at me with wide, scared eyes. I glance over at the clock and realize less than a minute has passed since Ella first started screaming.

"You saw it too?" she whispers.

I nod, not sure how to answer, much less describe what I just saw. How is it possible that I just found myself in Ella's dream?

Someone knocks on the door and without waiting for an answer, Sarah pokes her head in. I can see Sam standing behind her in the hallway. They both look concerned.

"Is everything all—?"

Before Sarah can finish, Ella makes a sudden motion towards the door, slamming it shut with her telekinesis.

"Ella! Why'd you do that?"

"They shouldn't be near me," she replies, her eyes wide and frantic.

Someone tugs at the door, but it won't budge. Now I hear John's voice, probably drawn by all the screaming and commotion. "Marina? Everything all right in there?"

"We're okay!" I yell through the door. "Just give us a minute."

Ella pulls a blanket around herself and curls up at the head of the bed, pressing her back to the wall. Her eyes are still wide and she's shaking like a leaf. When I try to touch her, she flinches away from me.

"Don't!" she snaps. "What if I send you back there again?"

"Calm down, Ella," I say soothingly. "It's over now. The dreams can't hurt you, especially when you're awake."

She lets me hold her hand. There's no telepathic jolt this time, which I'm thankful for. Whatever strange effect the nightmare had on Ella's telepathy is over now.

"How—how much did you see?" she asks, her eyes darting around the room, like there could still be some leftover nightmare lurking in the shadows to get her.

"I don't even know what I saw, exactly," I answer. "It was the city. It looked like something terrible happened."

Ella nods. "It's after they come."

"Who?" I ask, but I already have a good idea who Ella means.

"The Mogadorians. He's showing me what happens after they come. He—he made me hold his hand and walk through it all." Ella shudders and lunges away from the wall, into my arms. I feel like shuddering too. The thought of having to walk through that carnage hand in hand with Setrákus Ra is enough to get me rattled. I try to put on a strong face for Ella.

"Shh," I whisper. "It's okay now. It's over."

"It's going to happen," Ella cries. "We can't stop him."

"That's not true," I reply, squeezing her tight. I try to think of what John or Six might say in this situation. "The nightmares are lies, Ella."

"How do you know?"

"Remember those cave paintings Eight showed us in India? The one of Eight dying? That was supposed to be a prophecy, but we broke it. There's no set future, only the one we make."

Ella lets go of me and takes a deep breath, pulling herself together.

"I just want the nightmares to stop," Ella says. "I don't know why it's happening to me."

"It's Setrákus Ra trying to scare you," I tell her. "He's trying to scare you because he's scared of us."

I'm glad I was able to calm her down, to sound

confident doing so, because I'm actually pretty freaked out. Sunlight is starting to peek through the curtains, and outside that window is a beautiful city full of innocent people that I just saw ravaged. That dream seemed so real, I can't just shake it off. What if we aren't able to stop what's coming?

CHAPTER
TWENTY

LATER THAT MORNING, I GATHER EVERYONE IN the living room for what I hope will be a strategy session. Some important things got brought up at dinner last night and it's time we planned our next move. However, the first order of business for our tired group, many of whom were woken up by screaming a few hours ago, is this issue of Ella's nightmares.

Malcolm strokes his beard thoughtfully. "Let's assume that these nightmares are being caused by Setrákus Ra. I find it extremely troubling that he's able to transmit them somehow, presumably through some form of Mogadorian telepathy, without knowing our exact location. In fact, you said you saw Chicago burning, correct?"

Ella nods, not looking eager to revisit her latest nightmare. Bernie Kosar, curled up at her feet, nuzzles against her.

"It was Chicago after a major battle," Marina clarifies.

"Is he taunting us?" Six asks. "Or is it like some kind of prophecy?"

"I thought we were done with prophecies," Eight says, rolling his eyes.

"Sometimes there's a little bit of truth in the nightmares," I say.

"Like when we had that vision about New Mexico," Nine chimes in.

"Yeah, but other times, it's like he's just trying to screw with us."

"The content doesn't worry me so much as the fact that Setrákus Ra is able to transmit them at all," says Malcolm, deep lines forming in his face as he thinks this through. "Do you think it's possible he's tracking us through the dreams?"

"If he could do that, wouldn't we already be fighting off Mogs?" Eight replies. "Why even bother drawing John and Nine off to New Mexico?"

I nod in agreement, thinking back to the visions Nine and I shared. "Even though the nightmares can be creepily specific, I don't think he knows where we are. It's more like he's trying to make us slip up."

"The question, then, is how do we stop the nightmares?" Malcolm asks.

"I've got a solution," Six says, and everyone looks in

her direction. She takes a considering sip from a mug of coffee. "Let's go kill Setrákus Ra."

Nine claps his hands and points at Six. "I like the way this chick thinks."

"Oh, is it that easy?" Five asks, speaking up for the first time. "You make it sound like taking out the trash."

"I wish it were so simple," I say. "But we don't know where he is and, even if we could find him, that's not going to be an easy fight. The last time we went up against him almost killed us."

"We could get him to come to us," Nine suggests, glancing over at Five. "Maybe fire up some more crop circles."

"You can't be serious," Sam says. I noticed him shifting in his seat at the mention of Setrákus Ra.

"He's not serious," Five says, glaring in Nine's direction. "He's mocking me."

Nine shrugs and feigns a yawn. "Whatever. I really do think we should go fight something."

"That's all you ever want to do," Eight cuts in.

"Yeah, it's my thing."

"For the first time ever, we're together," I say, keeping my voice measured. "We have the element of surprise on our side. We've got an opportunity to prepare and pick our next battle. Let's not rush into anything."

"John's right," Marina says. "There's still so much we don't know about ourselves, our powers, our Chests."

"It'd be good to know exactly what we're working with," Eight says. "We did some training with Nine in the Lecture Hall the other day. It was helpful. Surprisingly so."

Nine grins. "Compliment taken, insult ignored."

"Yeah," Sarah chimes in. "I think I speak for all of us humans when I say a little more combat training wouldn't hurt."

"Learning what our Chests contain would help too," I offer. "Maybe we could figure out which items are those Phoenix Stones that Malcolm was talking about."

"An inventory seems to be in order," Malcolm says.

"Which means we need to make finding your Chest a top priority," I say, looking over at Five.

"Absolutely," Five replies, seeming about as certain as I've ever seen him. "I know exactly where to go. We can do that whenever you want."

"That might make a good first mission," Eight says. "Especially if we could get it done under the Mog radar."

"I still think we should just blow up their freaking radar," Nine grumbles.

"Soon, buddy," I reply. "For now, we need to play it safe. Gather our strength. Malcolm, what about the Mogadorian guy? Adam?"

Malcolm shakes his head, his features sagging. "I've hooked up a tracker so we'll be alerted if his cell phone turns on, but nothing yet. I fear the worst."

"Maybe he just ditched his phone," suggests Sam, trying to cheer up his forlorn-looking dad.

"We got a bit off topic here, didn't we?" Six puts in. "What about Ella's nightmares?"

It's Ella, who has been listening quietly, that responds. "I'll tough them out. The next time that big freak gets into my head, I'm going to punch him in the balls."

"Whoa!"

"All right," I say, grinning. "Meeting adjourned."

CHAPTER TWENTY-ONE

LATER, THE FOUR OF US THAT STILL HAVE OUR Chests gather in the workshop with Malcolm. I'm happy to help out—I'm just not sure how much use I'll be. Adelina wasn't around enough to explain what any of the stuff in my Chest does.

From the Lecture Hall comes the muffled sound of Six training marksmanship with Sam, Sarah and Ella. I think Five is in there too, although he didn't look too thrilled about the prospect of learning to shoot. Nine stares longingly at the door to the Lecture Hall. Sighing dramatically, he starts rummaging through his Chest.

"Check this out," Nine says. He holds up a small purple stone and then places it on the back of his hand. The stone slides into his hand—through it. Nine turns his hand over just as the stone pops out in his palm. "Pretty cool, right?" he asks me, waggling his eyebrows.

"Uh, but what is it supposed to do?" Eight asks,

looking up from his own Chest.

"I dunno. Impress girls?" Nine looks over at me. "Did it work?"

"Um . . ." I hesitate, trying not to roll my eyes too hard. "Not really. But, I've seen guys teleport so I'm kind of hard to impress."

"Tough crowd."

"What does it feel like when it passes through your hand?" Malcolm asks. He holds a pen poised over a clipboard.

"Uh, kinda weird, I guess. My hand goes numb until the stone passes through." Nine shrugs, glancing around. "You guys want a try?"

"Yes, actually," Malcolm says. When he puts the stone on his hand, nothing happens. "Hmm. I guess it's Loric only."

Malcolm hands the stone back to Nine. Instead of putting it back into his Chest, Nine shoves the purple stone into his pocket. Maybe he's going to go out and try to impress some ladies later.

John holds up a collection of brittle-looking leaves, the bundle held together by some yellowed twine. He cradles them gently in his hands, unsure what to make of them.

"This has to be something to do with Lorien, right?"

"Maybe it's a reminder from Henri that you're supposed to rake the lawn," Nine says, digging through his own Chest again. "I don't have any dumb leaves in here."

Malcolm peers at the bundle in John's hands. Gently, he runs his index finger along the edge of a leaf. I almost expect the delicate little thing to crumble. Suddenly, the sound of a gentle breeze fills the room. It stops as soon as Malcolm pulls back his finger.

"You all heard that?" he asks.

"Sounded like someone left a window open," Eight says, looking around at the four walls cluttered with equipment. Not a shred of daylight comes through any-where.

"It was the sound of wind on Lorien," John says, his eyes getting distant. "Somehow, I know that's what it was."

"Do it again," Nine says, and I'm a little surprised by the sincerity in his voice. But then, I really want to hear the wind again too. There was something comforting about it.

John brushes his hands through the leaves and this time the sound is fuller. My skin prickles; it's almost as if I can feel the fresh Loric air on my skin. It's beautiful.

"Amazing," Eight says.

"But what is it for?" Nine asks, returning to his usual bluntness.

"It's a reminder," John replies, his voice low, like he's a little choked up and trying to hide it. "A reminder of what we've left behind. What we're fighting for."

"Interesting." Malcolm makes a note on his clipboard.

"Further study will be required."

One by one, Malcolm stands over our shoulders as we empty out our Chests. He writes down everything, making notes for the objects we know how to work and underlining the ones that we don't. From the dark gloves that shimmer when I touch them to the circular device that looks sort of like a compass, pretty much every item in my Inheritance gets underlined.

"What do you think this does?" Eight asks, holding up a curved antler that looks like it was snapped off the head of a small deer. "It's the only thing in here I don't know how to work."

Five seconds after Eight held up the antler, Bernie Kosar bolts through the workshop door with his snout in the air. He looks thrilled, his tail wagging. He jumps right on Eight, pawing at him.

"He wants the antler," says John. "In case you couldn't tell."

Shrugging, Eight lowers the antler and BK takes it in his jaws. He flops over onto his back and begins to roll back and forth. He emits a happy purring sound that definitely doesn't go with his dog form. In fact, his form begins to flicker in and out, almost as if he's having trouble controlling himself.

"He's so weird!" Nine is laughing hysterically. "If we weren't on the run, I would totally put this on the internet."

"Whoa, whoa," John says, rubbing his temples. "Calm down, BK."

Malcolm looks from BK to John. "You can communicate with him?"

"Yeah," John answers. "Telepathically. So can Nine. He's pretty wound up. He says the antler is—I don't know how to put it, it's coming through in a weird language—like, a totem or something. For Chimæra."

"Well, he's our only Chimæra, so he can keep it," says Eight, grinning as he crouches down to rub BK's belly.

"Ella came here on a ship filled with Chimæra," I say. "Do you think we could use that to attract them? Maybe they're lost and need to know where to find us."

Malcolm immediately starts writing on his clipboard. "Very good thought, Marina."

I smile, feeling a little swell of pride. Now if I could only figure out what the stuff in my Chest does.

"If you're looking for boring nature-themed crap, I've got this," Nine says, holding up a small leather pouch. He passes it around and we each look inside. It's filled with rich, chocolate-brown soil. "When Sandor was explaining my Inheritance, he told me it was meant for growing things. But that we wouldn't need it for a long while."

Nine reties the leather strings at the top of the pouch and dismissively tosses it back in his Chest. I guess he's not all that interested in things that can't kill Mogadorians. I look through my Chest, brushing aside the assortment of gems that could've funded my Spanish version of Nine's penthouse if Adelina had cared, looking for anything that might have to do with restarting Lorien.

"What about this?" I ask, holding up a slim vial of crystal-clear water. The glass is cool to the touch beneath my fingers.

"Drink it," suggests Nine.

Malcolm shakes his head. "I'd advise against ingesting any of the items in your Chests until we know what they do."

"You listening?" Eight elbows Nine. "Don't eat any of the rocks."

I uncork the vial. As soon as the air touches it, the liquid transforms to a shade of blue exactly the same as the Loralite stones. It's only a brief reaction, though, the blue quickly fading back to the clear water. I drag my finger down the side of the vial and a trail of bright blue appears in the liquid, then fades as I lift my finger away. I notice little tendrils of blue swirling about beneath the tips of my fingers where I'm holding the vial.

"Do you see that?" I exclaim.

"It's like the liquid can feel your touch through the glass," says John.

"May I?" asks Malcolm.

I hand it over to Malcolm. When he holds the vial, the color of the liquid doesn't change. "Hmm," he says, and holds the vial out to John. "You try."

As soon as John takes the vial from Malcolm, the

liquid again flashes the brilliant cobalt shade of Loralite. We all watch as it slowly fades away, except where John is touching it. The way the liquid pulses, it's like it wants out of the vial, like it's eager to be in contact with us.

"So, it detects Loric," Eight says, "but what good is that if we're the only ones left?"

"I'm going to try something," I say, taking the vial back from John. Carefully, I tip the vial so that just a single drop spills into the palm of my hand. The liquid turns blue and a tickling sensation spreads across my palm. Then, the single droplet quivers and expands, gaining mass and density until I'm holding in my hand a smooth nugget of Loralite.

"Whoa," Eight says, taking the stone out of my hand and turning it over, examining it.

"Whoa, indeed." Malcolm bends down, gazing in amazement at the stone. "Whatever that material is, it defies the laws of physics."

"So we can create Loralite with that," John muses. "Nine and I both have something that looks like it could be used for farming or planting, and Eight has an object that can summon Chimæra. Doesn't it seem like that's the stuff that can help us jumpstart Lorien?"

"It does indeed," says Malcolm.

I put the stopper back into the vial, not wanting to waste any more of our precious liquid Loralite.

The inventorying goes on for a little while longer with

Malcolm taking really meticulous notes. We're all eager to learn as much as we can about our Inheritances—well, except for Nine. He keeps gazing towards the door of the Lecture Hall. He makes us promise to train with him after we're done with all "the brainy stuff." In truth, I'm looking forward to another session in there myself. I feel like I've got a lot of catching up to do before I'm at the same level of combat readiness as the others.

When the others leave, Eight and I linger, putting the last few items back into our Chests. I put the Loralite stone that I created in there as well, but Eight plucks it out. He squeezes it tightly in his fist and concentrates.

"What're you doing?"

He opens his eyes and sighs. "I wanted to see if I could use this to teleport to one of the other Loralite stones. I've tried using my pendant before and that didn't work either. They must not be big enough chunks."

"What? You wanted to take a quick jaunt to Stonehenge? Maybe Somalia?" I take back the stone and put it in my Chest, locking it up.

"Things are going to be moving fast now, that's all. I just wish we had more time to do some of that exploring."

"We?" I reply, feeling a sudden heat rising in my face. "You were going to teleport me away with you?"

Eight flashes me that disarming smile. "Just for a quick breather. You telling me you couldn't use one?"

Eight's right, obviously. After getting woken up before

dawn by Ella's screaming and witnessing that horrific vision of Chicago, I could definitely use a time-out from Loric business. But there's no time for that now. I touch Eight on the arm.

"Sorry," I tell him. "We've gotta be serious. Like Nine said, no time for gallivanting off to foreign lands or even the waterfront."

Eight sighs with good-natured disappointment. "Ah well," he says, "we'll always have pizza." He pauses for a moment, looking like he wants to say something more, but then Nine bursts into the room. He's already changed into workout clothes.

"You suckers ready to work?"

CHAPTER
TWENTY-TWO

"LET'S GRAB FIVE," NINE SAYS GRUFFLY, AFTER EIGHT and I have gotten changed. "That dude could use a workout."

We find Five stretched out on one of the couches in Nine's living room. He's fired up some video game from Nine's collection on the big-screen television. I don't have any experience with the things and watching Five play makes me sort of dizzy. The game is in first-person perspective, Five's character running around a battlefield with a machine gun, mowing down soldiers. Five doesn't even acknowledge us entering the room until Eight loudly clears his throat.

"Oh, hey guys," Five says, not bothering to pause the game. "This thing is freaking amazing. We never had anything like it on the islands. Watch this."

On screen, Five's character launches a grenade. A group of enemy soldiers hiding behind a pile of sandbags explodes in a shower of dismembered limbs. I look away. After seeing into Ella's dream this morning, the video game just seems a little too realistic.

"Cool," Eight says politely.

Nine yawns. He stands right in front of the television so that Five is finally forced to pause the game. "I used to be really into these when I was a kid," Nine says. "Now I'm more into the real thing. You want to join us?"

Five raises an eyebrow. "The real thing? We're going to go kill some soldiers in um—?" He squints at the open case for the video game. "World War Two. I guess my Earth history must be spotty because I thought that was all over."

"We're going to train," Nine replies, unamused. "From what I heard about Arkansas, it sounds like your game could use some work."

I notice a flash of anger in Five's eyes and for a moment I think he might leap off the couch. But then he settles back, crossing his arms and making a concerted effort to keep his features neutral.

"I'm not really feeling it right now," Five says. He makes a show of stretching out further on the couch. "Anyway, this game is good for my hand-eye coordination. Probably the best training I'll get around here."

I'm realizing now that this might have been a bad idea. Nine's about the least diplomatic person I've ever met. After spending some time around him, I've learned not to take him too seriously. I can tell Five hasn't quite worked up that same tolerance yet.

"It's really surprisingly fun," I say, trying to smooth things over. If Five doesn't feel like we're pushing him, maybe he'd be more likely to train with us. "It gives us a chance to work together as a team. Also, we'd really like the chance to get to know you better."

For a moment, Five's look softens. It's like I figured; if you're nice to him, he lets his guard down. Nobody likes to be told what to do, especially when they've been alone for as long as Five has. I can tell he's going to cave in and come train with us.

Unfortunately, Nine's not so good at picking up signals, or maybe he's just impatient. He casually walks behind Five's couch and, with one hand, flips it over. Five is unceremoniously dumped onto the floor.

Eight shakes his head, although there's a small smile playing at the corner of his lips. I know Five didn't make the best first impression on him, dredging up all those memories of what Eight did in India. Still, this is no way to treat our newest Garde.

"Come on, Nine," I say, using that disappointed-but-not-angry tone I used to get from the nuns. "You're being a bully."

Nine ignores me. Five has already jumped back to his feet, glaring at Nine.

"What'd you do that for?"

"My couch," says Nine. "I can do whatever I want with it."

Five makes a disgusted snort. "That is so childish. You're ridiculous."

"Maybe," Nine replies, shrugging blithely. "You can show me how ridiculous I am in training."

So this is all one of Nine's little motivational tools, trying to get Five mad at him so that he'll come fight in the Lecture Hall. Such a boy's plan. We could've just asked Five nicely. Five keeps right on staring at Nine, sizing him up. He smirks, a glint of something mischievous in his eyes, and I get the impression that Five has seen right through Nine's ploy.

"Tell you what," says Five. "I'll give you a free shot right here. If you can hurt me, I'll come train with you. If you can't hurt me, you take the overcompensating macho stuff out of my face for the rest of the day."

Nine's face lights up in a wolfish grin. "You want me to hit you, little guy?"

"Sure," Five replies, his hands in his pockets, chin jutting out. "Give it a shot."

"This is dumb, you guys," I say, trying to defuse what has suddenly become a really absurd situation. Both Five and Nine are so involved in this pissing contest when we should be learning to work together. I glance over at Eight for some support. A small smile tugs at the corners of his lips, almost like he's amused by this whole thing. When he catches my look of disapproval, Eight's smile turns sheepish and he places a hand on Nine's shoulder.

"Let's just go train," Eight says, keeping his voice light. "Five can come by when he's ready."

Nine shrugs off Eight's hand and cocks his fist back. He raises his eyebrows at Five. "You sure you wanna test me, Frodo?"

"I hope your punches are better than your insults," Five snaps back. I have to admit, I sort of admire his spirit. Of course, this all could've been avoided if he'd just swallowed his pride to begin with. The way both Five and Nine are acting is pathetic. Two of the last remaining Loric in the universe need to be given a time-out.

Like me, Eight has resigned himself to letting this play out. We both take a step back.

Nine really takes his time, drawing it out. He cracks his knuckles, rolls his neck, makes sure his shoulders are square. I think I'm more nervous than Five is; he just stands there passively, waiting for Nine to throw his punch.

Finally, Nine takes a swing. It's a big overhand blow and even though it's definitely enough to knock some-one out, I think I've seen Nine throw punches harder and faster. I guess he took a little off the punch, not wanting to hurt Five that bad.

In midswing, Five's skin transforms into glistening steel. Nine's fist crunches against Five's metallic jaw and he cries out immediately. It's like hitting a metal girder. I put a hand over my mouth to stifle a cry of surprise. Next to me, Eight has to cut off a surprised laugh when he realizes that Nine's hand is definitely broken. He spins away from Five, clutching his hand against his chest.

Five's skin returns to normal. "Is that it?"

Nine growls a series of curses. I rush over to take a look at his hand but he pushes me away and stalks out of the room, heading towards the Lecture Hall. I'm sure he'll want me to heal that hand as soon as he cools down. Anyway, after acting like a jerk, he deserves a little pain.

"If he really listened to Four talking about our battle in Arkansas, he would've seen that coming," Five says as he watches Nine storm off, his voice wooden, almost bored.

"He's not exactly the master technician," Eight replies, coolly. "Well, welcome to the team. Enjoy your video games, I guess."

Eight follows Nine out of the room. Five watches him go, looking a little baffled that Eight would just brush him off. I help him return the couch that Nine flipped over to its normal position.

"I'm not sure what I did wrong here," Five says quietly. "How am I the bad guy?"

"You're not," I reply. "Things just got out of hand. You were both being pretty stupid."

"He's been picking on me since I walked in the door," Five continues. "I figured if I didn't stand up to him, it would just keep happening."

I sit on the couch next to Five. "I understand," I tell him. "Nine has a way of getting under people's skin. John told me a story about how him and Nine almost tore each other apart once. You'll get used to it."

"That's the thing. I don't want to get used to it." Five picks up the video-game controller, but he doesn't start playing again. He clicks a few buttons and the screen goes dark. "And the thing is, I wanted to train with you guys. I don't want to be left out. I want to see what you guys can do and learn to work together. It was just the way he asked. I couldn't stop myself from reacting."

I pat Five gently on the shoulder. "You know, you and Nine aren't all that different."

He seems to consider this, gazing down at the carpet. "No. I guess we aren't. Should I apologize for hurting his hand?"

I shake my head, chuckling a little. "It's probably his pride that's hurting more, but you shouldn't apologize for that either." I stand up and grab Five's arm, tugging him to his feet. "Come on. Let's get to training."

Five hesitates. "After that, you really think I'd be welcome?"

"You're one of us, aren't you?" I say decisively. "What better time to learn teamwork than after punching a teammate in the face?"

Five almost allows himself a laugh. He nods and we walk towards the Lecture Hall together. "Thanks, Marina," he says. "You know, you're the first person to really make me feel welcome here."

Well, at least there's that. I might not be able to help Ella with her dreams, or identify half the objects in my Inheritance, or fight as well as the others. But at least I'm good at coaxing jerks into being more personable. I wonder if that's a Legacy.

CHAPTER
TWENTY-THREE

JOHN HOLDS THE ILLINOIS ID CARD UP TO THE light. He bends it between his fingers and picks at the picture with his thumbnail. Then, he turns to me, smiling wide.

"This is great work, Sam. As good as the ones Henri used to make."

"Finally." I sigh, relieved. A dozen similar ID cards, all with some minor defects, sit in a pile next to Sandor's main computer. All of them have John's face along with the name John Kent.

"You should make one for yourself," John says. "Maybe your alias could be Sam Wayne."

"Sam Wayne?"

"Yeah, like Bruce Wayne. Superman's buddy without any powers. That's why you chose Kent for my last name, right? It's a Superman reference."

"I didn't think you'd catch that," I reply. "Never knew you were into comics."

"I'm not, but we aliens like to keep tabs on each other." John comes around to the other side of the desk, skirting one of the workshop's many junk piles, to look at the screen over my shoulder. "All this was already on Sandor's computer?"

"Yep," I reply, guiding the cursor across the various forgery programs and government database hacks installed on Sandor's machine. "It was just a matter of accessing them. And, uh, figuring out how to use them right . . ." I point to the pile of screwed-up IDs.

"Awesome," John says. "Let's get new identities ready for everyone. It'll make traveling to pick up Five's Chest easier."

"Can't Eight just teleport you down there?"

John shakes his head. "He can only do long ranges between those massive Loralite stones he mentioned last night. And with short range there's too much risk of being spotted appearing from thin air. Or of him teleporting us into a wall."

"Yeah, that would hurt." I adjust the webcam that's hooked onto the monitor so that it's pointing at me. When my image appears on screen, I take a second to fix my hair and then flash my corniest smile.

"Nice," John says, still watching.

"What can I say? I'm photogenic."

"I always wondered why picture day at Paradise High was called Sam Goode Appreciation Day."

"And now you know."

I drag and drop the picture into one of the programs Sandor installed and it immediately gets to work resizing my pic for a new driver's license. "So," I begin lamely, not having a better segue prepared. "There's something I've wanted to ask you."

"Yeah?"

"What's going on with you and Six now that Sarah's, uh, not a traitor?"

John laughs. "We actually talked about it on the way to Arkansas. I think we're cool now. It was kinda awkward for a while. I'm with Sarah, though. One hundred percent."

"Okay, cool," I reply, keeping things nonchalant. Although that doesn't stop John from elbowing me.

"She's all yours," he says, and my face gets hot right away.

"That's not why I was asking."

"Uh-huh, sure," John says, picking up a loose bolt from the desk and tossing it at me. "You're gonna act like you forgot about what happened before she went to Spain? Her saying she like-likes you? Her kissing you?"

I shrug, flicking the bolt back in John's direction. "Hmm, that sounds familiar, but it wasn't on my mind at all." Even as I say this, I think back to that hug Six gave me when we were reunited in Arkansas. My face gets even hotter.

Luckily, before John can mess with me further, my dad enters. He smiles at us as he wipes his greasy hands off on an old rag. He looks worn down from working on the machinery in the Lecture Hall, but there's a pleased smile on his face. Digging into some Loric-built technology sure beats wasting away in a Mogadorian prison.

"How'd it go?" I ask him.

"The human mind is an amazing thing, Sam," my dad muses. "When you have gaps in your memory like I do, you come to better appreciate the things you do remember. The way your hands just repeat a task you've done enough times, without even needing to think. Who needs Legacies when we have the infinite power of the human mind at our disposal, eh?"

"I wouldn't mind some Legacies, actually," I say, glancing over at John. "Sorry, he can get philosophical about science-y stuff."

"I don't mind at all," John says, his smile wistful as he looks between me and my dad.

"The repairs aren't easy," my dad continues. "Sandor's work is impressive and I've—ah—been out of the game for awhile. Everything works like I remember, it's all just much smaller. The Lectern might be too intricate for me to get fully operational. I've been able to make some repairs to the controls. Some of the booby traps should be operational as well. It's not perfect, by any means, but it's something."

"I'm sure it's great," John says. "Anything that could improve our training will help. I'd like to get a team session together before we go to Flo—"

Nine flings open the workshop door with enough force to almost tear it loose from its hinges. He takes one big stride forward and then violently kicks a stack of junk, sending circuit boards and scrap metal flying in our direction. I start to shield my face, but John catches the temper-tantrum shrapnel with his telekinesis.

"What the hell?" John yells. "Calm down!"

Nine looks up, startled, like he didn't even realize we were in here. "Sorry," he mutters, then stomps over to John. He holds out a hideously swollen right hand. "Heal this."

"Damn," I say. "What happened to you?"

"I punched Five in the head," Nine says matter-of-factly. "It didn't go well."

Well, that didn't take long, I think. Nine's been trying to get under Five's skin since we walked in the door. I'm actually more than a little surprised it's Nine in here needing the healing. That's not how I would've imagined that fight going. I keep my mouth shut, letting John deal with his wounded attack dog. He takes Nine's forearm, maybe with a little more force than necessary, and holds his hand out over Nine's messed-up fist. But he doesn't heal him.

"You've gotta chill out," John says, locking eyes with Nine. "No punching our friends. No challenging them to rooftop fights. No bullshit."

Nine stares John down and, for a second, I think he might take a swing at him too. He doesn't. Instead, he slaps on a big grin, as if the whole thing was one big joke. "I'm like the shittiest welcoming committee ever, huh?"

"Back in Paradise, Sarah's mom used to bake stuff for anyone new that moved into the neighborhood. Maybe you should have to bake some cookies every time you punch someone," I suggest.

John laughs as he sets about healing Nine's hand. "I love that idea, Sam."

"I am not baking," Nine growls, fixing me with a death stare.

My dad clears his throat. We all look over at him. Standing straight, his hands folded behind his back; it's the same look I'm sure his students at the university used to get. "Nine, I was wondering if you might want to assist me in the Lecture Hall?"

"With what?"

"Your Cêpan built the equipment. I was hoping you might have some insight into how it works."

Nine laughs with disbelief. "Yeah, uh, sorry, dude. I left the nerd stuff to him."

"I see," my dad replies, undeterred by Nine's bluster. "In that case, perhaps we could figure out how it works as a team? Unless you're too busy punching things."

To my surprise, Nine actually considers this. I see the same wistful look on his face that I noticed on John's face earlier and it occurs to me that they're both thinking about their Cêpans. I realize then what my dad is doing, reaching out to the angry guy, trying to get him involved in a project, *Afterschool Special* style. It's a total parent move, but I admire it.

"All right, yeah," Nine says. "It's my shit. I should know how it works. Lead the way."

As Nine and my dad head into the Lecture Hall, John turns to me.

"Your dad's a good guy," he says. "We might have to make him an honorary Cêpan."

"Thanks," I reply, my smile brittle. A cold knot of dread forms in my stomach, because I know what happens to Cêpan around the Garde, what happens to adults. It's a dark thought, I know, but I can't suppress it. I've only just reunited with my dad––I don't want to lose him. Without realizing it, I've started rubbing the scars on my wrists. John must intuit what I'm feeling because he puts a hand on my shoulder.

"Don't worry, Sam," he says. "We're not going to lose anyone else."

I hope he's right.

CHAPTER TWENTY-FOUR

"SO WHEN ARE YOU GUYS GOING TO FLORIDA?"
Sarah asks me casually, like it's a vacation I've been
planning.

I'm beat. It's a good kind of tired, though—today
was a productive day. No time spent running and hiding, no time wasted. We cataloged the contents of our
Chests, Sam managed to print up some solid fake IDs,
and I got some training time in the newly refurbished
Lecture Hall.

"Two days from now, I hope," I answer Sarah, dropping down to the floor to knock out a quick set of
push-ups before bed. "I want to get everyone together
in the Lecture Hall tomorrow, see how the team looks.
I don't expect much trouble recovering Five's Chest, but
you never know. It'll be good to have everyone get some
experience together. And then we're off."

Sarah's gone quiet. I look up at her. She sits on the

edge of the bed—our bed, still weird to even think that—her legs curled beneath her. She wears her pajamas—a V-neck gray T-shirt and a pair of my boxers. She's watching me, but isn't paying attention to a word I'm saying. I clear my throat and she blinks her eyes, flashing a lopsided smile. "Sorry, you distracted me with push-ups. What were we talking about?"

I sit down on the bed next to her, curling my fingers through her just-brushed hair. She smiles at me and suddenly I'm not so tired anymore. I'd be lying if I said I hadn't thought about what could happen with us sharing a bed. Things have been hectic since we've been in Chicago, between Ella's nightmares, Five's call for help, and my own insomnia. Plus with everyone else sleeping in the next rooms, it hasn't felt right.

"Florida," I remind her.

"Oh yeah," Sarah says. "You lived there for a while, didn't you?"

"Yeah, a few months. Why?"

"Just trying to fill in some blanks. There's still a lot I don't know about you, John Smith." She puts her hand on my cheek, lets her fingers run down my neck, and then along my shoulder. "Also, talking helps distract me from what I really want to do."

My hand slips through her hair, down the back of her neck, and slowly dances across her spine. Sarah shivers a little and I slide closer, bending my head down towards hers. "You know, it seems pretty quiet tonight. I think everyone's asleep."

Right on cue, someone knocks on our door. Sarah's eyes widen and she laughs, her face flushed. "Is horrible timing one of your Legacies?"

I open the door to find Six waiting, her coat on, like she's just come in from outside. She glances over my shoulder at Sarah, then catches my exasperated look, and cracks a devilish smirk. "Oops," she says, "interrupting?"

"It's cool," I say, playing it off. "What's up?"

"You need to come to the roof and see this. BK's going nuts."

We pull on some clothes over our pajamas and then race down the hall after Six. I can hear BK before I'm even at the staircase leading to the roof. The sound he makes is like a cross between a wolf howling and an elephant blowing through its trunk—it's loud and soulful, not a bad sound at all, but totally not of Earth.

"He won't shut up," Nine says, as soon as I emerge onto the roof. He rubs his temples, probably exhausted from using his telepathy to try calming BK.

He is still pretty much in beagle form, although his shape bulges and stretches erratically, like he might change into something else at any second. The antler from Eight's Chest is clenched in his teeth, the sound not at all muffled by it. Flecks of drool drip down the antler and into BK's fur. He stands up on his hind legs, his snout pointed at the moon, the oddly melodic noise flowing out of him. It looks like he's in some kind of trance.

Eight teleports in from downstairs. "I've got Sam and Malcolm monitoring emergency channels, just in case some nosy neighbor calls the cops," he says. "I don't know what's gotten into him, John, but I think it's got something to do with that antler."

"No shit," Six says. She snaps her fingers at BK. "Quiet, Bernie Kosar!"

BK doesn't even seem to notice. I spot Marina over at the edge of the rooftop, using her night vision to keep an eye out for anyone that might spot us. Luckily, we're high enough and Chicago is loud enough that I don't think anyone will hear BK. Even so, I don't want to take any chances.

"Did you try taking the antler from him?" I ask.

"Yeah," Nine replies. "He didn't like that. Growled at me and wouldn't let go. I didn't want to hurt him."

"That doesn't sound like BK," Sarah says, her eyes widening with concern.

"Think this is some kind of Chimæra nightmare?" Six suggests.

I shake my head. All this weirdness with BK started when he got hold of that antler. It doesn't seem like anything in our Chests should work against us. Even my bracelet, which hurt like hell initially, turned out to be helpful. There should be a rational explanation for this.

"Where is Ella?" Sarah asks. "Could this be like what's happening with her, but for Chimæra?"

"Sleeping right through it," Marina replies. "And this seems totally different."

I reach out with my telepathy—*Bernie Kosar, you need to be quiet now*—but don't get any response. Not seeing any other option but to try and wrestle the antler away from him, I step forward. Before I take a second step, Bernie drops onto all fours, letting go of the antler. His howling echoes in my ears for a few seconds after it's over. I grab the antler with my telekinesis and pluck the slobber-covered thing out of the air. BK pants happily, looking around at everyone.

I make eye contact with Nine, both of us patched into BK telepathically. "It's like he doesn't know what just happened," I say.

"Are you drunk, BK?" Nine asks, mystified.

BK bounds over to us, tail wagging. He's got the same look of dog euphoria that he gets when we've just come back from a really satisfying run outside.

"You freaked us out," I tell him. "You know you were up here making all kinds of noise, right?"

BK sits down at my feet. Sarah crouches down to scratch his ears.

"Can you ask him what he was doing?" Sarah says,

looking up at me and Nine.

"Trying," I reply, and Nine nods too, squinting at BK. "It's a lot of images and feelings, you know? Not exactly words."

"Telepathic barking," Eight observes.

"Pretty much," replies Nine.

"He says—" I pause, wanting to make sure I'm getting my interpretation of BK's thoughts right. "He says he was calling the others." I hold up the antler. "I guess that's what this is for."

"The others?" Marina asks. "You mean the Chimæra from Ella's ship?"

"I guess so," I reply, looking down at BK. *Do you think they heard you?*

BK rolls over onto his back, asking Sarah to rub his belly. I guess that's the Chimæra equivalent of a shrug.

"He doesn't know," I say.

Nine shakes his head. "Well, crisis averted. I'm going to bed. Can we have a night without screaming or howling, please?"

Everyone else follows Nine downstairs, leaving just Sarah, BK and me. The night air is cool and, now that BK has stopped with the noise, it's peaceful. I kneel down next to Sarah and put my arms around her. "Cold?"

"Not really," she says, smiling. "But you can leave your arms. I see why you like it so much up here."

We sit like that for a while, Sarah in my arms, both of us gazing out over the Chicago skyline. This is one of those perfect moments, the kind I need to save up and remember for when things get bleak.

And then, because maybe Sarah is right and bad timing is one of my Legacies, a dark shape detaches from the night sky and zooms towards us.

CHAPTER
TWENTY-FIVE

"WHAT IS THAT?" SARAH CRIES.

"I don't know," I reply, springing to my feet and instinctively putting myself between Sarah and the black blur that's descending on us. I fire up my Lumen, feeling some comfort in the fresh heat, ready for anything.

The dark form slows down. It's definitely a person, I realize. The shape lands gracefully on the other side of the roof, its arms raised in a gesture of peace.

"Five."

"Hey, guys," Five says. "You're up late. Did I scare you?"

"What do you think?" Sarah asks, gesturing at the fireballs still held in my hands. On edge, I finally let them dissipate. Five, wearing a black sweatshirt and pants, pulls down his hood so I can see his apologetic face.

"Shoot. Sorry. I didn't think anyone would notice."

I legitimately thought we were under attack for a

second there, so my words come out harsher than I mean them to. "What the hell were you doing?"

"Just flying around. Sometimes I like to see how high I can go."

I try to think of a response that won't make me sound too bossy. I'm all for training, but flying around the city of Chicago seems like a pretty stupid idea. Hiding in plain sight is one thing; hiding while teenagers soar through the air around your base is another.

"Aren't you worried someone might see you?" Sarah asks, taking the words right out of my mouth.

Five shakes his head. "No offense, Sarah, but you'd be surprised how little your people bother to look up. Anyway, it's night and I'm in dark clothes. Trust me, guys, I'm cautious."

"Still, there are cameras to think about, airplanes, who knows what else," I say, trying not to sound like I'm lecturing.

Five sighs deeply and holds out his hands, like he's sick of arguing. On the heels of his run-in with Nine earlier, I guess he doesn't want to make any more trouble. "I'll stop if you want me to," he says. "You should know that I'm getting better at it, though. Covering more distance. In fact, I could probably just swoop down to the Everglades and pick up my Chest, be back before breakfast."

I like this can-do attitude from Five; he suddenly

doesn't seem like the kind of guy we need to worry about passing up training for video games. Still, I shake my head. "We'll go as a team, Five. We don't need to do anything alone ever again."

"Safety in numbers. You're right." Five yawns, stretching his arms out. "All right, I'm gonna turn in. The Lecture Hall first thing tomorrow, right?"

"Right."

Once Five has marched downstairs, I turn to Sarah. She's gazing up at the night sky, a tiny smile playing at her lips. I take her hand.

"What do you make of that?" I ask her.

She shrugs. "If you could fly like that, wouldn't you?"

"Only if you could fly with me."

Sarah rolls her eyes, elbowing me gently in the ribs. "Okay, cornball. Let's get to bed before anything else crazy happens."

CHAPTER
TWENTY-SIX

"ARE YOU SURE YOU'RE UP FOR THIS?"

Ella nods her head as we walk towards the Lecture Hall together. She looks pale, dark circles under her wide eyes, like she's just gotten over a horrible illness. She made it through last night without any nightmares or screaming fits, but she still looks drained.

"I can do it," Ella says, straightening up.

"No one will think any less of you if you sit out," I tell her.

"You don't have to baby me," she replies sharply. "I can train just as hard as the rest of you guys."

I nod, dropping the argument. Maybe some physical activity will be good for Ella. At the very least, it should tire her out enough so that she'll get some real rest.

We're the last two to arrive in the Lecture Hall. Everyone stands in the middle of the room, dressed in workout clothes. Malcolm sits behind the Lectern's console, examining the glowing buttons and levers through his glasses.

Nine claps his hands when he sees us. "All right! Let's get started! Capture the flag time, baby! The ultimate test of teamwork and, um, ass-kicking ability."

Six rolls her eyes and Five stifles a groan. I stand next to Eight, who flashes me a quick smile. I hope we end up on the same team.

"The rules are simple," Nine says. He gestures to the opposite ends of the gym where he's mounted a pair of makeshift flags made out of old Chicago Bulls T-shirts. "The first team to grab the other team's flag and bring it back to their side is the winner. You've gotta be holding the flag at all times, no telekinesis. Also, no teleporting the flag back to your own side—ahem, that means you, Eight."

Eight smirks. "No problem. I like a challenge."

Piled on the floor are four Mogadorian rifles that I grabbed on our way out of Arkansas. Figured we might want them for just this kind of exercise. I notice Sam eyeing them hesitantly. "What are those for?" he asks.

"Each team is going to get two guns," explains John, jumping in. "Malcolm has modified them so they're nonlethal. Like stun guns. We always end up using their own guns against the Mogs in battle; I figured this would be good practice."

"Also, we wanted to give you non-Garde a fighting chance," says Nine, glancing at Sam and Sarah.

Malcolm strides over from the Lectern, his hands clasped behind his back. "I'll be using the Lecture Hall's systems to throw in some obstacles," he says. "Remember, if anyone gets hurt, it's okay to call a timeout so Marina or John can heal you."

Nine sighs, annoyed. "There're no timeouts in a real fight, so let's try to keep wimping out to a minimum."

John glances around, taking a less cavalier approach. "Remember, this is just practice. We're not really trying to kill each other."

John and Nine are captains, dividing us into two teams. John chooses Six with his first pick, and Nine selects Eight. Next, John takes Five and Nine picks Marina. John's third pick is Bernie Kosar, and then Nine surprises everyone by choosing Sarah. I expected to go in the last round; there's no shame in it when the rest of the players are packing superpowers. John picks me, probably wanting to divide the humans up evenly, which leaves Ella to join Nine's team.

We huddle up at our end of the gym.

"I'm going to turn invisible right away," Six says. "If you guys can keep the rest of them busy, I should be able to make it to their flag no problem."

John nods in agreement. "I'm mostly worried about Eight. He's probably going to teleport to our side right away and make a go for the flag. Sam, I want you and Bernie Kosar on guard duty."

I pat Bernie Kosar on the head. His beagle fur transforms under my fingers into the smooth coat of a tiger. "Um, yeah. We can handle it."

"Five, you and I will go on offense. Keep them busy while Six makes a break for it."

Five looks over his shoulder to where the other team is having their own huddle. "I want to take on Nine."

John and I exchange a quick look, both of us remembering yesterday's incident. It's not every day that someone volunteers to go head to head with the Garde's battle-crazy lunatic. John shrugs. "Sure. I'll have your back. Take it easy on him this time, okay?"

Five smiles, a cavalier look in his eyes. "No promises."

As our huddle breaks, I smile at Six. "Good luck out there. They'll never see you coming."

So cheesy. *Ugh, way to go, Sam.* Six returns my smile quickly. She picks up one of the Mog blasters and tosses it to me. "Thanks, Sam. I'm counting on you to keep me covered, okay?"

⊏⊐

"I'll teleport over there, grab their flag, and make a break for it," Eight says, snapping his fingers. "We won't even break a sweat."

Nine shakes his head. "That's exactly what they'll be expecting. So yeah, do that. But it's just going to be a diversion."

Sarah raises her hand, interrupting. "Sorry, Nine, I just have to ask. Why did you pick me?"

Nine grins at her. "You're my secret weapon, Hart. There's no way John's going to be effective with you making kissy faces at him."

"Kissy faces?" Sarah repeats dryly, cocking the Mog blaster she picked up. "Do you want me to shoot you?"

"I've seen her shooting. She won't miss," I put in. I've watched Sarah shooting during training. I'm envious of her aim. I haven't been able to adapt to firearms nearly as quick as she has. They just make me nervous.

"I know she won't," Nine replies, getting serious. "That's why she's gonna be on Six patrol."

"You know she's going to go invisible," Eight says. "How are we supposed to stop that?"

"That's where Ella comes in," Nine answers. Ella looks up from the blaster she's fiddling with, startled to hear her name. I think she was a little hurt at being picked last.

"Me?" she asks, incredulous.

"Hell yeah, you," Nine replies. "You're gonna use your telepathic mojo to pinpoint Six's location when she's invisible. Then, you and Sarah light her up."

"Um, I'm not sure if I can do that."

"You located her in a big-ass base in New Mexico. This is just one room." Nine shakes Ella's shoulder encouragingly. "Just try for me, all right?"

"What am I going to be doing?" I ask.

Nine's got that proud look on his face—I think I heard John refer to it as "shit-eating"—that he gets when he thinks he's come up with something really juicy. He grabs my hand and the little hairs on my arm stand up, an electric shock shooting through me. "You, Marina, are my real secret weapon."

"Are both sides ready?" Malcolm shouts from the Lectern.

The two teams stand about ten yards away from each other, close to the halfway point of the Lecture Hall. I glance around. Everyone on my side looks determined. Sam has already started sweating a bit, constantly adjusting his grip on his blaster. Across from me, Sarah shoots me an innocent smile as she brandishes her own blaster. My heart actually flutters in response, but I try to keep a serious face.

"Ready!" I shout to Malcolm.

"Let's kick some ass!" Nine shouts.

Malcolm hits a few buttons on the Lectern. The room hums to life around us. Sections of the floor begin to rise, creating blocks of cover for people to hide behind. A pair of medicine balls on chains swing loose from the ceiling. Nozzles protrude from the walls, emitting bursts of smoke.

"Begin!" Malcolm yells.

For a moment, no one makes a move. Then, suddenly, my bracelet tingles to life. My red shield deploys just in time to block a burst of blaster fire. I look across the gym to see Sarah grinning at me, the muzzle of her blaster smoking.

"Sorry, baby!" she yells, before diving behind a piece of cover.

On one side of me, I see Six disappear into the thin air. On the other side, Sam falls back towards our flag. Everyone is moving and suddenly it's just like a real battle. Chaos.

And there's Nine. Coming right for me.

He's so fast that I barely have time to fire up my Lumen and toss a small fireball his way. He leaps over it and crashes down on top of me. I fall backwards, my shield between the two of us as he pins me to the ground. Nine pounds down on the shield with all his might. Dents forms in the red material, but the shield holds. Frustrated, Nine leaps off me, and my shield immediately retracts into my bracelet. I get back to my feet as quickly as I can, but even blocked by my shield, Nine's tackle knocked the wind out of me. I'm slower than I should be.

"You and your damn jewelry, Johnny," Nine grunts. "I've been thinking about that thing ever since the last time we fought. It shocked me when I tried to yank it off by hand, so I wonder what'd happen if—"

I feel his telekinesis working. It's too late to do anything about it. He rips the bracelet right off my arm and flings it to the sideline.

"Ha!" Nine yells, gleeful. "What's up now?"

Just as Nine's about to charge me, Five's rubbery arm slithers around his waist and flings him to the side. Nine springs right back to his feet. Five stands in front of him, his rubber bouncy ball and chrome ball bearing turning over in his palm. His skin transforms from rubber to solid steel.

"Ready to take another shot?" Five asks.

"Oh, you have no idea," Nine growls back.

It happens just like John said it would. Almost as soon as I've taken cover by our flag, Eight teleports into the vicinity. Remembering the rules, that he can't teleport the flag back across the room, I wait for Eight to snatch our flag off the wall. As soon as he does, I spray him with blaster fire.

Eight yelps in surprise as my first shot electrifies his back, knocking him off his feet. He rolls over. "Damn, Sam! Shooting a guy in the back. Not cool."

I level my blaster at him. "Drop the flag!"

"I don't think so," he says, and scrambles to his feet. I squeeze off a couple more shots but Eight nimbly dodges them, dancing behind a piece of cover. Even so, I've got him pinned down and he knows it. There's no way he's making it back across the room with our flag.

"Okay, Sam, try this on for size," Eight shouts. He shoves the flag into his mouth and shape shifts into the form of some freakish ten-armed lion creature. He lumbers over the barricade towards me, swatting my blaster out of my hands with one clawed paw.

"Get him, BK!" I yell.

Before Eight can make another move, Bernie Kosar crashes into him. BK has shape shifted as well. He's taken the form of a giant boa constrictor. He wraps his body around Eight, pinning Eight's arms to his sides. As Eight gasps for breath, the flag goes drifting out of his mouth. I snatch it up and pin it back to our wall.

I watch as Sarah and Ella, both of them crouched down behind cover close to our flag, point their blasters around the room. They're looking for a target they can't see.

"Come on, Ella," Sarah says hopefully. "You can do it."

Ella's face is pinched tight with concentration as she tries to locate Six telepathically. I hope this isn't too much exertion for her after yesterday's ordeal. Suddenly, Ella lights up.

"There!" she shouts, and starts shooting her blaster into thin air on the right. Sarah follows suit, not really aiming, just trying to cover the same area as Ella.

Most of the blasts sail harmlessly into the wall. After

a few shots, though, one of the electric currents seems to stop in midair. It sizzles for a moment and I see the outline of Six's skeleton, almost like an X-ray, as it's knocked to the ground. Six's form reappears, looking surprised and confused that she's been caught out. She has to crabwalk backwards to avoid another volley of shots from Sarah and Ella.

"Nice job, guys!" I yell. Ella and Sarah take a moment to high-five before going back to aiming at Six.

I slink along the wall, watching the action from the sideline. No one's paying any attention to me yet, and that's just the way our team wants it.

In the center of the room, Nine ducks under one of Five's steel-plated punches, grabbing Five's arm as it sails over his head and twisting it, wrenching it behind Five's back. He starts prying at Five's fingers.

"You might be made of metal," I hear Nine snarling, "but you're still not stronger than me."

Nine forces Five's hand open. I can hear the metallic clang as Five's ball bearing hits the floor. Immediately, Five's skin returns to normal. Nine shoves him away, right into one of the swinging medicine balls. It hits Five in the face, flipping him over. He groans, holding his head.

"Oops," says Nine. "Looks like somebody lost his balls."

I'm distracted by the fighting so I almost step right on the bracelet that Nine tore off John's wrist. Figuring that might come in handy, I pick it up and snap it on my own wrist. The icy feeling that spreads up my arm surprises me so much that I almost tear the thing off. I force myself to focus, sliding along the wall, staying out of view.

"Hey!" yells John, and it takes me a moment to realize he's talking to me. "You've got something that belongs to me!"

Both of John's fists glow with fire. He sends two burning orbs the size of basketballs sailing right towards me.

I wouldn't have lobbed fireballs that intense at Marina if I wasn't sure the bracelet could handle them. The shield deploys in time to absorb them, but the force still knocks her against the wall, stunning her. I don't know what she's up to, sneaking around on the sidelines, but I'm sure it's part of some plan their team concocted.

I glance over my shoulder to where Five is trying to scuttle backwards as Nine stalks him. Not good. I toss a fireball at Nine and he dives away. That gives Five a chance to regain his feet and create some distance between them. Of course, as soon as Five pops back to his feet, a bolt of blaster energy from Sarah puts him down again. Even though she's really screwing my team over, I can't help but be psyched at how well she's handling herself.

Five's going to have to fend for himself for now. I need to figure out what Marina's up to and get my bracelet back. I race over to her just as she's pushed herself away from the wall. Her eyes widen when she sees me coming and she lashes out with a kick to my legs. I deflect the blow and pin her up against the wall, trying to pry the bracelet off her.

"What's your plan, Marina?"

"I'll never talk!" she yells, getting into the spirit as she tries to head butt me. Somebody's definitely been taking dirty fighting lessons from Nine.

"John!" I hear Sam shout from the other side of the room. "Watch out!"

I know what's coming as soon as Sam yells, but there's no way to dodge it. Eight teleports next to me, socking me in the jaw and knocking me away from Marina. As I turn to face him, he teleports behind me, kicking me in the back with both his feet. I stagger onto one knee. How am I supposed to defeat a teleporter in hand-to-hand combat?

I try to line up a shot on Eight, but he's moving too fast. He keeps teleporting around John, hitting him with a quick punch and then disappearing before John can counterattack. Next to me, Bernie Kosar is still in the same boa form as when Eight teleported out of his clutches.

"BK, go help John! I'll hold down the fort."

He transforms into a huge hawk and soars out to help John. That leaves me alone guarding the flag.

Our best chance for victory is still Six. She's pinned down behind cover, with Sarah and Ella blasting away to keep her there. I can see her clearly from my position. She's crouched, concentrating, a gentle breeze blowing through her light hair.

Wait. Where is that breeze coming from?

Suddenly, I feel the air pressure change in the room. Six stands up from behind her barrier and thrusts her hands out towards Sarah and Ella. Ella is knocked backwards, somersaulting into the wall. Sarah falls back too, losing her grip on her blaster.

Before they've finished tumbling, Six is sprinting forward. Sarah reaches out to reclaim her blaster, but Six uses her telekinesis to send it skittering farther across the floor. Six jumps up, grabs the flag from the wall, and starts booking back to our side. "Go, Six!" I shout, feeling a swell of pride; no one else in here would make this distinction, but I think of me, John and Six as the originals competing against the newbies. And we're winning!

As Six races back towards our side of the Lecture Hall, I keep my blaster leveled, ready to lay down cover fire.

Eight is too busy trying to outmaneuver both John and BK to notice Six making a break for it. Nine, however, sees it happening. He tosses aside a battered and exhausted-looking Five and rushes to meet Six in the middle of the floor. I'm willing Six to turn invisible as Nine barrels towards her. She doesn't. In fact, it almost looks like she wants to take Nine on.

Nine swings first with a big overhand right hook that Six easily sidesteps. Quickly, she rabbit punches him twice in the side, then attempts to sweep his legs out from under him. Nine leaps over Six's leg and grabs her wrist when she tries to hit him with a palm strike to the nose. With his free hand, Nine fires off a punch, but Six blocks the blow and hooks his arm. They grapple like that, each of them controlling one of the other's arms. Six twists and struggles, but I can tell that Nine's starting to overpower her.

For a moment, I'm frozen watching Six and Nine fight. I guess it's just my natural instinct to stand back when the Garde do battle, whether against Mogs or each other. But then I realize that I've got a clear shot at Nine. His broad back presents a perfect target. I could end this game right now. With just one pull of the trigger, Nine will drop and Six will be home free to make it back to our side.

I line up my shot and fire.

I don't know how he does it. Maybe it's just my crappy luck. Nine spins Six around just as I fire. My blast hits Six in the back and she crumples, spasming, to the ground. The flag goes fluttering out of her grasp and Nine snatches it up.

"Six!" I yell, startled. "I'm sorry!"

I don't even see Marina coming.

Now is your chance, Marina. Go!

With Sam distracted, I sprint past him and grab their

flag off the wall. He notices me just as I start running back to my side, keeping close to the wall. He tries to take aim at me but I rip the blaster out of his hands using my telekinesis. He won't be a problem now. Five is laid out just a few yards away, looking groggy from tangling with Nine. He won't be a problem, either.

It's John and Bernie Kosar I have to worry about.

The two of them break away from Eight when they see me running with the flag. Eight quickly teleports into BK's path, tackles him, and teleports with him to the other side of the room. That just leaves John.

Nine tries to intercept him but even though she's barely shaken off the effects of the blaster shot, Six manages to jut her leg out and trip Nine up. That gives John a clear path towards me. I'm still wearing his bracelet, so he must know that shooting his fireballs at me won't work. Instead, he makes a beeline to cut me off.

It's disorienting at first, using the antigravity Legacy that Nine transferred to me at the start of the game. It's odd to feel the world shift sideways as I run up the side of the wall, my feet landing where it should be impossible. John's coming on so fast that he doesn't have time to adjust and crashes into the wall beneath me.

I sprint across the ceiling to our home-base wall and drop back down to the floor, holding the flag aloft. Part of me can't believe it, even when Malcolm blows a whistle signaling an end to the game. I did it. We won!

"Damn," I say, rubbing my head where it bounced off the wall. "Didn't see that coming."

I can't help but smile as I watch Marina celebrate. Eight teleports across the room to wrap her in a big hug and Ella runs over to join in. Nine limps over to me, extending a hand.

"Good game, boss," he says.

"Yeah, you too," I say, clasping his hand. A couple weeks ago the idea of losing to Nine would've made me nuts. Now, it doesn't seem to matter as much. The important thing is that both sides worked well together. The Legacies on display, the fighting skills, everyone watching one another's backs—I know it's only a game, but it makes me believe we can take on anything.

Nine steps away from me to go help Five back to his feet. Five looks pretty beat up, bruises all down the side of his face, one of his arms hanging limp at his side. Nine makes a show of brushing him off.

"No hard feelings," Nine says, smirking.

"Yeah, sure," Five replies sullenly.

I watch as Sam kneels down next to Six. She's still shaking off the electric jolt of the blaster. I can tell Sam is feeling guilty.

"Six," he begins, "I'm sorry, I didn't mean to."

Six waves him off. "Forget it, Sam. It was an accident."

"Not really," interrupts Nine, strolling back over. "Ella warned me it was coming telepathically. That's how I knew to turn you around."

We all turn to look at Ella. Her face is flushed from the excitement. She looks healthier than she did when we started. And more awake.

As the others cross the room to congratulate Marina and get themselves healed, Malcolm strides over to me. He pats me on the back.

"Well done," he says.

"Not exactly. We lost."

Malcolm shakes his head. "That's not what I meant. Well done bringing this all together. You know what I saw while watching all this, John?"

I look at Malcolm, waiting for an answer.

"A force to be reckoned with."

CHAPTER
TWENTY-SEVEN

AFTER TRAINING, WHEN I EMERGE FROM THE shower, Sam is waiting for me in the hallway outside the bathroom. He's frowning, pretty much the same look he's had since after capture the flag, like he just single-handedly lost the war for us instead of making one mistake in a training game.

"I really screwed up out there," he says. "I can see why you're not bringing me to the Everglades."

Once everyone was healed, the group came together to unanimously vote on flying to the Everglades tomorrow. Sam staying behind has nothing to do with his performance in the Lecture Hall; it just makes sense to have him and Malcolm in Chicago, using the tablet to coordinate if we should get separated, and monitor news feeds in case of trouble. It's an important task, but not something I was going to try talking any of the others into doing. No one wants to stay behind on our first mission as a unified Garde.

"You know that's not why, Sam."

"Yeah, yeah," he replies half-heartedly.

"Come on, it was just a game. Forget about it," I reply, punching him on the arm.

He sighs. "I was a freaking embarrassment out there, dude. In front of Six."

"Ohhh," I reply, catching on. "So, you shot the girl you like in the back. Big deal."

"It is a big deal," Sam insists. "I looked like a fool that can't protect himself. Or even worse, like someone that'll get the people he cares about hurt."

I don't know what to tell Sam. He's never had a girl-friend before. Trying to get with Six is like deciding to take up mountain climbing and choosing Everest as your first mountain.

"Look, I wish I had something useful to tell you, buddy. Honestly, though? Six confuses the hell out of me. If you really do like her, just be honest with her. She appreciates honesty. Or, like, directness. Bluntness."

"Bluntness makes me think of cavemen."

I pat Sam on the back. "Be direct but, you know, don't club her or anything. You won't survive that."

I'm joking, but Sam's frown only deepens. "What chance do I even have, John? She'll be hooking up with Nine in no time, probably. At least he can fight."

"Nine?!" That makes me laugh. I pat Sam on the

shoulder. "Come on, man. And Six can't stand Nine."

"Really?" Sam looks at me. His smile is more relaxed now, if still a little embarrassed. "Sorry to bug you with all this," he says. "Guess I just need a confidence boost or something."

We're standing in front of my door now. I put my hands on Sam's shoulders, looking him in the eyes. "Sam, just go for it. What have you got to lose?"

I leave Sam in the hallway to ponder his next move. I hope it works out for him. In a way, I think he and Six would work really well together, but I don't want to spend any more time trying to play matchmaker. I've got more important things to worry about. Not to mention a girlfriend of my own to think about.

Sarah is waiting in my room, drying her hair with a towel. She gives me a knowing look after I've closed the door behind me, her face lit up by a playful smile.

"That was some good advice," she says.

I glance over my shoulder towards the hallway, wondering how much of my conversation with Sam she overhead. "You think so?"

She nods. "Sam, all grown up. Emily would be heartbroken."

It takes me a moment to remember Sarah's friend from Paradise, the one Sam had a crush on when we took that hayride together. It seems like such a long time ago. "I hope I didn't just set Sam up to get his heart broken. You think he really has a shot with Six?"

"Maybe," Sarah replies, walking over to me. "Beneath that tough exterior, she's still a girl. Sam's cute and funny, and he obviously cares about her. What's not to like?"

She tosses her arms around my neck and I pull her close. "Maybe you should give him some advice on how to charm us Loric. You're pretty good at it."

"Am I?" she replies, wiggling her eyebrows. She presses a lingering kiss to my lips, her fingers curling through my hair. In that moment, I totally forget about Sam and all the serious problems we're facing. It's amazing; I wish I could live in that kiss. Sarah slowly pulls away and looks up at me, smiling. "That's for shooting at you."

"If that's what I get, you can shoot at me anytime."

"So, what's next today?" Sarah asks, ticking my usual tasks off on her fingers. "More planning? Map drawing? World saving?"

I shake my head. "I was thinking we could get out of here."

Sarah and I end up walking over to the Lincoln Park Zoo. I've spent plenty of time on the roof of the John Hancock Center, so it's not like I've been totally cooped up since we returned to Chicago. Still, it's different to experience the city down here, with the people. Even with all the car fumes and trash smells you get in a big city, the air still seems fresher somehow. Maybe it's just that I feel free, more alive down here than when I'm up on the roof with my troubles. With Sarah's hand in the crook of my elbow, it's possible to imagine we're just a normal couple on a date.

That's not to say I'm not cautious. I'm wearing my bracelet underneath a light jacket, just in case it should pick up any signs of danger. We stop in front of the lion enclosure, but we can't see anything except the golden furred butt of a lion dozing off behind a chewed-up tire.

"That's the bummer about zoos," Sarah says. "The animals get so lazy and sleepy, sometimes you don't even get to see them."

"That shouldn't be a problem for us," I tell her. I reach out with my telepathy, gently coaxing the lion to wake up. It climbs to its feet, shaking out its mane, and then saunters right towards us. He stares up at us from next to his watering hole, his black eyes blinking curiously.

I ask it to roar and it does, a big hearty growl that makes some little kids nearby run away from the enclosure shrieking and laughing.

"Good boy," I whisper. Sarah squeezes my arm.

"You're a regular Dr. Doolittle," she says. "If you ever need to go into hiding again, the circus would be perfect."

I use my animal telepathy at a few other cages. I

encourage a bored-looking seal to put on an impromptu show with a beach ball. I ask the monkeys to come right up and press their hands against the glass so that Sarah can give them little high fives. It's good practice for a Legacy that I usually only use to communicate with BK.

The zoo starts closing around sunset. As Sarah and I wander towards the exit, she puts her head on my shoulder and sighs. I can tell there's something on her mind.

"I need more days like this with you," she says.

"I know. I want that too. Once we've defeated the Mogs, I promise, we'll have all the time in the world."

Sarah gets a distant look on her face, almost as if she's imagining that future and it doesn't necessarily excite her. "What happens after, though? You go back to Lorien, right?"

"Hopefully. We still need to find a way back. And we need to hope Malcolm is right about these Phoenix things contained in our Chests, that we have enough of them and that they're capable of restoring our planet."

"And you want me to come with you?"

"Of course," I reply instantly. "I don't want to go anywhere without you."

Sarah smiles at me with an edge of sadness that I didn't expect. "You're sweet, John, but I don't mean this like our road-trip game with Six. I mean for real. Would we ever come back?" Sarah asks. "To Earth?"

"Yeah, of course," I say, because I know that's what

I should say in this situation, even though I'm not sure it's actually true. I look down at my feet. "I'm sure we'd come back."

"Seriously? Years in a spaceship, John. Don't get me wrong, part of me really wants to go. It's not every girl that has a boyfriend asking to take her to another galaxy. But I have a family here, John. I know they're not, like, on the level of restoring an entire planet to its former glory, but they're pretty important to me."

I'm frowning now, my good mood turning into something else. It's a sad feeling; a lost feeling. "I don't want to take you away from your family, Sarah. Returning to Lorien, it's supposed to be a good thing, a triumphant thing." I hesitate, trying to find words to articulate what I'm feeling. "I've always thought of it as what happens at the end, you know? After all the fighting, we'd return there and find a way to start over. It's like destiny, but it's also never actually felt truly possible, if that makes sense. I've never stopped to think out the details. I guess maybe I should."

We stop walking and she reaches up to touch my face. "I don't want to take you away from your destiny. Please don't think I'm trying to do that."

"No, of course not. But I don't want to go back to Lorien without you."

"I'm not sure I'd want to stay on Earth without you," she replies.

"So where does that leave us?"

"I don't know what the future holds," Sarah says. "But I love you, John. For now, that's all that matters. We'll figure the rest out when we get there."

"I love you too," I reply, pulling her close and kissing her.

Just then my bracelet begins to tingle.

CHAPTER TWENTY-EIGHT

"WHAT'S WRONG?" SARAH ASKS WHEN I SUDDENLY pull away from her.

"My bracelet's warning me. Something's up," I reply, spinning around, trying to take in everything around us at once. "Something bad."

"This seriously can't keep happening," Sarah says with disbelief, referring to last night's BK emergency.

"No, this is different. Worse."

Instinctively I touch my bracelet as it sends icicles up and down my arm. We're on a pretty crowded street in downtown Chicago. I scan the faces around us; people walking home from work, couples heading out for dinner, humans all of them. Not a pale face with a penchant for dark clothing to be seen. Yet the bracelet has never steered me wrong in the past. There's danger nearby.

"We should get back home," Sarah says. "Warn the others."

I shake my head. "No. If they're following us and we don't flush them out, we could end up leading them to the others."

"Crap, you're right. So what do we do?"

"We have to find them." I grab Sarah's hand and walk a few steps down the block. The pins-and-needles sensation on my wrist begins to fade, which means the danger is in the other direction. I turn back around and head that way, although I don't see anything out of the ordinary.

"John . . . ," Sarah says warningly, clutching my hand in both of hers. She's trying to hide the glow that my skin is suddenly giving off. My Lumen has triggered, both my hands lighting up, ready for a fight. I take a deep breath and calm myself, willing my hands to go back to normal. Luckily, no one around us seems to notice.

"Over here," I say, and lead Sarah towards the mouth of a dark back alley. The bracelet is practically screaming at me now, my entire arm numb from the pins and needles. I slide up against the wall and poke my head around the corner of the alley.

There are three of them. Mogadorian scouts by the look of them. They're not even making much effort to pass as human, their pale heads clean shaven but without tattoos, dressed in the dark trench coats that would spook just about anyone. Whatever they're doing here, it's pretty clear they aren't expecting to be spotted. Two of them are keeping watch while the third runs his hands underneath a Dumpster. He yanks something free from beneath the metal, an envelope of some kind.

"There're three," I whisper to Sarah. She's standing next to me, her back against the wall. "They must be the vat-grown ones Malcolm was talking about. Pale and ugly, as usual."

"What're they doing here?"

"Don't know," I reply. "But they're easy targets."

"I didn't bring a gun on our date," she whispers back. "I should've known better."

"It's okay," I tell her. "They haven't spotted us."

Sarah looks down at my hands. "We can't just let them do whatever they're doing, can we?"

"Hell no," I reply, realizing that my fists have clenched. For once, I've got the drop on Mogadorians. I want to know what they're up to. No more running scared. "If things go bad, you run for help."

"Things won't go bad," Sarah says firmly, and confidence flows through me. "Light those assholes up."

I step into the alley and walk right towards the Mogs. Their hollow eyes focus on me in unison. For a moment, that old familiar chill runs through me, that fugitive feeling. I shove it down; this time, I'm choosing fight over flight.

"You guys lost?" I ask casually, striding closer.

"Get outta here, kid," one of them hisses, flashing a row of tiny teeth. The Mog next to him opens up his coat, showing me the handle of a blaster tucked into his pants. They're trying to scare me off like I'm just some human taking a really ill-advised shortcut home. They don't recognize me for what I am. That means whatever they're doing here, it isn't hunting me.

"Getting kinda chilly," I say, stopping about ten yards away from them. "You warm enough?"

Without waiting for a response, I trigger my Lumen. A fireball swirls into existence over my palm and I lob it at the closest Mog. He doesn't even have a chance to react before it envelops his face, lighting him up like a matchstick for a moment before he disintegrates to ash.

The second Mog at least manages to reach for his blaster but that's as far as he gets. I hit him with a fireball right in the chest. He lets loose a short scream and then joins the first Mog as dust on the dirty alley ground.

I don't hit the final Mog with my Lumen. He's the one holding that envelope and I don't want to risk torching it. I want to see what the Mogs are after, what secret mission has these Mogadorians skulking around Chicago. He stares at me, almost as if he's waiting for me to dispatch him as easily as I did the others, the envelope clutched to his chest. When he realizes that I'm hesitating, he takes off, sprinting down the alley.

A Mogadorian running from me. Now there's a welcome change of pace.

I grab the Dumpster with my telekinesis and launch it at the Mog before he can get too far. The Dumpster's metal sides screech as they grind against the alley wall. It hits the Mog and pins him up against the wall, his bones crunching.

"Tell me what you're doing here and I'll make this quick," I say, walking over to him. To demonstrate, I put a little telekinetic pressure on the Dumpster, grinding it farther into his mangled body. A bubble of dark blood dribbles down the Mog's chin. His scream of frustration and pain makes me hesitate. I've never done anything like this before. The Mogs I've killed have all been quick and in self-defense. I hope I'm not going too far.

"You—you're all going to die," spits the Mog.

I'm wasting my time. I'm not likely to learn anything important from some lowly scout. I shove the Dumpster one last time with my telekinesis, finishing him off. Then I pull the Dumpster away from the wall and pluck the envelope from the pile of Mogadorian ash. I turn it over in my hands—it's stuffed with papers.

"What is it?" Sarah asks, approaching cautiously from the mouth of the alley.

I light up one of my hands so I can see the papers in the darkness. I'm holding three pages covered in rigid script that looks like a cross between hieroglyphics and

Chinese. Written in Mogadorian, of course. I guess it'd be too lucky to catch the Mogs sending secret orders in English. I hold up the papers so that Sarah can see.

"Know any good Mogadorian translators?" I ask.

Back at the penthouse, I gather everyone in the dining room to describe my encounter with the Mogs. Nine pats me on the back when I get to the part about killing the three Mogadorians.

"You should've brought that last one back here," he says. "We could've tortured something out of him like they did to us."

I shake my head. I glance over at Sam, who has begun surreptitiously rubbing his scarred wrists. "That's not what we do," I say. "We're better than that."

"It's a war, Johnny," Nine replies.

"What does this mean?" Marina asks. "Do they know where we are?"

"I doubt it," I say. "If they were here for us, they'd have sent more than three. They didn't even recognize me when I approached."

"Yeah, and you're a famous Mogadorian killer," says Eight. "Weird."

"They'd have come by now if they were coming," Six adds. "They aren't exactly known for their subtlety. We need to figure out what these papers say. It could be some kind of invasion plan."

"Just like my dream," whispers Ella.

The papers in question are being passed around the table, everyone taking a look at the meaningless symbols on the pages.

Malcolm takes the papers, frowning. "I spent time in captivity, but I never learned their language."

"Pretty sure there's some translating software on Sandor's computer," offers Nine. "Doubt it has Mogadorian, though."

Malcolm runs a hand over his beard, still looking over the papers. "There are patterns here, like with all languages. This can be cracked. If you show me that software, I may be able to use it."

Everyone around the table looks nervous. It's the first whiff of the Mogadorians we've had since battling them in Arkansas.

"This doesn't change anything," I say. "Whatever is in those documents, I'm sure it's something the Mogadorians don't want us to know. It's something we can use to our advantage. But, until we know for sure, we press on with the plan we've already made. Get some rest, everyone; we leave for Florida in the morning."

CHAPTER
TWENTY-NINE

I STAND OVER MY FATHER'S SHOULDER AS HE scans the Mogadorian documents into Sandor's computer system. Once the documents are scanned, my dad loads up some translating software along with some kind of hacker program that's supposed to be able to crack through firewalls and crap like that.

"Do you think you'll be able to translate it?" I ask.

"The first step was figuring out which program to use."

"And did you?" I notice that my dad's opened and minimized a copy of iTunes. I tap the screen. "Were you going to listen to some music?"

"I—they didn't have iTunes when I was taken. I thought it might . . ." My dad shrugs self-deprecatingly. "I'll admit to some trial and error, okay?"

"So now what?"

"I'm approaching it from every angle. All languages— even alien ones—share some commonalities. It's just a matter of isolating one and using it to decode the rest of the writing." He looks over his shoulder at me. "This is pretty boring stuff, Sam. You don't need to keep me company."

"No, it's cool," I say. "I want to."

"Really?" he asks, looking me over. "It looks to me like you had other plans."

Observant as always. I'm dressed in what passes as my best outfit considering I've only got like three options. It's just a boring gray sweater and my least grungy pair of jeans. I'd been psyching myself up to do like John said, to try to have a conversation with Six about my feelings, carpe diem and all that. This latest crisis, even if it just involves paperwork, is a pretty good excuse to put that off.

"They can wait," I say lamely, making a show of studying the computer screen as various language samples scroll by.

"Hmm." My dad smiles gently, looking back to the screen himself. "You know, they're off to Florida tomorrow. After that, there will surely be another mission. And who knows what intel we might glean from these documents. A lot happening."

"What's your point?"

"It might be awhile before we have another quiet night like this one," he says. "Don't put it off, Sam."

I find Six on the penthouse roof, which is apparently the hot spot for Garde who want to be alone. It's night and the wind is stronger up here than normal, probably on account of Six messing with the weather. Both her hands are raised and as she moves them back and forth the sky responds; it reminds me of art class, the way paint would swirl together when we mixed watercolors. Six is doing that to the clouds. If there are any weathermen watching the skies tonight, they're probably pretty freaked out.

I don't say anything at first, not wanting to interrupt. I stand next to Six and watch her, the wind whipping her blond hair across her face, bathed in the blinking red lights that line the roof. There's a small smile creeping up on the corners of her mouth. If I didn't know her better, I'd say Six was actually feeling content.

Slowly, almost like she regrets stopping, Six lowers her hands and looks at me. The wind dies down immediately, the clouds resuming their normal lazy course across the night sky. I feel like I'm interrupting something.

"Hey. You didn't have to stop."

"It's cool. What's up?" she says. "Did your dad figure out those documents already?"

"Um, no, nothing's up. I just wanted to talk to you."

"Oh," Six replies, looking back up at the sky. "Sure."

"It's no big deal," I say hurriedly, feeling stupid. "You can go back to practicing or whatever. I'll leave you alone."

"No, stay," she says suddenly. "Being cooped up in that

penthouse all the time is hard for me. Ever since I developed this Legacy, I've felt connected to the weather. I like to keep in touch with it, if that makes sense."

"Yeah, totally," I reply, as if I understand the first thing about being connected to the weather. "You did really great in training today. I'm sorry I screwed up."

"Come on, Sam," she says, rolling her eyes. "Enough apologizing already. Is that really what you came up here to talk about?"

"No," I reply, sighing. Screw it. I decide to just take John's advice and go for it. "I was wondering if you'd like to—uh, I don't know—hang out sometime?"

So, maybe not my smoothest attempt at asking someone out. Six playfully arches an eyebrow. "Hang out? We practically live on top of each other in there. We hang out all the time."

"I mean, like, hang out by ourselves."

"Aren't we doing that right now?"

"Yeah—I mean, uh—," I stammer, then notice the wicked smile on Six's face. "Are you messing with me?"

"A little," she says, crossing her arms. "So you're asking me on a date? Is that it?"

"Yeah, and I'm doing an amazing job at it."

"You're not doing so bad," she says gently, moving a little closer to me. "But we're fighting a war here, Sam. There's not a ton of time for hanging out. You know that."

"Um, John and Sarah went to the zoo today."

"But I don't want to have a John-and-Sarah thing with you," Six says, like it's the most obvious thing in the world.

"Oh." I shrink back, feeling gut punched. "I just thought—when you went to Spain, John told me how you felt about me, and back in Arkansas the way we hugged—uh, crap, I'm an idiot. I should've known you wouldn't be interested in someone like me."

"Whoa, there," Six says, grabbing my hand before I can make a break for the door. "I'm sorry, Sam. I didn't mean it like that. I do like you."

"You just don't like me that way," I say, filling in the rest of the classic line.

"I didn't say that. I do. Well, I might." Six throws her hands up. "I don't know! Look, it's just, John and Sarah, they think it makes things easier for them, but it doesn't. It just causes trouble."

"They seem happy to me," I reply.

"Sure, right now," Six says. "But what about when something happens? You know, John's a good leader and all, but he's not a realist. Do you think we're going to fight an entire army of Mogadorians without some casualties?"

"Jeez, that's dark."

"It's the truth. Everything's gonna go to shit eventually, Sam." She reaches out and plucks a loose thread off the front of my sweater. "I wish you'd stay away from us. Go somewhere safe. When it's over, maybe things could be different . . ."

I let loose with an incredulous laugh. "Ugh, seriously? That's, like, the kind of crap that Spider-Man tells Mary Jane when he's trying to break it off with her. Do you know how embarrassing it is to be talked to like I'm some superhero's girlfriend?"

Six laughs too, shaking her head. "I'm sorry. I didn't mean it that way. I'm just realizing what a hypocrite I'm being. This is exactly the opposite of the advice I gave to John about Sarah."

"Maybe you're right and things are going to get bad," I say. "But that doesn't mean you should cut yourself off. Being all about the war all the time? That can't be good. Maybe you should spend like ninety-five percent of your time as Six and, uh, five percent with me, being Maren."

I didn't plan that little speech; Six's old human name just pops out. Her mouth opens a bit, but she doesn't say anything at first, the name catching her off guard.

"Maren," she whispers. "I'm not sure I even remember how to be her."

There's something in the way she's looking at me now, almost like she's throwing caution to the wind. It's not the sort of devil-may-care look I'd expect from Six, but it's something more vulnerable, like she's decided to drop her guard just a little. I don't let go of her hand.

"Promise me you won't die," she says, bluntly.

In that moment I'd promise her just about anything. "I promise."

Her grip on my hand tightens, her fingers intertwined with mine. She steps closer. The wind picks up again and I reach up to brush some hair out of her face, holding my hand there against her cheek.

And that's when Eight teleports onto the roof.

Six jumps away from me like she's been scalded. I could pretty much strangle Eight right then and not feel any remorse. I expect Eight to crack some joke, but his face is set and serious.

"Guys, we need you downstairs!"

"What is it?" Six asks, starting towards Eight. "Mogs?"

Eight shakes his head. "It's Ella."

I guess my dad was wrong about this being one of those quiet nights.

Eight takes our hands and I immediately get the disorienting feeling of having the world yanked out from under me. I blink my eyes and we're suddenly standing in the room that Marina shares with Ella.

Ella is on her back in bed, all the blankets kicked off, rigid as a board. Her eyes are squeezed shut. Perhaps the most frightening thing is the small trickle of blood dribbling down from the corner of her mouth. She's bitten down on her lip, hard enough to draw blood.

Marina kneels next to the bed, dabbing at Ella's mouth with a tissue. She keeps whispering Ella's name over and over, trying to wake her up. Ella doesn't move except to clench and unclench her fists in the sheets.

"How long has she been like this?" my dad asks.

"I don't know," says Marina, sounding panicked. "She went to bed before me, said she was tired from training. I found her like this and she won't wake up."

I look around, not really sure what I should be doing. Pretty much everyone seems to be sharing that feeling. Everyone has crowded into the room or is standing in the doorway, everyone sharing a look of uncertainty.

"This has never happened before?" I ask Marina.

"You were here for the worst one, when she was screaming," she answers. "She's always woken up before."

"I don't like this," grumbles Nine from the doorway. Bernie Kosar seems to agree; he stands at the foot of the bed, sniffing the air like a guard dog catching a bad scent.

"She's sweating so much," says Marina.

"Some kind of fever?" John asks.

"It was never like this during my visions," Eight says. "You guys?"

John and Nine both shake their heads.

Marina grabs a towel from a nightstand drawer and begins to dab at Ella's forehead. Her hands are shaking so badly that Sarah eases the towel away from her. "Here," she says, "let me do it."

Eight puts his arm around Marina as she steps back from the bed, rubbing her back. Marina leans against him gratefully.

"Should we try healing her?" Six asks. "Or using one of the healing stones?"

"There's nothing to heal," John replies. "Not that we can see, anyway. And using the stone . . . who knows what might happen, what with it doubling the pain and all."

"Did you try just prying her eyes open?" suggests Five. Everyone gives him a strange look, like it's a callous suggestion, but it actually doesn't seem much worse than letting Ella suffer through whatever nightmare she's having. "What? You guys have better ideas?"

Gently, my father peels back one of Ella's eyelids. Her eye is completely rolled back in her head; we can only see the whites. I remember the time I got knocked off the rope in gym class by Mark James and had to get a concussion test. They shined a flashlight in my eyes.

"John, maybe you could use your Lumen?" I suggest. "It's bright, it might wake her up."

John reaches over, lighting up his hand like a flashlight and shining it into Ella's eye. For a moment, her body stops its constant twitching and she seems to relax.

"Something's happening," I breathe.

"Ella, wake up," urges Marina.

Ella's hand snaps upwards, grabbing John's wrist with a force that startles him. It reminds me of one of those scary movies where the little girl is possessed by a demon. Her hand glows red where it touches John's skin.

"What's she doing?" Sarah gasps.

For a moment, John looks puzzled. He starts to say something, but his eyes roll back in his head and his body contorts, like all his muscles are cramping up at once— then, as if all the tension goes out of him, he collapses like a puppet with his strings cut, right onto the floor next to Ella's bed.

"John!" Sarah shouts.

Ella's hand is still clamped around John's wrist. Nine lunges into the room. "Get her off him!"

Marina blocks Nine's way. "Wait! Don't touch her!"

Not listening, Sarah reaches down and pries Ella's hand off John's wrist. He doesn't move, doesn't come to at all, even when Sarah rolls him over and shakes him. Whatever Ella's touch did to John, apparently it doesn't have the same effect on humans because Sarah is unaffected.

Six steps forward to look closer, and I see Ella's hand reaching up towards her, fingers clenching and unclenching.

"Watch it," I say, and grab Six by the back of the shirt, pulling her backwards. The rest of the Garde notice Ella's grasping hand and everyone takes a cautious step away from the bed. As soon as there aren't any Garde within reach, her hand drops lifelessly back to the bed. She looks just like she did before, trapped in a nightmare. Except now, John has joined her.

"What the hell is going on?" Nine asks.

"She did something to him," breathes Five.

Sarah cradles John's head in her lap, stroking his hair. Nearby, my dad gently lifts Ella's hands and tucks them under the covers. I look over at the Garde. They're used to being on the run, to physical threats that they can fight and destroy. But how are they supposed to escape— or defeat—something that attacks them from within?

CHAPTER THIRTY

NOBODY GETS ANY SLEEP THAT NIGHT. WELL, except for the two of us that can't be woken up, and that's a sleep I don't think anyone is eager to join.

My dad and I lifted John onto the bed next to Ella, laying them side by side, the two of them sporadically thrashing. Sarah refuses to leave the room; she holds John's hand, stroking it gently, trying to coax him awake. Bernie Kosar won't leave either; he lies curled up at the foot of the bed, whining occasionally, nuzzling John and Ella's feet.

I poke my head into the room a few hours after John first collapsed. Sarah has her head down, pressed to the back of John's hand. I'm not sure if she's asleep or not and I don't want to disturb her. Nothing has changed with John and Ella. Their facial muscles twitch, and their bodies occasionally lurch as if they've just tripped in a dream and are scrambling for their balance. I've had those dreams before, the ones where you trip or fall off a bike, and I always wake up before I hit the ground. That doesn't seem to be the case for John and Ella.

I take a closer look at John. It has only been a few hours, but already his skin has taken on a pallor similar to Ella's, dark circles forming around his eyes. It's almost as if he's being drained somehow. Now that I think about it, Ella looked pretty washed out before training this morning. I'm worried there's some kind of physical aspect to the nightmares, like they're weakening John and Ella, or worse.

"Sarah?" I whisper, and then realize there's no point in keeping quiet. We want these two to wake up. I should be banging on pots and pans. "Everyone's getting together in the living room."

Sarah stirs, shaking her head. "I'm going to stay here," she says quietly. "I don't want to leave them."

I nod and don't press the issue. I leave the room and head over to the workshop, where my dad has spent the rest of the night hunched over a computer. When I enter, language samples are scrolling by on the screen, but it doesn't look like he's any closer to cracking those Mogadorian documents.

"Anything?" I ask.

"Not yet," he replies, turning to face me. He has to blink a few times, his eyes dilated from staring at the screen. "I've worked up an auto decoder so I don't have to sit here monitoring the progress. It's pretty, ah, old school. I'm a little behind the times when it comes to software, but it should be able to crack it eventually. I only hope it's quick enough."

I glance at the scanned Mogadorian pages. "You think any of this is related to the nightmares?"

"I don't know. The timing certainly seems convenient."

"Yeah." I notice my dad's cell phone sitting out on the desk. I tap it. "Were you trying Adam again?"

I didn't think it was possible, but my dad's face droops even farther. "Yes. No progress there either."

I pat him on the shoulder. "Come on. The others are meeting and want us to join them."

The remaining Garde are waiting in the penthouse living room. They're already discussing the nightmare situation, which is pretty much what we've been doing for the last couple hours without making any progress.

"Ella did that to me before," Marina is saying, her voice hushed. "Sucked me into her dream. I should have warned him, should've warned everyone. But I was touching her before, when I first tried to wake her up, and nothing happened. I was in such a panic. . . ."

Sitting next to her on the couch, Eight puts his arm around Marina's shoulders. She leans against him as he says, "It's okay. You couldn't have known this would happen."

Nine is pacing back and forth across the length of the room, which is actually an improvement over him pacing across the ceiling. He'd probably still be wearing a track into the space around the chandelier if Six hadn't snapped at him for being annoying. For once, he didn't bother with a comeback and simply resumed his pacing somewhere less obtrusive. He looks up at me hopefully when I reenter.

"Well?" Nine asks.

I shake my head. "No change. They still haven't woken up."

Five slaps his hands on his legs in frustration. "This sucks. I feel useless sitting here."

Six's brow was knit in consternation when I first entered, but she looks up when Five speaks. She nods her head slowly, considering. "We should talk about that."

"About what?" Marina asks.

"About continuing on with the mission. Five's Chest isn't going to recover itself."

Nine stops pacing, considering what Six has just said. Marina looks aghast at the notion of going on a mission.

"You want to leave now?" Marina asks. "Have you gone crazy?"

"Six is right," Five jumps in. "We're not doing any good sitting around here."

"Our friends are in there comatose and you just want to leave them?" hisses Marina.

"You make it sound cold, but I'm just trying to be practical," Six says. It sounds similar to what she was telling me on the roof, how she's reluctant to start a relationship because of that moment where things go to shit. It seems like that moment is here.

"It is practical, but that doesn't mean it's right," I murmur. I don't mean to say that out loud, but it's been a long night and there's a lot on my mind.

A shadow of hurt passes over Six's face, but it's gone as soon as she looks away from me. She turns to Nine. "What do you think?"

"I don't know," Nine says. "I don't like abandoning John and the squirt."

"If even Nine's backing down from a mission, then you know it's not the right idea," snaps Marina, sounding exasperated. "What if they need us, Six?"

"We wouldn't be abandoning them," Five says, his voice level. "At least, we wouldn't be abandoning them any more than we are by sitting out here having this pointless discussion. The humans will take care of them, just like they are now."

"Absolutely," my dad says. "We'll do everything we can."

"We need to figure out why this is happening," Marina says. "If not what's causing the nightmares, then what Ella did to knock out John."

"Did you guys notice the way her hand glowed when she touched him?" I ask. "It was like a Legacy or something."

"What kind of Legacy does that?" Nine asks, pointing towards the bedroom.

"John thought she used some new Legacy to scare off Setrákus Ra in New Mexico," Marina says, thinking this through. "We never had a chance to test it."

"Or it could be her telepathy gone crazy. Maybe she got in his head and lost control," suggests Eight. "She's only just started getting her Legacies. Who knows what she might be capable of?"

I think back to our time in Paradise, remembering how much work it took John to control his Lumen over those first few weeks. It seems like Ella's telepathy would be an even more difficult Legacy to master. I notice Five nodding his head slowly as if he's remembering something too.

"Back when I first developed my Externa, I had problems changing my skin back to normal," Five says. "Albert used this prism thing from my Chest and it helped, I don't know, relax me somehow. I was able to change my skin back."

Six points at Five. "There you go. Another argument for going to the Everglades, to get whatever that was."

Nine nods in agreement. "I can't believe it, but you actually might be on to something, Five."

Five holds his hands up. "Well, wait, I don't even know if it would work on Ella. Or how it works."

"I still don't think we should leave them like this," says Marina.

"Actually, I think separating all of you from John and Ella is a good idea," my dad says. "Who's to say this couldn't start spreading somehow, especially if it's related to her telepathy? We can't afford to have any more of you in a catatonic state."

"How do we fight this?" Nine asks gruffly, his brow furrowed, probably having exhausted all the possible ways to punch out a nightmare. "I mean, if Setrákus Ra can just put us into some dream coma, how are we supposed to fight back against that?"

"He's come at us with these dreams before," says Eight. "We woke up, no problem."

"It's different this time," Marina insists.

"Last time Johnny woke up," Nine says. "That means this shit got stronger."

"Or maybe the difference is Ella," says Six. "Maybe Setrákus Ra has been focusing on her because he knew it would make her psychic powers go haywire."

I look over at Five. "And you think this prism thing from your Chest can help?"

He shrugs in response. "I'm not even sure what it does exactly, only that it helped me. Going after it seems more productive than sitting around here."

Nine claps his hands. "I'm with Five. Let's get the hell out of here."

Marina has been quiet since initially arguing against the Everglades. Now Six reaches over and puts a hand on her arm. "Are you all right with this?" she asks.

Marina nods slowly. "If you believe this is the best way to help them, then I'm with you."

I head down to the parking garage to see the Garde off. Sarah won't be budged from John's side and my dad has gone back to check on the Mogadorian translator. I'm holding a folder full of documents that John had me prepare using Sandor's computer—fake driver's licenses for each of the Garde, some paperwork documenting a phony school trip, the itinerary of their direct flight from Chicago to Orlando. They should be able to travel undetected.

I fish John's documents out of the file and stick them in my pocket. "Guess you won't need these," I say, handing the rest over to Six. I hold on to the file a second too long and Six ends up having to tug it loose from my hand. "Sorry. Just nervous about this."

"It's the right move, Sam. It'll be okay."

Nine pats me on the shoulder and goes off to pick out a car to drive to the airport. Five follows him, not bothering with a good-bye. To my surprise, Marina wraps me in a hug.

"Take care of them, okay?" she says.

"Of course," I reply, trying to sound reassuring. "They'll be fine. You guys just hurry back."

Eight nods to me and then he and Marina follow after Nine. That leaves just Six and me. She's making a show of thumbing through the documents I handed her, but I can tell she's lingering because she wants to say something.

"Everything's there," I tell her.

"I know. Just double-checking," she replies, looking up at me. "We should be back by tomorrow night at the latest."

"Be careful," I say.

"Thanks," she says, touching me on the arm.

There's an awkward pause, neither of us really sure what to do. I wish we could've had just fifteen minutes more alone on the rooftop. I feel like that would've been enough to figure out whatever is going on between us. Now, we're standing here like a couple just back from a really bizarre first date, neither sure what the other is thinking nor whether it's an appropriate time to make a move. Well, maybe Six knows exactly what I'm thinking and just doesn't know what to do with that information. I certainly don't have a clue what's going through her mind. I feel like I should say or do something, but then the moment passes, her hand drops away from my arm, and she turns to join the others. Whatever is between us, it'll have to wait.

Nine's penthouse seems even bigger now that it's emptied out. I wander through the deserted halls and lavish rooms, not really sure what to do with myself. I end up going back to Ella's room to check in, just as Sarah is leaving. It's the first time that she's been away from John since he went down.

"Your dad is making me eat something," she explains

sullenly, looking exhausted from staying awake for the entire night.

"Yeah, he's got this thing about people not starving to death," I reply. Sarah gives me a weak smile and I put my hand on her back, guiding her towards the kitchen. She rests her head on my shoulder as we walk.

"We've had so many arguments about one of us getting hurt. It's like the most frequent fight of our relationship." She laughs bitterly. "Funny thing is, I always thought it'd be me, not John. He's supposed to be untouchable."

"Geez, Sarah, you're acting like he's been chopped in half or something. He'll probably pop awake in an hour and be mad they went on the mission without him." I try to sound optimistic. Sarah is probably too tired to notice the uncertainty in my voice.

"If he was chopped in half, they could probably heal him," she says. "This is something else. I can see the pain on his face. It's like he's being tortured in front of me and there's nothing I can do about it."

I pour Sarah a glass of water and take some leftover Chinese food out of the fridge. I don't bother heating it up. We eat in silence, picking at cold fried rice and boneless spareribs straight from the cartons. I repeat the phrase *he'll be fine* over and over in my head, like a mantra, until I'm confident that I can say it with conviction, even if I'm not entirely convinced it's true.

"He'll be fine," I tell Sarah firmly.

While Sarah goes back to watch over John and Ella, I try to get some rest in the living room. I guess when you've just recently seen your best friend sucked into a state of perpetual sleep, naptime can be a little nerve-racking. Still, my body is more exhausted than my anxiety is strong, and I must fall asleep for at least a few hours.

The first thing I do upon waking up is check on John and Ella. There's still no change.

I wander down to the Lecture Hall thinking that some kind of workout will do me good. Maybe if I pick out the noisiest guns in Nine's arsenal to use in target practice, I'll disrupt John and Ella's slumber.

I stop through the workshop on my way. It's empty. My dad must be in his room getting some rest.

The tablet is still plugged in and I can see that five blue dots have made it to Florida, currently moving slowly across the southern tip. That's good. It means Six and the others didn't have any problems using their new fake IDs at the airport and that there weren't any Mogadorian scouts waiting to pick them off. Everything appears to be going just the way John planned. If only he was awake to see it.

I notice something blinking in the corner of one of the computer screens. It's the translator program my dad set up. It must have been on autopilot this entire time. I restore the window, a dialogue box popping up.

TRANSLATION COMPLETE. PRINT NOW?

I swallow hard, not sure if it's my place to be the first one viewing these Mogadorian translations, but clicking YES anyway. A printer beneath the desk hisses to life, spitting out the document. I grab the first page before the rest have even finished printing.

Some of the words are jumbled or mixed up, making it clear that the translation program is not 100 percent accurate. But even with the occasional misplaced word, I recognize the document immediately. I've seen it before.

I realize that I'm holding my breath, that my fingers have clenched the papers tight enough to wrinkle and bend them. I'm rooted in place, disbelief and fear shutting down my much-needed motor functions.

I'm holding in my hands a copy of the notes my father took on the Garde's Inheritance. Tacked onto the end is the address of the John Hancock Center.

CHAPTER THIRTY-ONE

I BURST OUT OF THE WORKSHOP, THE DOOR sharply clanging behind me. My palms are sweating, almost like the documents I'm holding are radiating heat. My mind races.

What would the Mogadorians be doing with copies of my father's notes? How would they even have gotten them?

I think back to dinner that first night when my dad laid out the details of his long Mogadorian imprisonment. I remember some of the Garde seeming suspicious, especially when my dad talked about the tinkering the Mogadorians did with his mind. Nine even came right out and said that it could be a trap.

But that wasn't possible. He's my father. We could trust him.

I race down the hallway to my dad's room. I'm not even sure what I'm going to do when I find him. Confront him? Tell him we need to get the hell out of here?

His room is empty. I find myself taking a quick glance around, not even sure what I'm looking for. Some kind of Mogadorian communicator? A Mog-English dictionary? Nothing looks out of the ordinary.

There has to be a rational explanation for this, right?

Hadn't I seen with my own eyes the kind of literal mind games the Mogadorians are capable of? I'd seen Adam use a Legacy that was apparently the side effect of the Mogs ripping out the memories from a dead Garde. Even now, John and Ella were comatose thanks to some telepathic assault perpetuated by Setrákus Ra. The Mogadorians held on to my dad for years and ran unspeakable experiments on his mind.

Was it really outside the realm of possibility that the Mogs could've brainwashed him?

My dad might not even be aware they're controlling him. They might have done something to his brain and then let him escape on purpose, knowing that he'd be more valuable out in the world, gathering intelligence. The Mogs could've programmed him in a way that he's secretly reporting to them while he sleeps—I remember reading something about how double agents could be hypnotized into forgetting their own subterfuge. Was that a real article or a comic book? I couldn't remember.

Back in the hallway, I yell, "Dad? Where are you?" I try to keep my voice normal and steady. Because what if he is a Mogadorian spy? I don't want to tip him off.

"In here," my dad yells back from Ella and John's room.

My dad the alien spy? Come on. Get a grip, Sam. That's the kind of conspiracy theory I might've found in *They Walk Among Us*. It's ridiculous. More importantly, I know in my heart that it isn't true.

So why do I feel so nervous?

I stand in the doorway to Ella's room clutching the translated documents. Sarah has gone to her own room to get some sleep, so it's just him and Bernie Kosar standing watch over John and Ella. BK is curled up, asleep, my dad idly scratching behind his ears.

"What is it, Sam?" he asks.

My dad must know by my wide-eyed look that something's wrong. He leaves BK and walks towards me, but I find myself stepping instinctively backwards into the hallway. I'm keeping a safe distance from the loving father who rescued me from a prison cell. Great.

I thrust the documents at him. "Why would the Mogadorians have these?"

He flips through the papers, turning the pages more rapidly as he realizes what they are. "These—these are my notes."

"I know. How did the Mogadorians get their hands on them?"

He must realize the implication of my question because a hurt expression briefly clouds his face.

"Sam, I did not do this," he says, trying to sound convincing, but there's a note of uncertainty in his voice.

"Can you be sure? What if—what if they did something to you, Dad? Something that you don't remember?"

"No. Impossible," he says, shaking his head, almost as if he's trying to convince himself. I can tell by his tone that he doesn't truly believe it's impossible. In fact, I think he's frightened by the thought. "Are the originals still in my room?"

· Together, we run back to his room. The notebook is on his bureau, right where it's supposed to be. My dad flips through it, like he's looking for some sign it's been tampered with. His features tighten like they do when he's trying to remember something. I think he's realizing that he can't trust himself, that the Mogadorians could've done something to him.

He turns to me with a grim look on his face. "If my notes have gotten into Mogadorian hands, we have to assume this place is compromised. You should arm yourself, Sam. Sarah too."

"What about you?" I ask, my stomach turning over.

"I—I can't be trusted," he stammers. "You should lock me in here, until the Garde return."

"There has to be another explanation," I say, my voice cracking. I'm not sure if I really believe that or if I just want it to be true.

"I don't remember leaving," he says. "But I suppose my memory isn't worth much, at this point."

He drops heavily onto the bed in his room. He folds his hands in his lap and stares down at them. He looks defeated somehow, undermined by both his mind and his son.

I start towards the door. "Look, I'm going to go get Sarah and some guns. But I'm not going to lock you in here. Just stay here, okay?"

"Wait." He stops me, holding up a hand. "What is that?"

I hear it too. A low rumbling sound, coming from the drawer of his nightstand. I get there first, flinging open the drawer.

It's the phone he was using to communicate with Adam. The screen is lit up, a phone call coming in from a blocked number. In the corner of the screen, I see that the phone has nineteen missed calls. I hold it up to my father. His face lights up, but I feel increasingly nervous. Too much is happening all at once. It feels like the walls are closing in on me.

I hit the button and press the phone to my ear, my voice shaky. "Hello?"

"Malcolm!" the breathless voice on the phone shouts. "Where have you been?!"

"This is Sam," I correct, a feeling of dread rising in my stomach as I recognize the voice. "Adam, is that you?"

My dad jumps up and squeezes my shoulders, excited that Adam is still alive. I wish I could feel relieved, but the way he sounds on the phone, it's like more bad news is on the way.

"Sam? Sam! Where's your father?"

"He's—"

"Never mind! It doesn't matter!" he shouts. "Listen to me, Sam. You're in Chicago, right? The John Hancock Center?"

"How—how did you know that?"

"They know, Sam!" Adam yells. "They know and they're coming for you!"

CHAPTER
THIRTY-TWO

"HOLD ON!"

We all lurch to one side as Nine haphazardly steers our fan boat—exactly what it sounds like, a small boat propelled by a giant fan on the back—around an overturned log floating in the murky brown swamp water. Eight nearly loses his balance and has to grab on to my arm to steady himself. He flashes me a sheepish smile as he lets me go to swat a mosquito. The air is thick and humid, buzzing with insects that can be heard even above the roar of our boat's propeller. This place smells of rich soil, of nature overgrown.

"Look at that!" Eight shouts to be heard over the boat. I peer over the side to where a massing of lily pads is disturbed by something drifting through the water. At first I think it's another log, but then I notice the rough scales of a tail swaying across the water and know it's an alligator. "Keep your hands inside the ride," Eight yells.

I watch as the alligator disappears into an outgrowth of trees to our left. I can see why Five thought the Everglades would be a safe place to hide his Inheritance; it's a maze of tall grasses and muddy water, deserted except for the bugs and the lurking animals.

We're traveling down what is basically a road in the water, a place where the dense saw grass and trees that sprout up on either side of us part to allow boat traffic. Not that there's anyone else out here—we haven't seen a single human being since picking up our boat from the rental place an hour ago. Even that was just a ramshackle cabin stuck between the end of a country road and the edge of the swamp. We had our pick of three rusted fan boats lashed to the rickety dock. The solitary man living out there, sunburned and smelling like a combination of alcohol and jet fuel, hiccupped his way through a tutorial on boat operation before accepting some cash in exchange for a dog-eared map of the area and the keys to the boat. He didn't ask any questions, which we were all thankful for.

It's the local man's map that Six is concerning herself with. She's comparing it to the map of the Everglades that we printed off the internet, the one Five marked with the location of his Chest. She keeps switching between our map and the smudged but more detailed map of local tributaries and bayou backwaters. She holds the papers away from her, annoyed. "I can't make sense of this," she grumbles.

"Don't worry about it," Nine replies, steering us forward, towards the sunset. "Five said he knows where we're going. Let him be useful for a change."

I glance to the sky, looking for Five. He flew off about fifteen minutes ago, claiming he could better find his Chest from above. The edge of the sky is starting to turn a shade of pink that I'd normally find beautiful, but out here seems somehow ominous.

"I don't mean to sound like a chicken," I say warily, pushing a wet strand of hair behind my ear, "but I seriously don't want to be out here after the sun sets."

"Me neither," adds Eight, flicking the map in Six's hands. "Especially if our esteemed navigator doesn't know how to get us back to civilization."

Six narrows her eyes at Eight but doesn't reply. Nine just laughs. Huge sweat stains darken his shirt and bugs buzz around him incessantly, but he doesn't seem to notice. In fact, Nine seems to be enjoying this—the humidity, the stickiness, the sense of danger. It's his natural element. "I was thinking we might go camping after," he says.

Eight and I groan. If there weren't alligators drifting around in the water beneath us, I'd definitely take this opportunity to splash Nine. I look to the skies again, keeping my eyes peeled for Five.

"I'm sure he'll be back soon," I say. There's no reason not to be optimistic. So far, this mission has run smoothly with no sign of any trouble. I still don't feel right about leaving John and Ella behind, but the others were right. There's nothing we could do for them in Chicago. I haven't quite reached the levels of enthusiasm Nine has, but it definitely feels better to be out here doing something, searching for a way to help our friends and win this war.

Just as long as we don't get lost in this swamp. No good could come from that.

A shadow passes overhead. Five. He hovers over the boat for a moment before gently dropping down beside us. He's dripping sweat, his white T-shirt soaked through.

Nine snickers. "Probably gonna lose some weight if we hang down here long enough, huh, big boy?"

Five grits his teeth, pulling his wet shirt away from his body self-consciously. We're all sweaty and gross, but for some reason Nine just can't resist picking on Five. I had dared to hope that maybe the game of capture the flag helped them work out some of their issues, but there's still tension festering between them.

"Ignore him," I say to Five. "Did you find your Chest?"

Five nods, pointing in the direction we're already going. "There's a patch of solid ground about a mile farther. It's there."

Nine sighs. "Why didn't you just grab the Chest and fly it back here, man?"

Five smirks at Nine. "You didn't listen to the plan, did

you? We voted that you should handle all manual labor and grunt work."

"Huh?" Confused, Nine looks over at Eight. "Is he serious?"

Eight shrugs, playing along.

Six makes an exasperated noise. "Just drive the damn boat, Nine."

"Aye-aye, captain," Nine says, wiggling his fingers. "One Chest, coming right up."

Six turns her gaze to Five. She's been more quiet than usual. "Why didn't you grab the Chest?" she asks sharply.

Five shrugs. "It's getting dark and it's a good place to rest, if we need to."

"See?" Nine shouts, delighted. "Camping!"

"No way," says Eight, shaking his head vehemently. "Drive this thing faster so we can get out of here."

Nine accelerates the boat, spray kicking up over the side as a result.

I guess where Five leads us could charitably be described as an island. Really, it's just a pile of mud in the middle of the swamp, the support system for one massive and gnarled tree that looks like it has been growing since the dawn of time. The tree's roots are so huge and outstretched that Nine has to drive the boat up cautiously, not wanting to get stuck on any of them. We climb out of the boat, our feet squishing through mud and slipping across the uneven protrusions of the tree. There's a ring of tall grass growing from the water around us and the tree's branches above are so numerous and thick that the entire little island is thrown into shadow almost as soon as you step onto it. It's actually almost ten degrees cooler here than it was on the water.

"This is actually a pretty great spot," I tell Five.

Five's chest puffs out a little at the rare compliment. "Yeah. I camped here one night. This old tree is amazing. Figured I wouldn't have any problems finding it again."

"Congratulations," grumbles Nine, swatting at a bug on his neck. "So where's your damn Chest?"

Five leads us right to the base of the tree. Under our feet is a complicated lattice of roots; it's like the tree is a fist plunged into the earth and the roots are its fingers, mud squeezing out from in between the tree's tight grasp. Five kneels down under a knot of roots, a place where they've bunched up a bit, almost like a knuckle. He reaches underneath the roots where a soft pocket of mud waits.

"It's under here," Five says, feeling around. "Almost got it."

The mud makes a wet sucking noise when Five pulls the Chest free, as if it's reluctant to give up our prize. Five kneels in front of it, wiping muck off the familiar wooden surface.

Eight taps on my shoulder and points to a place where the tall grass is parting. I can see the flat head and yellow eyes of an alligator, maybe the same one as before. "Looks like someone's hungry," Eight jokes.

"Is he following us?" I ask, partly kidding around, but also a little creeped out. I inch closer to Eight.

"Lots of gators down here," says Five absently, hefting his Chest up.

"You talk to animals, don't you?" I ask Nine. "Tell that beast we don't want any trouble."

"Maybe I'll keep it as a pet. Or make a sweet-ass coat out of it," Nine replies, squinting as he focuses on the approaching animal. Something in his face suddenly changes. "Hold up—"

A second alligator's head appears next to the first, and then seconds later a third head also emerges from the muck. At first, I think we're being stalked by a pack of gators, if such a thing is even possible. But then the three heads rise out of the water as one, a thick scale-covered neck connecting them all to a single body. The scales disappear beneath a soaked coat of oily black fur on the beast's torso, droplets of water violently shaking loose as it stretches a pair of leathery bat wings. It ends up standing almost fifteen feet tall on a pair of almost humanoid legs. It hunches forward, six pairs of jaundiced eyes staring at us hungrily.

"Look out!" shouts Six, just as the creature flaps its wings and takes to the air.

The creature looms in the air over me. It's funny the

things you notice in a moment like that. The monster's feet are huge, curled talons extending from each foot's three toes as well as from the heels. But the pads of the monster's feet look almost soft, a pair of S-shaped scars carved into the tissue there, like some Mogadorian scientist signed his work.

I see all that in the moment before it tries to stomp down on me.

"Watch out!" Eight grabs me around the waist and we teleport backwards. The mutant gator's clawed toes shear a chunk out of the root I was standing on.

"How the hell did they find us?" Nine snarls, extending his pipe staff.

"I don't see any Mogs," I shout, spinning around, trying to take in the entire swamp. "Could it be alone?"

"I'll go ask it."

Nine charges in. The beast snaps at him with one of its three mouths. Nine brings his pipe-staff up and jams it right into the closest mouth, knocking out a couple of yellowed fangs. With one head roaring in pain, the monster lashes out with a wing, forcing Nine backwards.

Five drops his Chest on the ground and unlocks it. Six grabs his shoulder. "What the hell?" she yells. "You didn't see this thing when you scouted?"

"It came from underwater. How could I see it?" Five's voice is calm, he doesn't seem rattled at all, unlike how John described him in their last battle. "Don't worry," he continues. "I've got just the thing in here."

"A little help?!" Nine shouts as he jumps away from one of the monster's snapping mouths.

Eight teleports right above the creature's three heads. He kicks it hard in one of its snouts, then teleports away so he's side by side with Nine. The thing lets loose a frustrated roar, flapping its wings and trying to take to the air. Nine and Eight separate, trying to flank the beast.

As Five rummages through his Chest, Six thrusts her hands in the air. "Marina, watch my back while I do this." I hear the first droplets of a rainstorm working their way through the foliage.

Five pulls some kind of leather sleeve out of his Chest. He slides it over his forearm. When he flexes, a sleek one-foot blade extends from the underside of his wrist. Five grins. "Missed you," he says to the sleeve contraption, the blade sliding back down when he flexes again.

"Let's hurry up on that lightning, Six!" yells Nine. The monster is bearing down on him. It's everything he can do to get his staff up, deflecting a series of bites from the trio of fanged mouths. Backpedaling blind, Nine trips over a branch and goes toppling onto his butt. The beast is about to leap right on top of him when Eight shape shifts, assuming the form of a massive half-man, half-boar, one of the avatars of Vishnu, I presume. He grabs the creature by its alligator tail and yanks it backwards, keeping it from devouring Nine.

The beast swivels around and sinks its teeth into

Eight's shoulder. He bellows through his boar snout and his form begins to flicker. I can see he's having trouble keeping his concentration with the pain from the bite.

"Eight!" I scream. I want to go to him, to heal him, but I can't leave Six while she's focusing on creating a storm.

"Go help him," she says through gritted teeth. "I'm good to go."

I race forward, intent on getting to Eight. Before the flying gator can take another chunk out of him, a lightning bolt slices down from the heavens. It strikes the creature and knocks it flat, the thing convulsing and smoking. It's raining harder now, Six really amping up the storm.

Nine is back on his feet. He barrels forward while the beast is still struggling to get its two legs under it. Nine bludgeons the creature with his staff but the blows hardly make a dent in the scale-covered hide.

With Nine back on the attack, Eight staggers away from the monster, still in his Vishnu form. He transforms back to normal when I reach him and I can see deep and jagged lacerations covering his right shoulder. I press my hands to Eight's shoulder, let the icy feeling flow through me and into him, and watch as his wounds close up.

"I could kiss you," Eight says.

"After we kill this thing, maybe," I reply.

The monster rears back and swings one of its leathery wings at Nine, knocking him backwards. As soon as

Nine is out of the way, Six calls down two more lightning strikes. The lightning knocks the beast down again and tears a hole in the membrane of its wing, but it just struggles back to his feet again and roars. It seems like we're only making it angrier.

"What does it take to stop this fucker?" shouts Nine.

A high-pitched whistle fills the air, so loud and sharp that it causes my skin to crawl, like fingernails on a chalkboard. I spin around to see Five blowing into an intricate flute carved from solid obsidian. As the shrill note fills the air, he stares unblinking at the monster.

All at once, it's like the fight goes out of the thing. It folds its huge wings around its body and sinks to the ground, its three heads tucked against its chest, almost like it's bowing.

"Whoa," breathes Eight.

"See?" says Five, lowering the whistle and glancing around. "Easy."

"If you had that thing the entire time, why didn't you use it?" Nine snaps.

"I thought you might want a workout," Five says, smiling coldly at Nine.

Six shakes her head. "Would one of you just kill that thing so we can get out of here?"

"Gladly," says Five, his skin turning into glittering steel. He takes two steps towards the genuflecting beast, but stops right next to Six. "I made the damn thing," Five says, absently. "The least I can do is put it down."

"You what?" I ask with disbelief.

Five's steel-plated fist shoots forward with a force I've never seen from him before, hitting Six with an uppercut.

The force sends Six's entire body into the air and she lands at my feet; I can see her eyes are rolled into the back of her head and twin tendrils of blood are leaking out of her nostrils. A concussion at best, a fractured skull at worst. Instinctively, I move to heal her, but when I try to crouch down something hits me in the chest—not hard, not even with enough force to knock the wind out of me—but I can't move forward. It's telekinesis. Five is gently keeping me at bay. I look up at him, confused tears filling my eyes.

Eight breaks the stunned moment of silence, yelling, "Why'd you do that?!" He's drowned out by Nine's scream.

Five's body has taken on the consistency of rubber and his arm stretches like a tentacle, wrapping twice around Nine's throat. Nine struggles, but Five lifts him off his feet with ease. His arm stretches further, hanging Nine ten feet off the ground, and then plunges downward. He dunks Nine in the swamp and holds him there. Drowning him.

Both Eight and I are frozen as Five turns to look at us. His expression is disconcertingly friendly considering his stretched-out appendage is currently holding Nine under water and Six is lying unconscious at my feet thanks to a vicious sucker punch. I can see vibrations spread up Five's arm from where Nine must be punching at it, trying to free himself. The blows must not be giving Five any pain because he hardly seems to notice.

He sits down on his Chest and looks at us.

"The three of us should probably talk," Five says calmly.

CHAPTER
THIRTY-THREE

THE CONNECTION TO ADAM ABRUPTLY GOES DEAD.
I glance down at the phone's screen, but Adam called
from a blocked number. There's no way to call him back.
Wherever he was, Adam sounded like he was moving fast,
practically shouting over the wind whipping around in the
background. On the run and sounding panicked. I'm the
exact opposite: rooted in place and feeling almost numb.

What would John do in this situation? Get moving,
that's what. I shove the phone into my back pocket and
move past my dad, heading for the hallway.

"He said the Mogadorians know where we are, and that
they're on their way. We need to get out of here. Now!"
I call back to my dad.

When I glance over my shoulder, he's still standing next
to the bed.

"Come on," I say. "What're you waiting for?"

"What if—" My dad squeezes the bridge of his nose.

"What if I can't be trusted?"

Oh, right. The whole possibility that my dad could be some kind of unwitting double agent for the Mogadorians. There has to be a better explanation for how his notes fell into their hands. Maybe he's not sure if he can trust himself, maybe he's worried that his memory is failing or working against him. It doesn't matter. I make up my mind right then and there. I trust him.

"Remember outside of the Dulce Base when I wanted to rush back inside to go help the Garde fight? You told me there would be other moments to make myself useful to the Loric. Well, I think this is one of those times. I trust you, Dad. I can't do this without you."

He nods solemnly. Without another word, he reaches under his bed and pulls out the rifle that he used to take down that monster in Arkansas, pumping a shell into place.

"Did Adam tell you how long we have?" he asks.

As if in answer, the building shakes, all the lights flickering. An engine flares outside, the noise above us and dangerously close, followed by a sharp metallic grinding. Something just landed on the roof.

"Apparently, not long at all."

We dart into the hallway where Sarah has just emerged from her room. Her eyes widen as she notices my dad carrying a rifle. "What was that sound?" she asks. "What's happening?"

"The Mogs are here," I answer.

"Oh, no," Sarah says, backing towards the room where John and Ella are laid out defenseless.

From the hallway, I have a clear view of the floor-to-ceiling windows that line the penthouse living room. A half dozen ropes come slithering down from the rooftops, the Mogadorians rappelling down the side of the building.

"I have to get to John!" Sarah says.

I grab her by the wrist. "We don't stand a chance if we don't get to the weapons."

The windows shatter, blown open by a synchronized series of blasts from Mogadorian cannons. A rush of cold air flows through the penthouse. The Mogs swing inside, swiftly detach from their rappelling wires and start scanning the space around them for targets. They're in the living room, standing between us and the penthouse elevator—our only exit. I'm surprised there aren't more of them. If I was attacking a hideout for the Garde, I'd have sent an entire army. It's almost as if they aren't expecting a lot of resistance.

The three of us duck back into my dad's room.

"I'll get to John and Ella," says my dad. "You two make a break for the Lecture Hall."

I can hear the Mogs moving out of the living room, starting down our hallway. "Here they come. Let's go on three. One—"

Before I hit two, a ferocious roar erupts from the hallway, immediately answered by wild Mogadorian blaster fire. I poke my head into the hallway in time to see Bernie Kosar, in the shape of a grizzly bear, mauling a pair of Mogadorians. I'd forgotten all about BK! Maybe things aren't as desperate as they seem.

"Go!" my dad shouts as he makes a break towards Ella's room. "Get weapons and we'll hold them here."

BK lunges from Mog to Mog, tearing through them with his claws, tossing aside the furniture that they try to hide behind. He takes a few blaster shots in the side and the air fills with the smell of burned hair, but that only seems to make him angrier. Crouched in the doorway of Ella's room, my dad takes aim and starts picking off Mogs.

Sarah and I take off in the opposite direction, towards the Lecture Hall and the armory. Behind me, I can hear blaster fire sizzling into the walls, my dad's rifle answering back. We have to be quick. More will surely be dropping in from the roof and they won't be able to hold them off forever.

Suddenly, the bedroom door on my right swings open. I have a second to feel the rush of cool air from the broken window, and then there's a Mogadorian on top of me. He drives his shoulder into my side, pinning me up against the wall. His forearm presses into my throat and he puts his pale face close to mine, his lifeless black eyes filling my vision.

"Human," the Mog hisses. "Tell me where the girl is and I'll kill you quick."

Before I can ask which girl he's talking about, Sarah cracks the Mogadorian over the head with an empty vase. The Mog shakes off the blow and spins on Sarah. An anger wells up in me—for all that time in captivity, for what they've done to John and Ella. I grab the handle of the Mog's sword and rip it loose from his sheath. With a scream, I drive it through his chest, turning him to ash.

"Whoa!" Sarah cheers.

I can hear glass shattering from all around the penthouse. Doors to bedrooms all along the hallway are thrown open and Mogs come charging into sight, cutting me and Sarah off from my dad and Bernie Kosar. I remember thinking the empty penthouse was spooky before, but this is horrifying. I've lost sight of my dad at the other end of the hall. I can still hear his rifle working, the shots getting more and more frequent. I hear a loud crash, the sound of something tipping over in Ella's room.

"You're after the girl?" I yell, getting their attention, hopefully taking some of the pressure off my dad. "She's this way!"

Sarah and I sprint into the workshop, ten or so Mogs charging down the hallway after us.

Together, we shove over a stack of old appliances and engine parts that are next to the doorway, Sandor's accumulated clutter coming in handy. A Mog tries to force open the door, but it's jammed up against all the crap on the floor.

"That'll slow them down for a second," I say.

"Do they think I'm this girl they're after?" Sarah asks breathlessly. "Or do you think they're here for Ella?"

A chunk of the workshop door explodes in a burst of blaster fire, hot splinters flecking across my cheek and almost into my eye. I guess our second is up. Sarah grabs me by the arm and we stagger through the workshop, the door behind us being pulverized by the invading Mogs.

A stray blast hits the floor between us, knocking us apart, and sending Sarah falling over a table. More blasts are getting through now. I duck low and grab Sarah's hand, helping her stand up. "I'm okay!" she yells, and we run, hunched over, towards the Lecture Hall.

The workshop door is now just a smoking hole in the wall thanks to all the Mogadorian shooting. They're shoving in, tripping over the junk we knocked over, but advancing all the same. Next to me, the monitor that's displaying the location of the Garde explodes in a shower of sparks, a Mog blaster just narrowly missing me.

"How are we going to fight this many off?" Sarah yells as we burst into the Lecture Hall. "I've been practicing, but not against ten targets at once!"

"We've got the home field advantage."

Inside the Lecture Hall proper, Sarah makes a break for the gun rack and I climb into the Lectern. The first Mogs burst into the room just as I fire up the Lecture Hall's programming, keying up one of Sandor's old training routines—the one with difficulty marked insanity. The Mogs aren't even paying any attention to me just yet, seated behind the metallic console, tapping buttons. They're more focused on Sarah. Even if they realize she's not the girl they're looking for, she's still the most obvious threat, out in the open and pointing a pair of pistols at the Mogs. Obvious threat and also an easy target.

"Sarah! To your left!" I shout, raising a block of cover from the floor for her to hide behind. She dives to safety just as the Mogadorians open fire.

Smoke starts filling the room from the nozzles along the walls. Some of the Mogs look confused; most are only interested in blasting away at Sarah. A few shots begin ricocheting off the front of the Lectern and I hunker down in the seat, trying to make myself small. I hope this thing is strong enough to withstand some blaster fire. Above the shooting, I can hear the Lecture Hall whirring to life.

A half dozen panels along all four walls slide open, turrets loaded with ball bearings coming into view.

"Stay down!" I yell at Sarah. "It's starting!"

A crossfire erupts through the Lecture Hall, the Mogs caught in the middle. This drill is meant to help the Garde practice their telekinesis, not maim them, so the marble-sized ammo being shot out of the walls doesn't travel fast enough to kill the Mogs. Still, it has to sting like hell. Between that and the medicine balls suddenly swinging from the ceiling, I'd say they have their hands full.

I dive out of the Lectern. A ball bearing smacks me hard in the shoulder before I can make it to the ground. My arm is sore, but I manage to press myself flat, watching as the Mogs are bludgeoned from all angles. Seeing me, Sarah sends one of her guns sliding across the floor. I pick it up and crouch down behind the Lectern. Sarah and I have the only two pieces of cover in the room.

We open fire. It doesn't matter that we don't have the best aim. The Mogadorians are basically sitting ducks. With all the shooting coming from the walls, they're starting to panic. Many of them are knocked down to their knees by the turrets or the medicine balls, at which point Sarah and I pick them off. Some make a break for the door. If they manage to stagger that far, all they get for their trouble is a bullet in the back.

Only a minute has passed in the Lecture Hall's training routine before the room has completely cleared of Mogs. The Garde usually have to endure seven minutes before they get a break during the training portion. I guess they don't have anyone shooting real bullets at them, though. I reach up and slap the controls on the Lectern until the system shuts down.

"That worked!" Sarah yells, sounding almost surprised. "We got them, Sam!"

As Sarah stands up, I notice a burn mark on the outside of her left leg. Her jeans are torn, the skin beneath them a burned pinkish where it isn't bleeding. "You've been shot," I exclaim.

Sarah looks down. "Crap. I didn't even notice. Must have just grazed me."

As the adrenaline dies down, Sarah limps over to me. I put my arm around her for support and we move as fast as we can out of the Lecture Hall. We grab more guns on our way out. I tuck a second pistol into the back of my jeans just in case I run out of ammo. Sarah drops her spent handgun and grabs some crazy-looking lightweight machine gun, the kind of thing I used to believe didn't exist outside of action movies.

"You know how to use that thing?" I ask.

"They all work pretty much the same," she replies. "You just point and click."

I could almost laugh if I wasn't so worried about my dad and the comatose John and Ella. We don't hear any sounds of fighting as we pass through the wrecked workshop, picking our way carefully over the junk we knocked over. The penthouse is eerily quiet. I'm not sure if that's a good sign or a bad sign.

I poke my head into the hallway. There's no sign of anyone. The floor is covered with Mogadorian ash, but otherwise all is quiet. The loudest sound is the wind blowing through the building thanks to the Mogs having broken every single window on their way in.

"Do you think we got them all?" Sarah whispers.

In answer, we hear a shuffling noise from the roof that sounds like boots running across it. There must be more Mogadorians still up there and they'll be massing for a second wave any second now, as soon as they figure out their first group has failed.

"We need to get out of here now," I say, helping Sarah limp along. We hurry down the hallway.

Bernie Kosar lumbers into view, still in bear form. He looks wounded, his entire right side smoking from blaster burns. He stares at me as if he's trying to communicate something. I wish I had John's animal telepathy. He seems sad, somehow. Sad, but determined.

"You okay, Bernie?" Sarah asks.

BK grunts and takes the shape of a falcon. He soars towards the window and out, flying up. He must be going to hold off the remaining Mogs on the roof while we evacuate John and Ella. I realize now what that look BK was giving me meant; he was saying good-bye, just in case it's the last we see of him. I suck in a deep breath.

"Come on, let's go," I say, quietly.

There's an overturned bookshelf blocking the doorway to Ella's room. It's peppered with bullet holes. Obviously this was what my dad used for cover.

"Dad?" I whisper. "It's clear, let's go."

No response.

"Dad?!" I say, louder, a tremor in my voice.

Still nothing. I slam my shoulder hard against the bookshelf, but it's wedged tight. I feel sick, desperate. Why isn't he answering?

"Up there!" Sarah says, pointing. There's a space large enough to crawl through between the bookshelf and the top of the doorframe. I clamber up and over, scraping my knees on the protruding shelves, landing awkwardly on the other side. It only takes seconds, but that's time enough to imagine my dad riddled with blaster fire, John and Ella murdered in their sleep.

"Dad—?" My breath catches. It feels like time slows down. I stagger towards the bed on wobbly legs. "Dad?"

John and Ella look unharmed, and still in their comatose state, completely unaware of the chaos unfolding around them. And completely unaware that my father's body is draped across them.

His eyes are closed. He's bleeding from a gaping wound over his abdomen. Both of his hands are clenched there, like he's trying to hold himself together. His spent rifle is discarded on the floor, his bloody handprints running up and down the handle. I wonder how long he kept fighting after he was shot.

Sarah gasps as she climbs over the bookshelf. "Oh no. Sam . . ."

I don't know what to do except take his hand. It's cold.

Tears start filling my eyes. I realize that in one of the last conversations I had with my father, I basically called him a traitor. "I'm so sorry," I whisper.

I almost jump out of my skin when my dad squeezes my hand.

His eyes are open. I can tell he's having trouble focusing on me and realize that his glasses are gone, smashed somewhere during the fight.

"I protected them as long as I could," my dad says, his voice strangled, fluid bubbling up from inside him and trickling from the corner of his mouth.

"Come on, we're getting out of here," I reply, kneeling down next to him.

A shadow of pain crosses his face. He shakes his head. "Not me, Sam. You have to go on your own."

A howl rises above the fighting on the roof. Bernie Kosar, desperate and in agony.

Sarah touches my shoulder gently. "Sam, I'm sorry. We don't have long."

I shrug away from Sarah's hand, shaking my head. I glare at my dad, tears now running freely down my cheeks. "No," I hiss angrily, "you're not leaving me again."

Sarah tries to squeeze past me and drag Ella's body out from beneath him. I don't help. I know I'm being stupid and selfish, but I can't let him go this easily. I've spent my entire life looking for him and now it's all falling apart.

"Sam . . . go," he whispers.

"Sam," Sarah pleads, cradling Ella in her arms. "You have to grab John and we have to go."

I stare at him. He nods slowly, more blood spilling out from the side of his mouth. "Go, Sam," he says.

"I won't," I say, shaking my head, knowing it's the wrong thing and not caring. "Not unless you come too."

But it's too late anyway. The wire hanging outside the window goes taut as a Mogadorian rappels inside. We've taken too long and Bernie Kosar wasn't able to stop them. The second wave is upon us.

CHAPTER THIRTY-FOUR

BUBBLES BREAK THE SURFACE OF THE SWAMP WHERE Nine is still under water. He's been pinned down there for almost a minute. I take a step towards the edge, wanting to dive in and save Nine, but not sure if Five will let me. He's watching me closely, an eyebrow raised, like he's wondering how Eight and I will react.

"Where's the real Number Five?" asks Eight, his voice low. "What did you do with him?"

Five's brow furrows in confusion, then he smiles. "Oh, you think I'm Setrákus Ra," Five says, shaking his head. "It's cool, Eight. I'm the real deal. No shape-shifting tricks."

As if to demonstrate, Five reaches down with his free hand and opens the lock on his Chest. He clicks it shut again and glances over at us. "See?" Eight and I remain frozen in place, not sure what to do.

"Let Nine out of the water, Five," I say, trying to keep my voice level, as far from panic as possible.

"In a second," he replies. "I want to talk to you two without Six and Nine around to interrupt."

"Why—why would you attack us?" Eight asks, sounding angry and disbelieving. "We're your friends."

Five rolls his eyes. "You're my species," he replies. "That doesn't make us friends."

"Just let Nine out of the water and we'll talk," I plead.

Five sighs and lifts Nine up. He's gasping for air, his eyes fiery and enraged, still trapped in Five's strangling grip. Try as he might, Nine can't find any way loose.

"Not so strong now, huh?" taunts Five. "Okay, deep breath, bro."

He dunks Nine back under the water.

Meanwhile, Six is unmoving. Her head is cocked at an uncomfortable angle and a huge bruise is forming along her jaw. Her breath seems shallow. I start towards her, wanting to heal her, but feel Five's telekinesis gently shoving me back.

"Why are you doing this!" I shout at him, tears filling my eyes.

He looks almost taken aback when I yell at him. "Because you two were nice to me," he says, like it should be obvious. "Because unlike Nine and Six, I don't think you've been brainwashed by your Cêpans into thinking resistance is the only way forward. Eight, you proved that in India, when you let those soldiers die for you."

"Don't talk to me about that," hisses Eight. "I never meant for anyone to get hurt."

"Brainwashed?" I exclaim. "Did you say we're brain-washed?"

"It's okay," Five says, placating us. "The Beloved Leader is forgiving. He'll welcome you. There's still time to join the winning team."

The winning team? I can't believe what I'm hearing. My stomach turns over; I feel like I'm about to throw up. It can't be true— "You're working with them?"

"I'm sorry I lied to you about that, but it was necessary. I'd been on this planet for six months when they found me," says Five, sounding wistful. "My Cêpan was already dead of some vile human disease—that part was true, it just didn't happen when I said. The Mogadorians took me in. They helped me. Once you read the Good Book, you'll understand that we shouldn't be fighting them. This whole planet—the whole universe can be ours."

"They did something to you, Five," I say, almost whispering, feeling both sad for Five and horrified by him. "It's okay. We can help you."

"Just let Nine go," adds Eight. "We don't want to hurt you."

"Hurt me?" repeats Five, laughing. "That's a good one."

He yanks Nine out of the water and hurls his body against the gnarled tree. I try to use my telekinesis to stop Nine's flight, but it happens too quickly and Five is too powerful. Nine smacks spine first against the trunk with enough force to shake the uppermost branches. He cries out, his body contorted, and I can tell that he's broken some ribs, maybe even his back.

"Do you have any idea how dull it was pretending to be weak?" Five asks, his rubbery arm slithering back to his body, appearing normal again. "You were trained by pitiful Cêpans, if you were lucky. Mucking about with your Chests and your Legacies, always in the dark. I was trained by the most powerful fighting force in the universe and you're threatening to hurt me?"

"Pretty much, yeah," replies Eight.

Eight shape shifts into his ten-armed lion form, towering over Five. But before Eight can go on the attack, Five blows into his flute. The mutant gator, which had been waiting patiently, suddenly leaps into the air and slams into Eight. It's all thrashing wings and snapping jaws, Eight's clawed hands slashing in response, the two mammoth beasts crashing into the mud and rolling over each other. With a mildly entertained look on his face, Five turns to watch Eight scrapping with his pet monster.

"Don't hurt each other," Five calls to them. "We can all still be friends."

I'm not sure if Five is joking or if he's really that insane. The important part is that he's distracted. Nine moans from the base of the tree. He's trying to push himself upright, but his legs don't seem to be working. Meanwhile, Six still isn't moving. I'm not sure which one needs my care more urgently. Six is closer to me, so I scramble over and fall to my knees next to her, pressing my hands to her injured skull.

Suddenly, I'm lifted off the ground. My feet dangle in the air. It's Five. He's holding me up using his telekinesis.

"Stop!" I yell at him. "Just let me heal her!"

Five shakes his head, disappointed. "I don't want her healed. She's like Nine—she'll never understand. Don't fight me, Marina."

A branch strikes Five in the back of his head. He loses his concentration and I drop back to the ground. Five whips around just in time to see Nine tearing loose another branch with his telekinesis.

"Cute," Five says, easily deflecting Nine's next volley.

"Come on," growls Nine, who has managed to struggle into a sitting position against the tree. "I don't need my legs to kick your fat ass."

"Talking shit until the very end," sighs Five. "You know what's happening in Chicago right now? Your fancy suite is getting raided by Mogadorians. I want you to die knowing your bullshit palace is burning to the ground, Nine."

"You told them about Chicago?" I shout. My shock is real, but when Five glances back at me, I see an opportunity. He likes the sound of his own voice—well, I can use that to distract him. Nine is in no condition to fight. I need to buy him some time. "How could you do that? What about Ella and the others?"

"Ella will be fine," Five says. "The Beloved Leader wants her alive."

"He wants her alive? For what? I thought he wanted us all dead."

Five merely smiles. He turns back to Nine.

"What's he want with her, Five?!" I scream, feeling a fresh rush of panic. He ignores me and stalks towards Nine. I hope Nine can withstand him long enough for me to heal Six. I scramble back over to her and hold her head in my lap. Her skull is cracked, her nose and jaw broken. I try to concentrate and channel the icy energy of my Legacy.

I'm distracted by a feral shriek. Over in the mud, Eight has managed to pin down the monster. Two of its heads are already hanging limp. The middle head is still working, though, and it snaps violently at Eight. He manages to catch the jaws with six of his paws and wrenches its jaws open until they snap apart. The beast's head is practically torn in half; its monstrous wings thrash once more and then it finally goes completely still and slowly begins to disintegrate.

Five has turned to watch. "Well done!" he yells to Eight. "But believe me, there's more where that came from."

Eight is left kneeling in the mud. He's back to his normal shape, unable to hold on to the avatar form for any longer. I can tell he's wounded, bloody teeth marks up and down his chest and arms and even on the palms of his hands. He pushed himself hard to defeat that beast, but he still shakily picks himself back up.

Five looms over Nine, his steel skin glinting in the fading sunlight. Nine sneers up at him defiantly. "You going to hit an unarmed man, you traitorous shit?"

Before Five can reply, Nine reaches out with his telekinesis. His pipe-staff, which he must have dropped when Five first grabbed him, lifts out of the muck and comes zipping towards him.

Five snatches the staff out of the air. I make a mental note that he catches the staff with his right hand, which means the stones he's using to power his Legacy must be clutched in his left.

Five raises the staff and brings it down across his metallic knee, snapping it in half like a piece of kindling. "Yeah. I am."

Before Five can move, Eight teleports between them. He's hunched over, breathing heavily, and bleeding from multiple wounds. Even so, he stands his ground. "Stop this madness, Five."

I'm trying to keep an eye on the scene playing out next to the tree while also concentrating on Six. I can feel her skull starting to mend, the swelling on her face decreasing. I hope that I'm working fast enough. We need her badly.

"Come on, Six . . . ," I whisper. "Wake up."

Five has hesitated with Eight in front of him, some of the anger directed at Nine going out of him. "Get out of the way, Eight. My offer to you still stands, but only if you let me finish this loudmouth moron off."

"Let him take a shot, dude!" Nine shouts from the ground.

"Shut up," Eight snaps over his shoulder. He holds his hands up to Five. "You're not thinking straight, Five. They've done something to you. In your heart, you know this isn't right."

Five scoffs. "You want to talk about right? What's right about sending a bunch of children to a strange planet so they can fight a war they don't even understand? What's right about giving those children numbers instead of names? It's sick."

"So is invading another planet," counters Eight. "Wiping out an entire people."

"No! You understand so little," Five replies, laughing. "The Great Expansion had to happen."

"Genocide had to happen? That's insane."

Six stirs in my lap. She's not awake yet, but it seems like the healing has worked. I set her down gently and stand up, creeping closer to the others. Five doesn't notice me; he's ranting now, sounding almost frantic.

"You fight because your Cêpans told you that's what your Elders want! Have you ever questioned why? Or who your Elders really are? No, of course not! You just take orders from dead old men and never even question them! And I'm insane?"

"Yeah," growls Nine. "Are you even listening to yourself, bro?"

"You're confused. You've been their prisoner for years without even realizing it. Just calm down and we can discuss this," says Eight. "We shouldn't be fighting."

But Five isn't listening to Eight anymore. I thought he might have a chance of getting through to Five, but that last comment by Nine was enough to set him off again. Five drops his shoulder and attempts to barrel right through Eight.

I grab Five's left hand with my telekinesis, focusing on prying open his fingers so he'll drop those balls. He jerks away from Eight, surprised, struggling against me.

"His left hand!" I yell. "Help me get it open!"

I can tell by the looks on their faces that Eight and Nine have gotten the idea. Five screams in pain and frustration. I almost feel bad for a moment; we're just ganging up on him again. This must be what he's felt like since he joined us—an outsider. He's lost and confused and angry. But we can worry about mending fences and fixing his screwed-up worldview later. Right now, he needs to be stopped.

"Please don't fight us," I cry. "You're just making it worse."

Five screams again as his knuckles crack loudly. The small bones in his hand are probably shattered from our combined telekinetic assault. The two balls he was holding drop to the ground and roll beneath the roots of the tree. Five clutches his hand and drops down to his knees. He's looking at me, like he knows I was the first one to attack his hand and it makes this defeat all the more bitter.

"It's going to be all right," I tell him, but my words sound hollow. I'm trying to talk him down but, when I look at him, I get the same feeling of revulsion that I do with the Mogs. He was going to kill Nine—one of his own people, one of us. How can we bring him back from that?

Eight steps forward and puts a hand on Five's shoulder. It seems like the fight has gone out of him.

Five sobs, shaking his head. "It wasn't supposed to go like this . . . ," he says, quietly.

"Crying like a girl," Nine says.

Immediately, Five's expression darkens. Before we can stop him, he shoves Eight away from him. Eight stumbles, falls, and Five takes flight.

"Don't!" I scream, but Five is already shooting towards Nine. The wrist-mounted blade he grabbed from his Chest extends with a harsh screech of metal; it's a foot long and needle shaped, deadly and precise.

Nine tries to roll aside, but he's badly hurt and can't

move. The grass around Nine is flattened to the ground and I realize that Five is holding him in place with telekinesis.

I try to use my telekinesis to pull Nine towards me, but he doesn't budge. Five's telekinetic grip is too powerful.

It all happens so fast.

Five plummets down with blade extended. Nine, teeth gritted, unable to move, watches the fatal blow descend.

Suddenly Eight appears in front of Nine—he's teleported. "NO!" Nine screams.

Five's blade drives right into Eight's heart.

Five lurches backwards, shocked, as he realizes what he's done. Eight's eyes are wide, a spot of blood forming on his chest. He staggers away from Five, towards me, his hands outstretched. He tries to say something, but no words come out. He collapses.

I scream as the fresh scar burns across my ankle.

CHAPTER
THIRTY-FIVE

I WALK THROUGH A DECIMATED CITY. I'M RIGHT in the middle of the road, but there isn't any traffic. Totaled cars are piled up on the sidewalks, many of them just burned-out shells. The buildings nearby—the ones still standing, anyway—are crumbling and covered in scorch marks. My sneakers crunch across a blanket of broken glass.

The city isn't familiar to me. It isn't Chicago. I'm somewhere else. How did I get here?

The last thing I remember is Ella grabbing my arm and then . . . this place. An acrid burning smell fills the air, inescapable. My eyes burn from the clouds of ash blown through the empty streets. I can hear crackling in the distance; somewhere, a fire is still burning.

I keep moving forward through the deserted war zone. At first, I don't think there are any people. Then, I notice a handful of filthy men and women huddled inside the gutted remains of an apartment complex. They stand around a burning trash barrel, warming themselves. I raise my hand in greeting and shout.

"Hey! What happened here?"

Seeing me, the humans shrink back. They're frightened, one by one disappearing into the shadows of the building. I guess I'd be wary of strangers too if I lived through whatever happened here. I keep moving.

The wind howls through the broken windows and sagging doorways. My ears perk up; if I strain to listen, I can almost hear a voice carried on the wind.

John . . . Help me, John. . . .

The voice is thin and distant, but I still recognize it. Ella.

I realize where I am—well, not where I am geographically, but where my mind is. Somehow, I've been pulled into Ella's nightmare. It feels so real, but then so did those horrible taunting visions that Setrákus Ra used to inflict on me. I close my eyes, focus, and try to force myself awake. It doesn't work. When I open my eyes, I'm still standing in this broken city.

"Ella?" I say, feeling a little silly speaking to the thin air. "Where are you? How do we get out of here?"

There's no response.

A torn piece of newspaper blows across my path and I reach down to snatch it. It's the front page of the *Washington Post*, so that must be where I am. The paper is dated a few years from now. This is a vision of the future and it's one that I hope never comes to pass. I remind myself that this is how Setrákus Ra toys with us. Everything here is his creation.

Even knowing that, the picture on the front page causes my breath to catch. An armada of Mogadorian ships emerges from a cloudy Washington sky, hovering right over the White House. The headline is just one word, in bold capital letters.

INVASION.

I hear a rumbling sound from ahead of me, toss the newspaper away, and start jogging towards it. A dark military truck crosses through the intersection, moving slowly, flanked on all sides by Mogadorians. I quickly come to a stop and consider ducking into one of the nearby alleys for safety, but the Mogs don't seem to notice me.

A crowd of people shuffles along behind the truck. They're humans; gaunt and pale, their clothes torn rags, all of them looking dirty and hungry, many of them wounded. They walk along with their heads down, their faces grim, marching sullenly. Mogadorian warriors armed with cannons walk alongside them, the dark tattoos that cover their scalps displayed proudly. Unlike the humans, the Mogs are all smiling. Something is happening—an event of some kind, one that the Mogadorians want the humans to witness.

The wind picks up again. *John . . . this way . . .*

I slip into the crowd and walk along with the humans, keeping my head bowed. I steal an occasional glance around. The Washington Monument protrudes jaggedly on the horizon, the top half of it sheared off. A feeling of dread fills my stomach. This is what the future will look like if we fail.

The crowd is led to the steps of the Lincoln Memorial. There are other people already there, waiting for this sick Mogadorian sideshow to begin. The American flags that would normally hang above the Memorial have been taken down, replaced by black flags bearing a red Mogadorian symbol. Even worse are the chunks of stone piled along the sides of the road—well, I think they're stones at first. On closer inspection I make out the chiseled face of Lincoln, a huge crack running down the center of his forehead. The Mogadorians have broken down the statue and tossed it out of the Memorial.

I push my way to the front of the crowd. None of the humans seem all that eager to be at the front, so they let me through without a problem. A line of Mog warriors stands at the base of the steps, keeping watch on these dispirited people, their cannons pointed into the crowd.

Setrákus Ra lounges in a throne at the top of the Lincoln Memorial. His massive frame is clad in a black uniform, covered in epaulets and medals. A huge

Mogadorian sword protected by an ornamental scabbard is laid across his lap. Seven Loric pendants hang from around his neck, their cobalt surfaces shimmering in the afternoon light. His black eyes idly scan the crowd. They pass right over me and I flinch, ready to run, but he doesn't seem to notice me.

John . . . do you see me . . . ?

I have to stifle a gasp. Ella is seated in a smaller throne next to Setrákus Ra. She looks older and paler. Her hair is dyed jet black and bound in a tight braid worn down her shoulder. She's wearing a dress so elegant that it almost seems meant to taunt the tattered humans that stare at her in awe. Her face is stony, like she's long become immune to grim scenes like this one.

Setrákus Ra holds her hand.

I fight back the urge to rush up the steps and try to kill him, reminding myself that none of this is real. And anyway, even if it was, I wouldn't stand a chance. An entire army of Mogadorians stands between me and Setrákus Ra.

The crowd parts to let the military truck I saw before pull up to the Lincoln Memorial's steps. The back of the truck is open and I can see two prisoners huddled inside, their heads down and hands shackled. There's something familiar about them.

Setrákus Ra stands up when the truck parks. A hush falls across the crowd.

"Bring them forward," he shouts.

A stout Mogadorian warrior steps out of the ranks. He's not like the others; he's not so pale and the dark tattoos across his scalp seem almost new. He wears a patch over one eye and his working eye isn't the soulless black of a Mogadorian. I take an involuntary step backwards as I realize that I'm not looking at a Mogadorian at all.

It's Five. What the hell is going on here? Why is he wearing their uniform?

Five leads the first prisoner down from the back of the truck. He's a little older and there's a long scar running horizontal across his nose and cheeks, but I still immediately recognize Sam. He keeps his head down, not making eye contact with Five, looking haunted and defeated. I notice Sam has a bad limp that becomes all the more apparent when he's forced to climb the steps of the Lincoln Memorial. He stumbles, almost falls, and some of the Mogadorian onlookers chuckle at the humiliating display. I feel rage bubbling up inside me and have to take a deep breath as I feel my Lumen starting to activate.

The second prisoner doesn't go as meekly as Sam. Even with her hands and feet shackled, Six stands tall. Her blond hair has been shorn into boyish spikes and her face is contorted into a perpetual mask of anger, yet she's still strikingly beautiful. She sweeps her eyes across the crowd of humans and many of them look down in response, ashamed. Five says something to her that I can't hear, but his soft features are almost apologetic. In response, Six spits in his face. As Five wipes the spit off his cheek, a group of Mogadorian guards grab Six and drag her up the steps. She's a fighter until the very end.

Six and Sam are made to kneel before Setrákus Ra. He glowers at them for a moment, then turns to address the crowd.

"Behold," he shouts, his voice carrying above the silent masses. "The last of the Loric resistance! Today our society celebrates a great victory over those who would stand in the way of Mogadorian progress."

The Mogs all cheer. The humans stay quiet.

My mind is racing. If Six and Sam are the last remaining, then that means, in this future, I'm already dead and so are all the others. Those pendants dangling from Setrákus Ra's neck—one of those is mine. I remind myself again that none of this is real, but I feel terrified all the same.

Five walks up the steps and stands beside Setrákus Ra. He holds the ornamental sheath as Setrákus pulls free his glowing broadsword. Setrákus brandishes the sword for all to see, then takes a practice swing just above Sam's head. Someone in the crowd screams and is quickly silenced.

"Today, we cement a lasting peace between humans and Mogadorians," continues Setrákus. "At last, we will finally stamp out the final threat to our glorious existence."

This sure doesn't look glorious. The humans have clearly been beaten down over months and months of Mogadorian occupation. I wonder how many would join me if I tried to charge Setrákus Ra. Probably none. I don't feel angry at them, but angry at myself. I should've saved them, should've prepared them better for what's coming.

Setrákus isn't done giving his speech. "On this historic day, I have chosen to bestow the honor of sentencing to she who will one day succeed me as your Beloved Leader." With a grand gesture, Setrákus Ra motions to Ella. "Heir? How do you rule?"

Heir? That doesn't make any sense. Ella isn't a Mogadorian, she's one of us.

I don't have time to figure out what this all means. I watch as Ella rises shakily from her throne, seeming almost drugged. She stares down at Six and Sam, her eyes dark and impassive. Then, she gazes into the crowd, her eyes settling on me.

"Execute them," Ella says.

"Very well," Setrákus replies.

He bows deeply and then, in one fluid motion, chops off Six's head with his sword. The crowd is deathly silent as her body topples over, so quiet that I can hear Sam screaming. He falls across Six's body, crying and yelling.

I feel the searing pain on my ankle. A new scar is forming. I close my eyes as Five lifts up Sam, turning him towards Setrákus Ra's blade. I don't want to see what happens next, how badly I've failed them all. It's not real, I repeat to myself.

It's not real, it's not real, it's not real. . . .

CHAPTER THIRTY-SIX

I KNOW HE'S GONE. I CAN STILL FEEL THE LINGER-
ing pain from the new scar on my leg. I might never stop
feeling that; it could be with me for the rest of my life.

I have to try.

I fall to my knees in the mud next to Eight's body. The
wound doesn't even look so bad. There's not as much blood
as there was in New Mexico, and Eight lived through that.
I should be able to heal this, right? It should work. It has to
work. But this one is right on his heart, straight through.
I press my hands across the puncture and will my Legacy
to kick in. I did it before. I can do it again. I have to.

Nothing happens. I feel cold all over, but it's not the
iciness of my Legacy.

I wish I could lie down next to Eight here in the muck
and just shut out everything that's going on around me.
I'm not even crying—it's like the tears have gone out of
me and I just feel hollow.

Just a few yards away, Five is shouting but my mind can't process what he's saying. The blade he used to stab Eight has retracted back into its wrist-mounted sheath. His hands are on his head, like he can't believe what he's just done. At the base of the tree, Nine has fallen silent, in a state of shock. If only he'd shut up moments ago and not egged Five on. Six is finally struggling back to her feet, looking groggy, trying to make sense of the new scar on her ankle. Everything has fallen apart.

"It was an accident!" Five is babbling. "I didn't mean to do that! Marina, I'm sorry, I didn't mean it!"

"Be quiet," I hiss.

That's when I hear the dreaded hum of a Mogadorian ship's engine. The tall grass around us begins blowing wildly as the sleek silver vessel starts descending from the sky. This was all just a setup orchestrated by Five, so of course he'd have backup waiting in the wings.

I lean over and touch a gentle kiss to Eight's cheek. I want to say something, to tell him what an amazing person he was, how much better he made this terrifying life we're forced to lead. "I'll never forget you," I whisper.

I feel a hand on my shoulder. I whip around to find Five standing over me.

"It doesn't have to be this way," he's saying, pleading with me. "This was a horrible mistake, I know that! But everything I said is the truth."

He's insane. Insane to touch me. I can't believe he'd

even have the audacity to do that after what he just did. "Shut up," I warn him.

"You can't win, Marina!" he continues. "You're better off joining with me. You—you—" Five stammers as his breath mists in front of his mouth, the humidity around us cut by a sudden chill. His teeth chatter. "What are you doing?"

Something in me snaps. I've never felt anger like this before and it's almost comforting. The icy feeling of my healing Legacy spreads through me, but it's different somehow; freezing and bitter and dead. I'm radiating cold. Near Five and me, the murky swamp water crackles as the surface turns instantly to ice. The plants within my radius begin to wither, drooping under the flash freeze.

"Ma-Marina? Stop . . ." Five, hugging himself to keep warm, takes a step away from me. His feet nearly go out from under him as he slips on the ice.

With this new Legacy coursing through me, I act on pure furious instinct. I jerk my hand upwards and the ice takes shape beneath Five, a jagged icicle forming from the ground and thrusting upwards. He's not quick enough to get out of the way and the icicle stabs straight through his foot, pinning him to that spot. Five screams, but I don't care.

Five pitches forward and grabs at his impaled foot,

just as another icicle juts up from the ground. It strikes Five right in the face. If it was any larger, it would've probably killed him. Instead, it merely takes out one of his eyes.

Five falls to the frozen ground awkwardly, his foot still impaled. He clutches at his face, screaming. "Stop it! Please, stop it!"

He's a monster and he deserves this. But no. I can't do it. I'm not like him. I won't kill one of my own people in cold blood, even after what he's done.

"Marina!" Six shouts. "Come on!"

The Mogadorian ship has landed and its doors are opening. Over by the tree, its branches now sagging under the weight of fresh ice, Six has thrown Nine over her shoulder. She holds her hand out to me.

I take one last look at Five. He holds both his hands over his face, grasping at his ruined eye. He's crying, the tears turning to frost on his cheeks.

"If I see you again, you traitorous bastard," I yell, "I'll take the other fucking eye!"

Five makes a weak gurgling sound. Pathetic.

I'm about to run to Six, but stop. At my feet, encased in a solid chunk of ice, is Eight's body. As I realize what I've done, the air around me begins to warm up. I kneel down and press my hands to the sheet of melting ice that separates me from Eight. I want to take him with us, to keep him away from the Mogadorians and lay him to rest like he deserves, but there's no time to wait for the ice to melt. Six is shouting at me and the Mogs are closing in.

"I'm sorry," I whisper, feeling numb all over.

I race over to Six and grab her outstretched hand. We turn invisible.

CHAPTER
THIRTY-SEVEN

I SNAP AWAKE AND SIT UP RAMROD STRAIGHT IN a bed that isn't my own. I know immediately that I'm back in reality, the searing pain of a new scar burning into my ankle enough to wake me up. But wait—that nightmare wasn't supposed to be real, I shouldn't have actually gotten a scar. And yet, I can feel the burned skin, stinging and raw, the pain more than skin deep.

That part of the nightmare was real—we've lost someone.

I don't have time to think things through, barely even have time to assess my situation. Sam is shouting at me.

"JOHN! GET DOWN!"

There's a Mogadorian standing in front of the bedroom window—a broken window, cold air blowing in from outside. When did that happen? He's aiming a cannon at me. My instincts take over and I roll to my left, just as the Mog shoots the space where seconds ago I was comatose. From the floor next to the bed, I shove the Mog with my telekinesis. He flies backwards, out the window and into the empty air, and plummets to the street below.

It's bedlam, the chaos in the real world more intense than in Setrákus Ra's vivid nightmare. The bedroom has been completely torn apart by blaster fire. Sarah is standing in the doorway, using a broken bookshelf for cover. With one arm she cradles Ella's still unconscious body and with the other she haphazardly sprays machine gun fire into the hallway. Beneath the gunfire, with my enhanced hearing, I can hear Mogadorians swarming through the penthouse. There's so many of them, yet for some reason it doesn't seem like Sarah's taking any return fire.

It's because she's holding Ella, I realize. Setrákus Ra wants—I can't believe I'm even thinking this, haven't even had time to process what it means—his heir brought in alive. That's why the Mogs aren't shooting at Sarah; they're afraid to hit Ella.

Sam is on the floor next to me. He's cradling Malcolm, who has a massive blaster wound in his midsection. His breathing is shallow and he's barely conscious; it doesn't look like he has long left.

"What the hell happened here?" I shout to Sam.

"They found us," Sam replies. "Someone betrayed

us." I remember seeing Five in that Mogadorian uniform and I immediately know the truth.

"Where's everybody else?"

"They went to the Everglades for the mission." Sam points at my leg, his eyes wide and frightened. "I saw your ankle light up. What—what does that mean?"

Before I can answer, I hear Sarah scream. Her gun is making an empty clicking sound and, realizing that she's empty, the Mogs have descended on her. One of them reaches through the doorway and buries a dagger deep into her shoulder. She falls to the ground, grasping her shoulder as another Mog reaches in and yanks Ella violently from Sarah's arms.

I light up my Lumen, but it's too dangerous to launch a fireball while the Mogs are holding Ella. They're out of range quickly, disappearing down the hallway in retreat. I reach out with my telekinesis and drag Sarah over to us.

"Are you all right?" I ask, quickly looking over the wound in her shoulder. It looks bad, but not fatal. Sarah looks stunned and relieved to see me awake.

"John!" she exclaims, and yanks me in close with her good arm. It's not even a half-second hug, Sarah shoving me away, realizing the danger. "Go! You have to stop them!"

I leap to my feet, ready to tear off after the retreating Mogadorians. I stop myself, looking down at Sam and his father. Malcolm is still alive, but fading fast. The way Sam crouches over him, holding his hand, it reminds me of that night at Paradise High School when I was powerless to stop Henri from dying. I could save him, I realize.

Healing Malcolm would mean letting the Mogs escape with Ella, though. It would bring Setrákus Ra closer to what he wants—a future that I still don't entirely understand, but one where Ella rules over humanity alongside him.

Sam looks up at me, his cheeks wet with tears. "John! What're you waiting for? Go help Ella!"

I think of that Sam I saw in the nightmare, how tired and beaten down he looked, his spirit gone out of him. I think of how badly it hurt me to lose Henri. I can't let my friend go through all that, not after he and Malcolm have just found each other again.

Letting Ella go, the future I could be dooming her to—no, there will be time to stop that later, I tell myself. I have to help Malcolm now.

I kneel back down and press my hands to Malcolm's stomach and his wound begins to close slowly beneath my touch. Finally, some color begins to return to Malcolm's face, and his eyes open.

Sam is staring at me. "You let them take her."

"I made a choice," I reply. "They won't hurt her."

"How—how can you know that?" Sarah asks.

"Because Ella—" I shake my head. "We'll save her. We will stop them. All of us, together, I swear."

Sam grabs my shoulder. "Thank you, John."

As soon as I'm finished with Malcolm, I turn my attention to healing Sarah. The wound in her shoulder is clean. She brushes her fingers against my cheek while my Legacy is working.

"What happened to you?" she asks. "What did you see?"

I shake my head, not wanting to talk about the vision until I've really had time to figure out what's happened. Unlike Sam, I don't think Sarah noticed the new scar appear on my ankle, and I don't want to bring that up either. It's quiet now—the Mogs have retreated with Ella—but we still need to get out of here. There's no way the cops missed this battle. I just want to get Sarah healed and all of us somewhere safe. "Looks like you kicked some ass while I was out," I say.

"We did our best," she replies.

Sarah's wound all healed up, I glance around. "We need to move. Where's BK?"

I see Sarah and Sam exchange a grim look. My heart drops.

"He went to the roof to hold them off," Sam says. "He didn't come back."

"He's tough. He could still be alive," Sarah says.

"Yeah, definitely," Sam replies, but he doesn't sound confident.

Thinking about BK and whichever one of the Garde is dead in the Everglades almost makes me break down. I bite down hard on the inside of my cheek and focus on the pain. I stand up—there will be time for mourning later. Right now, we need to get out of here before the Mogs decide to come back and kill us.

"Time to go," I say, helping Malcolm to his feet.

"Thank you for saving my life, John," he says. "Now, let's get the hell out of this place."

The four of us rush out of the bedroom with Sam helping Malcolm along. The lights have all gone out, a circuit probably blown during the fighting. There aren't any Mogadorians waiting for us in the living room, but I can see by the destruction that they've definitely done some redecorating. For a moment, I imagine how mad Nine will be when he gets back. If he's even alive. And then I realize that we're never going to be able to come back to this place. It was a good home for a while, but now it's gone, destroyed like so much else by the Mogadorians.

Through the shattered windows, I can hear sirens wailing from the street below. This attack by the Mogadorians was way more brazen than usual. It's probably going to be pretty hard to sneak out undetected.

Amazingly, the penthouse elevator is still operational. I hustle Sarah, Sam and Malcolm inside and hit the button for the parking garage, but I don't get in the elevator.

"What're you doing?" Sarah cries, grabbing my arm.

"We won't be able to come back here. It's going to be crawling with cops and probably the feds that work for the Mogs. I have to get our Chests and see if I can find BK."

Sam steps forward. "I can help you."

"No," I reply. "Go with Sarah and your dad. With my telekinesis, I can carry them myself."

"You promised we'd stay together," Sarah says, her voice shaky.

I pull her close to me. "You're my getaway driver," I tell her. "Get the fastest of Nine's cars and meet me by the zoo. You guys shouldn't have a problem getting out, but they might be looking for me. I should be able to jump to the next roof and get down that way." I step back from the elevator, then lunge forward to plant one last kiss on Sarah. "I love you," I tell her.

"I love you too," she replies.

The elevator doors hiss closed. I race through the destroyed penthouse and back to the workshop. It's been wrecked too—all this hard work, the Lecture Hall never to be used again. I try to think only practical thoughts. What should I take with me? The first thing

I grab is the tablet that shows our locations. Four dots still displaying in Florida—damn it, that's one too few. I'm not ready to focus on the identity of the one we've lost or what to do about Ella or the fact that Setrákus Ra might actually be Loric.

I grab a stray duffel bag from beneath an overturned table and duck into the Lecture Hall to load it up with guns. I stow the tablet in there too and throw that over my shoulder. I want to keep my hands free, just in case any Mogs are still lurking around, so I levitate all of our Chests with my telekinesis. With all the windows blown out, I can easily hear the sirens wailing down below. This is all I'll be able to carry. It's time to get back on the run.

The Inheritances floating behind me, I run out of the workshop and back through the penthouse. I need to get to the roof and see if BK made it out alive.

Before I can reach the stairs, the elevator dings open. Damn it—I was too slow.

I look over my shoulder, expecting to see some of Chicago's finest with guns drawn. Instead, it's a lone Mogadorian. Pale as usual, dark hair in his face, younger than normal, and he looks different than other Mogs I've seen, more human. A gun pointed in front of him—at me.

All the Chests thunk to the floor as I redirect my

telekinesis, snatching the gun out of his hands. "Hey!" he screams, and if he says anything else, I'm not listening. I'm thinking about the friends I lost tonight. The dark future I had to suffer through. Killing this straggler Mogadorian won't change any of that, but it's a start.

I pitch a fireball in his direction, but he dives out of the way, hiding behind the torn-up husk of a couch. I lift it up with my telekinesis and fling it aside. He holds up his hands, surrendering. I'd probably think that was weird if I was thinking at all.

"Too late for that," I growl.

Just as I'm about to hurl another fireball at him, the Mog stomps on the floor. The whole room shakes, furniture tipping over, the carpet rippling like there's a wave passing underneath it. And then the seismic jolt knocks me backwards, stumbling, and I feel the cold fingers of open air clawing at my back. Stupid—I was standing right in front of a broken window. I swing my arms, desperately trying to regain my balance.

But I don't fall. He's got me. The Mogadorian has grabbed me by the front of the shirt.

"I don't want to fight you!" he shouts in my face. "Stop attacking me!"

As soon as he's reeled me back in, I shove him away. He doesn't come at me, but he remains crouched, ready to dodge anything I might throw at him.

"You're Four," he says.

"How do you know that?"

"They know what you look like, John Smith. What all of you look like. And so do I—" He hesitates. "Except I also remember seeing you as a child. Running for a ship while my people murdered yours."

"You're the one Malcolm and Sam talked about." My voice comes through gritted teeth. I can't shake the feeling that I should run or fight when faced with his kind. It's ingrained in me, but I try to keep it in check.

"Adamus Sutekh," the Mog introduces himself. "I prefer Adam."

"Your people killed a friend of mine tonight, Adam," I spit, knowing my anger is unreasonable, not able to help myself. "And they kidnapped another."

"I'm sorry," he says. "I came as quickly as I could. Are Malcolm and Sam safe?"

"I—" Well, I just don't know how to react to that. A Mog showing compassion. Even if Sam and Malcolm said it was true, I still never really imagined it. "Yeah, they're fine."

"Good," Adam replies. His voice still has the harshness of a Mogadorian. "We need to get out of here."

"We?"

"You're hurt, angry," Adam says, moving cautiously closer to me, like I might suddenly take a swing at him. "I get that. But if you want to hurt them back, I can help."

"I'm listening."

Adam extends his hand to me. "I know where they live."

Something recoils inside of me at the sight of that pale hand waiting for mine. But if what I saw in that vision was true—if Five is working for the Mogadorians—then why shouldn't we have one of them working with us? I take Adam's hand, squeezing hard. He doesn't cringe, only looks me right in the eye.

"All right, Adam," I say. "You're gonna help me win this war."

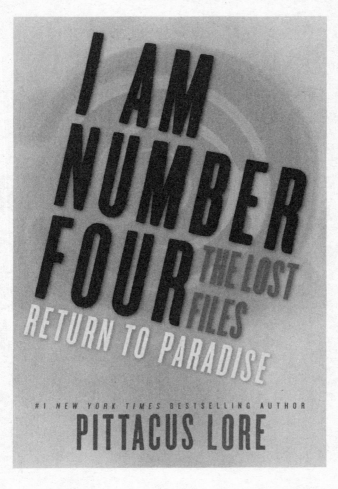

I AM NUMBER FOUR THE LOST FILES

RETURN TO PARADISE

#1 NEW YORK TIMES BESTSELLING AUTHOR

PITTACUS LORE

CHAPTER ONE

I HAVE TO KEEP REMINDING MYSELF WHO I AM the first week at the new school. Not, like, I lost my memory or something. I *know* who I am in a literal sense. But I have to keep forcing myself to remember what being me means. So all week I keep a single thought repeating through my head:

You are Mark James.

It's what I think on Monday when some douche bag trips me while I try to find an empty seat among a pre-calc classroom full of strangers.

You are Mark James, the guy everyone at your old school looked up to. These idiots will learn.

And Wednesday when someone loots my locker during weight training and forces me to walk around in sweaty gym clothes for the last two periods.

You are Mark James, all-conference quarterback. They're just jealous.

And at lunch on Thursday when I sit on the tailgate of my truck and someone in a loud old Camaro zips past, hurling an oversize Styrofoam cup of orange soda at me while yelling what I think is "ass pirate."

You are Mark James, and you are the best fucking athlete the Paradise High Pirates ever saw.

If someone had asked me a year ago what my future held, I'd probably have said something like "Mark James, Ohio State star quarterback." Maybe if I'd had a beer or two I'd go so far as to say, "Mark James, first-round NFL draft pick."

What I wouldn't have said—what I couldn't have even imagined thinking—was anything remotely close to "Mark James, survivor of an alien attack."

For my entire life, the future seemed set for me. As soon as I threw my first pass, I knew what I wanted to do. Paradise High QB, college football star, NFL hopeful. But now the future is this stupid, dark thing I can't predict, and I feel like my whole life has been heading towards something that doesn't even matter. Might not even exist if we end up conquered by a bunch of superpowered aliens. I mean, my all-conference trophy was used to *murder* an alien. A Mogadorian. A bunch of pale, janky-looking assholes from another planet came to Earth hunting for a very human-looking alien named John Smith—*ha*—and his invisible friend. Then they destroyed my school. My kingdom. Almost killing me in the process.

Some people did die. I guess I should count myself lucky, but I don't *feel* lucky. I feel like someone who's just found out that vampires exist or that reality is actually an elaborate video game. Everyone else keeps going on as usual, but the world has changed for me.

There are only a few people who know what really happened at Paradise High. Everyone thinks the school's in shambles because weirdo-drifter/new student John Smith went crazy and jumped through the principal's window one day, then came back that night and caused massive amounts of damage that took out half the building. Then he fled town. Word is that he's some kind of teenage terrorist or member of a sleeper cell or a psychopath—it depends on who is telling the story.

But one exploding school can't stand in the way of education, so now everyone from Paradise is being shipped to the next town over where there's an actual building for us to go to. It just so happens that the next school over is Helena High, our biggest rival, who I beat in the best football game of my life, capping off an undefeated season by completely annihilating their defense. So, yeah, I guess I can see why I'm not the most loved guy in school. I just never thought I'd spend my last semester of high school washing orange soda out of my hair. Maybe if I was still the same old Mark James I'd think it was kind of fun even. I'd be dreaming up ways to get back at the other students, ways for me and my football buddies to prank them and get the last laugh. But filling someone's locker full of manure isn't as high on my list of priorities now that I know beings from another world are walking among us and that a complete alien invasion is possible at any time. I *wish* manure were still higher on my to-do list.

A bunch of my teammates have told me I've gotten quiet and seem different since it happened, but I can't help it. It's kind of pointless to talk about cars and partying when I was literally almost squashed by some kind of extraterrestrial monster. How am I supposed to go back to being fun-loving, beer-chugging Mark James after all that? Now I'm "Paranoid That Aliens Are Going to Hunt Me Down" Mark James.

I can deal with the new school. Hell, I probably deserve it for the shit I put people like John through back in Paradise. It's only a semester, and then I'll have graduated. Maybe they'll even be able to fix up the school auditorium in time for me to walk the stage in Paradise. What sucks is that I can't tell everyone what's going on. They'd throw me in a mental institution. Or worse, those bad aliens—the Mogs—would be after me to try and shut me up.

At least I have Sarah to talk to. She was there. She fought with me, almost died beside me. As long I have Sarah, I don't feel like I'm going to go crazy.

CHAPTER TWO

THERE ARE BIG SCHOOL BUSES SHUTTLING KIDS back and forth between Helena and Paradise, but I was able to talk the principal into letting me drive myself. I told him I wanted to stay late and work out—that I didn't want what happened in Paradise to keep me from being an unstoppable college football machine. He said that was fine: I'm guessing partly because he hopes anything I do in the future will make Paradise High look good, and partly because everyone in town still feels kind of bad for me because I threw a party and some kids accidentally burned down my house.

I don't *think* that had anything to do with aliens. At least, I've made sure to tell everyone who insinuates that John blew up my house that it was really a couple of stoners down in the basement who were lighting stuff on fire for fun. That usually shuts people up— especially adults who like to pretend that stuff like that never happens in good old Paradise. Besides, John saved Sarah and both of my dogs. There's a YouTube video to prove it. No one should be giving him shit for that night. He gets a free pass on that one.

I meet Sarah in the parking lot after the last bell on the Friday of our first week in Helena. She waits for me at my truck. It's kind of gray outside, and she's got on a plaid sweater that makes her eyes look like they're practically glowing blue. She looks gorgeous.

She always does.

Sarah Hart was—*is*—the love of my life. Even after she dropped cheerleading and came back to school as some kind of emo hipster who suddenly didn't want to be dating the star QB. Even after she dumped me and started sorta dating an alien.

I smile at her as I approach, all teeth. It's a reflex. I can't help it. She smiles too but not as wide as I'd like.

Even with the "You are Mark James" mantra in my head all day, sometimes I don't feel like me at all. Instead of being the cool, put-together guy I've always been, I start worrying about intergalactic war and if Mogs are watching me have breakfast. But even when I start to wonder if I should be building a bomb shelter out in the middle of the woods or something, part of me wants to stay planted in the world I knew before there was definite proof of aliens on Earth, where I'm just a dude who's trying to win back his ex-girlfriend.

If this whole ordeal has had any bright side, it's that I see a lot more of Sarah than I did before. I like to think that me saving John's life impressed her, maybe even showed her that there's more to me than she thought. Someday when this is all said and done, Sarah is going to come to her senses and realize that even if John is a good alien, he's still freaking E.T. And I'll be waiting, even if it means fighting off space invaders to keep her safe and show her I'm better than he is.

The waiting totally blows.

"You're begging to get jumped, aren't you?" she says as I get closer.

At first I'm confused, but then I realize she's nodding at my chest, where my name is embroidered in gold over the heart on my Paradise High varsity letter jacket.

"What, this?" I ask, flexing a little and puffing out my chest. "I'm just repping our school. Trying to bring a little bit of Paradise to hell. That way we all feel like we're at home."

She rolls her eyes.

"You're provoking them."

"They're the least of my problems these days."

"Whatever," she says. "Your truck still smells like orange soda."

Once we're in my truck, Sarah leans her head against

the passenger window and exhales a long breath, as if she's been holding it in all day. She looks tired. Beautiful but tired.

"I got a new name in bio today," she says, her eyes closed.

"Oh yeah?"

"'Sarah Bleeding Heart.' I was trying to explain that John wasn't a terrorist who was going to try to blow up the White House. Like, literally, someone said that they heard he was going to blow up the White House."

"Now who's the one asking for it?"

She opens her eyes just enough to glare at me.

"I feel like all I do now is defend him, but everyone else refuses to listen. And every time I try to say something about how they don't know the whole story, I lose a friend. Did you know that Emily thinks he kidnapped Sam? And I can't even tell her that it's not true. All I can say is that John wouldn't do that, and then she looks at me like I'm part of some big plot to destroy America or something. Or worse, some lovesick loser who's in denial."

"Well, you've still got me," I say reassuringly. "And I try to defend John whenever I can. Though I don't think I've been very good at it. All the guys on the team think he was able to kick our asses after the hayride because he was trained as a special agent from Russia or something."

"Thanks, Mark," Sarah says. "I know I can count on you. It's just . . ."

She opens her eyes and looks out the window as we speed past a few empty fields, never finishing her sentence.

"Just what?" I ask, even though I know what's coming. I can feel the blood in my veins start to pump a little faster.

"Nothing."

"*What*, Sarah?" I ask.

"I just wish John was here." She gives me a sad smile. "To defend himself."

Of course, what she really means is that she wishes John was here because she misses him. That it's killing her not to know where he is or what he's doing. For a moment, I feel like my old self again as my hands tighten around the steering wheel. I want to find John Smith and punch him square in the jaw, then keep hitting him until my knuckles bleed. I want to go straight into a rant about how if he really loved her, he wouldn't have left her here to get picked on and laughed at. He would have manned up. Even if he did leave to find other aliens like him to save our planet. If I were in his shoes, I'd have figured out a way to keep Sarah *and* the world safe. And happy.

I can't believe these are the types of conversations I have with myself on a daily basis now.

Being super pissed at John just makes me sound like the Mark that Sarah broke up with. So instead of talking shit about him, I swallow my anger and change the subject.

"I've been thinking a lot about what's happened lately. How the FBI and stuff have been handling it. My dad says that it's kind of weird how they're keeping the local law enforcement in the dark. I mean, he's the sheriff and they aren't telling him anything about what's going on."

"Yeah, but isn't that so they can keep a lid on the investigation?" Sarah asks. "That's the FBI's *job*, right?"

"My dad doesn't think so. He should at least be kept in the loop, even if he can't tell the rest of his officers about what's happening. Plus, I know they found some bodies at the school and there was a lot of damage, but John got moved straight to the FBI's most-wanted list. That seems a little extreme, right? Especially considering there's no *actual* evidence that John was the one behind all this."

"So, what? Do you think this is some kind of government conspiracy?" She sits up straighter in the passenger seat, leaning towards me.

"I just think maybe they know more about what's going on with John's people than they let on. I'm *guessing* some of the people in black suits are smart enough to realize that it wasn't just some angry teenager who dug gigantic claw marks in the football field."

"Jesus, Mark, you're starting to sound like Sam," she says. Then she shrugs a little. "But I guess he was right about some of that stuff we all thought was crazy. That would make sense. I mean, if stuff like this is happening across the country, *someone* is keeping track of it all, right? The FBI swooped in here really fast. Maybe they're working with John's . . . species?"

I can't believe Sarah has fallen for someone who could be classified as another species.

"Or else they're working with the monsters with all the glowing swords," I say. "Which would mean we've just allowed the opposing team to set up shop in town."

Sarah lets her head fall against the window again.

"Where are you, John?" she whispers, her breath fogging up the glass in front of her. "Where are you?"

We're quiet for the rest of the drive home.

All I can think of is the promise I made to John when everything was going down at the school—that I would keep Sarah safe. Of course I'll do that. I'd be doing it even if he hadn't asked me to. But it makes my insides twist up to know that he's the one she's thinking of while *I'm* the one whose actually looking out for her.

CHAPTER ONE

"THE MOGS ARE HERE!"

My eyes shoot open as I jerk upright, hoping that sentence was just something from a bad dream.

But it's not.

"They're here," Rey whispers again as he crosses over the floor of our little shack to where I'm sleeping on top of a pallet of blankets.

I'm off the floor in seconds. Rey's solar-powered lantern swings in front of my face, and it blinds me. I flinch away and then he turns it off, leaving me in complete darkness. As he pushes me towards the back of our home, all I can make out is a sliver of silver light peeking through the window.

"Out the back." His voice is full of urgency and fear. "I'll hold them off. Go, go, go."

I start grabbing at the air where he'd stood moments before but find nothing. I can't see anything: My eyes still burn from the lantern.

"Rey—"

"No." He cuts me off from somewhere in the dark. "If you don't go now, we're *both* dead."

There's a clattering near the front of the shack, followed by the sound of something—or someone—slamming against the front door. Rey lets out a pained cry but the inside of the shack is still nothing but an abyss of black in my eyes. I know there's a metal bar over the door that's not going to hold up against much more than a little force. It's for show more than anything else. If someone *really* wanted into our shack, they could just blow through the flimsy wooden walls. And if it's the Mogs . . .

There's no time to think, only to react. It's *me* they're after. I've got to get to safety.

I rip away the piece of cloth that serves as a make-shift curtain and throw myself through the little window. I land with a plop in a three-inch puddle of mud, slop, and things I don't even want to imagine—I'm in the hog pen.

A single thought runs through my mind. *I'm going to die a thirteen-year-old boy covered in pig shit on an island in the middle of nowhere.*

Life is so unfair.

The hogs squeal—I've disturbed their sleep—and it snaps me back into the moment. Old training regimens and lectures from years before take over my brain and I'm moving again, checking my flanks to make sure there are no Mogs that have already made their way to the back of the hut. I start to think about what their plan of action might be. If the Mogs actually *knew* I was on the island, I'd be surrounded already. No, it must be a single scout that stumbled upon us by accident. Maybe he had time to report us to the others, maybe not. Whatever the case, I have to get out of the line of fire. Rey will take out the scout. He'll be fine. At least that's what I tell myself, choosing to ignore how frail Rey's looked lately.

He *has* to be okay. He always is.

I head for the jungle behind our shack. My bare feet sink into the sand, as if the island itself is trying to slow me down. I'm dressed only in dark athletic shorts, and branches and shrubs around me scratch at my bare chest and stomach as I enter the cover of the trees. I've done this sort of thing before, once, in Canada. Then, coats and a few bags weighed me down. But we'd had a little more warning. Now, in the sticky-hot night of the Caribbean, I'm weighed down only by my lack of stamina.

As I hurl myself through the dense vegetation, I think of all the mornings I was supposed to spend jogging along the beach or hiking through the forest that I *actually* spent playing solitaire or simply lazing around. Doing what I really wanted to do, like drawing little cartoons in the sand. Coming up with short stories told by stick figures. Rey always said I shouldn't actually write anything down—that any journal or notes I wrote could be found and used as proof of who I am. But writing and drawing in the sand was temporary. When the tide came in, my stories were gone. Even just doing that caused me to work up a sweat in this damned climate, and I'd return to Rey, pretending to be exhausted. He'd comment on the timing of my imaginary run and then treat me to a rich lunch as a reward. Rey is a taskmaster when it comes to doling out things to do, but his lungs are bad and he always trusted that I was doing the training he told me to do. He had no reason not to—no reason to think I wouldn't take our situation seriously.

It wasn't just the avoidance of having to work my ass off in the heat that kept me from training. It was the monotony of it all that I hated. Run, lift, stretch, aim, repeat—day in and day out. Plus, we're living out in the middle of nowhere. Our island isn't even on any maps. I never thought the Mogs would ever find us.

Now, I'm afraid that's coming back to haunt me. I wheeze as I run. I'm totally unprepared for this attack. Those mornings lazing around the beach are going to get me killed.

It doesn't take long before there's a stitch in my side

so sore that I think it's possible I've burst some kind of internal organ. I'm out of breath, and the humid air feels like it's trying to smother me. My hands grasp onto low-hanging branches as I half-pull my way through thick green foliage, the bottoms of my feet scraping against fallen limbs and razor-sharp shells. Within a few minutes the canopy above me is so dense that only pinpricks of the moonlight shine through. The jungle has given way to a full-blown rain forest.

I'm alone in the dark in a rain forest with alien monsters chasing after me.

I pause, panting and holding my side. Our island is small, but I'm only maybe a fifth of the way across it. On the other side of the island a small, hidden kayak is waiting for me, along with a pack of rations and first aid gear. The last-chance escape vessel, something that'll let me slip into the dark of the night and disappear on the ocean. But that seems so far away now, with my lungs screaming at me and my bare feet bleeding. I lean against a tree, trying to catch my breath. Something skitters across the forest floor a few feet away from me and I jump, but it's only one of the little green lizards that overrun the island. Still, my heart pounds. My head is dizzy.

The Mogadorians are here. I'm going to die.

I can't imagine what Rey is doing back at the shack. How many Mogs are here? How many can he take on?

I hope I'm right, and it's just a single scout. I realize I haven't heard any gunshots. Is that a good sign, or does it mean the bastards got to him before he was able to fire off a single round?

Keep going, I tell myself, and then start out again. My calves are burning and my lungs feel like they're about to split open every time I inhale. I stumble, hitting the ground hard and knocking what little breath I had out of me.

Somewhere behind me, I can hear movement in the trees.

I glance around. Without a clear view of the sky, I can't even tell which direction I'm going anymore. I'm totally screwed. I have to do something.

I abandon the plan to cross the island. I'm in no shape to do so. For a moment I think of burrowing down into the brush—maybe finding something to hide in until I can slip through the forest—but then I think of all the fist-sized spiders and ants and snakes that could be waiting there for me, and imagine a Mogadorian scout stepping on me by accident.

So I head up instead. Gathering every ounce of strength I have, I use a few sturdy vines to pull myself hand over hand up to a low branch on a nearby tree. All I can think of are the many different types of beasts Rey's told me the Mogs can command, any one of which would like nothing more than to tear me apart.

Why don't *we* have giant hell-beasts to fight for us?

My arms are shaking by the time I squat on the limb, the wood creaking under my weight as I stare into the blackness, hoping over and over again that nothing will emerge from it. That I can just wait this out.

That it will all just go *away*.

There's no telling how much time passes. If I'd been more put together or hadn't been so taken by surprise, I might have remembered to grab my watch on the way out the window. It's weird—time always seemed like it didn't mean anything on the island, and now it means everything. How many minutes before more of them arrive? How many seconds before they find me? I try to keep from trembling, and my stomach from turning over—between the running, my fear, and the damp smell of pig that clings to me in a thick coat of sludge, I'm teetering on the edge of vomiting. Maybe the stinking layer of crap will help keep me camouflaged, at least.

It's not a very reassuring silver lining.

Finally, a silhouette starts to take shape in the darkness. I draw in closer to the tree. The figure is human sized. Maybe even a little hunched over, leaning on a cane as he steps into the dim moonlight. He's wearing a blue linen shirt, khaki cargo pants, and sneakers that might have been white at some point. His beard is white, streaked with black, his wild hair almost silver.

I recognize him immediately, of course. Rey.

He's got something held against him, wrapped in a piece of cloth. I start to call down to him, but he's already staring holes into me, his lips quivering, as if he's fighting every urge to yell. He simply stands there, the silence hanging in the thick air between us. Finally, I break it.

"Well? Did you get him?"

Rey doesn't respond immediately, just looks away, staring down at the ground.

"What'd you forget?" His voice has a slight rattle to it.

"What?" I ask, my breath short.

He throws his parcel down on the ground. Part of the cloth falls back, and I can make out a familiar corner.

"The Chest?" I ask. My *Loric* Chest. The most sacred thing I own. The treasure I'm not actually allowed to look into. The container that supposedly holds my inheritance and the tools to rebuild my home planet, and I can't even peek inside until Rey thinks I'm ready to—whatever *that* means.

"The Chest." Rey nods.

I scramble down the tree, half falling to the earth.

"We should get going, right?" I ask. My words are spilling out now, my tongue stumbling over the letters as I try to say a million things at once. "You don't have any weapons? Or our food? Where are we going now? Shouldn't we be—"

"Your Chest is the second most important thing you have to protect after your own life. It was stupid to leave it. Next time, it's your priority to keep it safe."

"What are you—"

"You made it half a mile into the forest," he says, ignoring me. His voice is getting louder now, filled with barely restrained anger. "I didn't want to believe it, but I guess this is proof. You haven't been doing your training. You've been lying to me about it. Every day."

"Rey . . ."

"I already knew that, though." He sounds sad now. "I could tell just by looking at you."

My mind is racing, trying to figure out why we're still standing here. Why he's worried about my training when there could be a whole fleet of Mogs on their way after us. Unless . . .

"There aren't any Mogs here," I say quietly.

Rey just shakes his head and stares at the ground.

This was a test. No, worse than that: This was Rey's way of trapping me and catching me in a lie. And even though, yes, I technically have been less than honest about my training regimen, I can't believe Rey would scare me like this.

"Are you kidding me?" Unlike Rey, I don't have the power to keep my anger from clouding my voice. "I was running for my life. I thought I was going to *die*."

"Death is the least of your worries for now," he says, pointing at my ankle. Underneath the layer of mud and crap is an ugly red mark that appeared a few days ago. A mark that's starting to scab over, and will soon turn into a scar. The mark that—thanks to some otherworldly charm—shows me that another one of my fellow Garde has been murdered. Two is dead. Three and Four are all that stand between death and me.

I am Number Five.

I suddenly feel stupid for thinking I was about to be killed. Of course I wasn't. Numbers Three and Four have to die before I can. I *should* have been worried about being captured and tortured for information. Not that Rey ever tells me anything.

And I realize what this is about. Ever since the scar appeared, it's like something within Rey snapped. He's been getting sicker the last few years, and I'm not anywhere as strong as he thinks I should be. I haven't developed any of the magic powers I'm supposed to have. Neither of us can put up a good fight. That's why we're here on this stupid island, hiding.

Rey's eyes have been on the ground, but he finally raises them to mine, looking at me for a long moment. Then he nods at the Chest.

"Carry it back," he says. Then he's shuffling off into the darkness, leaving me in the sparse moonlight, staring at the duffel bag that contains my Chest.

We weren't under attack. It was only a test.

I'm not going to die on the island. At least, not tonight.

I pick up my Chest, hugging it close to me, letting the corners dig into my stomach.

I stare into the blackness that Rey has disappeared into, and in that moment there's only one emotion filling me. Not fear or relief or even shame for being found out. It's the feeling that the only person I have in this world has betrayed me.

CONTINUE FIVE'S STORY AND DISCOVER WHY HE
JOINS THE MOGADORIAN ARMY!

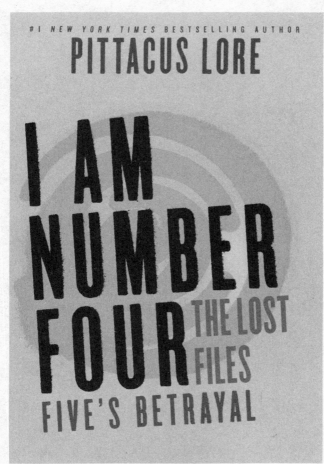

#1 NEW YORK TIMES BESTSELLING AUTHOR
PITTACUS LORE

I AM
NUMBER
FOUR THE LOST
FILES
FIVE'S BETRAYAL

CHAPTER
ONE

THERE WAS ONCE A PLACE THAT WAS BEAUTIFUL and lush and full of life and natural resources. Some people lived there for a long time, but then others came along who wanted or needed the land and everything on it. So they took it.

There is nothing special about this story. Open any history book on Earth—and probably every other planet—and you'll see a version of it play out continuously, on loop, over and over again. Sometimes the land is taken in the name of spreading a better way of life. Or for the sake of the native people. Occasionally the takers seize it based on some intangible reason—some divine right or destiny. But all of these reasons are lies. At the center of every conflict is power, and who will wield it. That's what wars are fought over, and why cities, countries and planets are conquered. And though most people—especially humans—like to pretend that gaining power is just an added bonus on top of whatever a conflict is *supposedly* about, power is the only thing that anyone is really after.

That's one great thing about the Mogadorians: they don't really bother with pretense. They believe in power. Even worship it. They see its potential to grow and serve their cause. So when you're someone like me who has extraordinary abilities, you become one of two things to the Mogs: a valuable asset, or an enemy who will eventually be destroyed.

Personally, I like being alive.

The Mogs don't pretend that they took my home planet of Lorien—which I barely remember—for any reason other than because they needed its resources. It's the same reason they're on Earth now. A planet as big as Earth will serve the Mogs well for decades before they have to go looking for another home—maybe even centuries. And the humans . . . well, it's not like there's anything really special about *them*. They're pretty weak for the most part and are only barely managing to keep the planet alive as it is. One day soon there will be a full-scale invasion, and all their petty problems won't mean anything, because suddenly there will be some incredibly powerful extraterrestrials lording over them. Showing them how to live. Giving their lives purpose.

And I'll be one of their new rulers. Because the Mogs

have seen the potential in me. They've promised me a spot as a commanding officer in the Mog ranks, with North America as my kingdom. My personal playground. And all I have to do is fight alongside them and help them capture the other Garde remaining on Earth. Then I can help the Garde see that there's no way the Loric are ever going to defeat the Mogs. I'm assuming they were spoon-fed the same stories Rey, my Cêpan, told me when I was growing up: that the Mogs were our enemies.

But that's not true. Or at least it doesn't *have* to be true. Not if we join them.

After sitting around training and waiting for almost my entire life, it feels good to finally have an actual mission. To have a purpose. To not just be hiding and waiting for something to happen to me. It makes me actually *want* to train and study and get better, because what I'm working towards now isn't some fairy tale Rey fed me over dinner on the island, but a future I can see.

I've learned a lot about the reasons why wars are fought and won in the last few weeks since I've been living in a Mog compound somewhere in the middle of West Virginia. In fact, most of my "research" hours are spent in an interrogation room that's been converted into a study for me, where I learn about famous battles and conflicts or read the Great Book, which is the story of the Mogadorians and how their intellect and abilities outgrew their planet and forced them to seek other worlds to rule and guide. About how the Loric refused to share their resources or listen to reason when it came to adopting the Mogs as rulers. It's a book written by Setrákus Ra, the unstoppable leader of the Mogs, and, well, let's just say if I'd read it earlier, I would have had a much clearer viewpoint of the fight between the Mogs and the Loric than I did when I was hiding in a lean-to shack on a deserted island. I've begun to wonder if all my memories of being so young and happy on Lorien are just because I was too dumb and little to know what was really going on. I mean, any civilization that puts their last hope in a bunch of toddlers on spaceships has got to be a little bit out of whack, right?

Ethan's helped me see these things. He's helped me realize that I have a choice in this war, even though the Elders didn't want me to have one. It was strange at first to find out that my best friend was working for the Mogs—and that I'd technically been under Mog care for the better part of a year without knowing it—but I can't blame Ethan for keeping things a secret from me at first. I'd been so brainwashed by my Cêpan's stories of the Garde triumphing over the armies of the Mogs and returning Lorien to its former glory that I probably wouldn't have seen reason if he'd been up front with me at the beginning. Ethan is what some of the

Mog commanders here have called a rare example of a human who has the intelligence to side with the winning team.

Still, it's so strange to be here underground. I'm technically an honored guest of Setrákus Ra, but I haven't proved myself yet. All they have is my word that I'm now loyal to them, but words don't carry a lot of weight with the Mogs. They believe in action, and results. And so I study and train and wait for the day when I get the chance to show them I am capable and ready to lead in their name. I follow orders. Because even though someday in the future I'll become invaluable to the Mogs, right now I'm just a former enemy living under their roof.

I'm buried in a book about the founding of America—particularly the expansion of European empires across the country—when Ethan comes into my study, flashing the toothy grin he always has plastered on his face.

"Good afternoon, Five," he says.

"Hey," I say, closing the book in front of me. Ethan's arrival means study time must be over. As much as I'm looking forward to being in charge of Canada and the United States, reading about the endless cycles of wars they've been caught up in can be monotonous. At least once the Mogs take over, war will be a thing of the past. There'll be no armies capable of standing up to them.

"How did you find today's reading?"

"There was some pretty dirty chemical warfare going on back when Columbus and other explorers were first coming over. Smallpox blankets? It's kind of insane."

Ethan's grin doesn't flinch.

"The beginning of every great empire is stained with a little blood," he says. "Wouldn't you say it was worth it?"

I don't answer immediately. Ethan's eyes shift almost imperceptibly, but I catch them. He's glanced at the one-way mirror at the other end of my desk. It's easy to see what he's getting at. Others are watching. Here in the Mog compound, someone is *always* watching.

I tense up a little. I'm still not used to being under constant surveillance. But it's necessary, as Ethan's explained, so that the Mogs know they can trust me. It makes me only want to say things that will impress whoever's watching, or show off how smart I am. I'm getting better at keeping my brain focused on that.

"Definitely," I say.

Ethan nods, looking pleased. "Of course it's worth it. Keep reading that book tomorrow and write down a few positive things about the conquerors' tactics."

"Whatever our Beloved Leader requires of me." I say this almost as a reflex. The first few days I was here, I heard it so many times that I just kind of adopted it. I probably say it ten times a day now without even realizing it half the time.

"Did you read the assigned passages from the Great Book?" Ethan asks.

"Of course. Those are the best parts of the study sessions." This is completely true. The other books are boring and make me suddenly understand why teenagers like me were always complaining about homework on TV shows I saw before coming to the Mog compound. But the Great Book is, well, great. Not only is it written much simpler than the other books, it also answers a lot of questions I've had throughout my life. Like why the Mogs went after Earth even though they had Lorien, and why they started hunting down the Loric once they got here, even though there were so few of us. The book explains that the Loric were weak but sneaky, and the Mogadorian belief that leaving even one enemy alive gives them the power to recruit others and multiply, gain power and one day rise against you.

Also, it's really bloody and violent, which makes it much more fun to read. I can see it play out in my head like one of the action movies I used to love to go see when I was still in Miami.

"And what did you learn about today?" Ethan asks.

"About how Setrákus Ra bravely fought our Elders.

How they tried to trick him and poison him, but our Beloved Leader was courageous and bested them, anyway."

"*Our* Elders?" Ethan asks, slight concern on his face.

I correct myself. "I mean the *Loric* Elders. It makes me even more excited to meet our Beloved Leader."

I have not had the pleasure of meeting Setrákus Ra in person yet. Apparently someone higher up thought it wasn't a good idea to give a superpowered guy like me an audience with the future ruler of the solar system until I've proved myself.

Ethan grins and pulls something out of his pocket. He tosses it on the table, and it bounces heavily a few times and then rolls. I stop it with my telekinetic Legacy and lift it in the air: a steel ball bearing almost as big as a Ping-Pong ball.

"What's this?" I ask.

"Consider it a gift. Use your power on it. See how it feels."

I float the ball over to the palm of my hand. With a little focus, my body suddenly takes on a metallic sheen. I drum my fingers on the table in front of me, and the sound of metal meeting metal fills the air. Ethan calls this Externa, the ability to take on the properties of whatever I touch. It's the newest of my abilities and the one that probably needs the most work.

I shrug as I crack a metallic knuckle.

"It feels like I'm made of steel. But I could have just touched the table and gotten the same kind of effect."

"But the table's not going to be with you all the time. From now on, this ball bearing should be. I don't want you to find yourself in the middle of a fight with nothing but sand or paper to turn into."

"Thanks." I smile. It's definitely not the flashiest or most expensive thing Ethan and the Mogs have given me, but I can see how it might end up being useful. I shove the ball bearing into my pocket, where it settles beside a red rubber ball I've carried with me for a long time—a trinket from a kid's vending machine.

Ethan tosses me a rolled-up sheet of paper. I push some books out of the way and spread it out in front of me. It's a map of the Western Hemisphere.

"What's this for?" I ask.

"I just wanted to make sure we had all the information correct on it. For record keeping and stuff like that."

The map includes a thick red line that zigzags across the United States and down into the Caribbean. There are dates printed along the markings.

"This is a map of all the places I lived growing up," I say.

"Correct. Just give it a once-over when you have a chance. I guessed on a lot of the dates based on stories you'd told me."

"But what good is any of this information?"

Ethan shrugs. "Just in case the Garde somehow caught your trail or tried to track you down, we'd know where they might be searching. We'll want to put a few scouts in those locations, just in case."

I nod, looking over the map. It's weird to think of myself as being young and powerless with Rey in all these places. Ethan comes up behind me and looks over my shoulder.

"Where was it that you said your guardian started to get so ill?" he asks.

I point to a place where the line dips into Pennsylvania.

"Around here somewhere. I'm not sure where exactly. We were camping in the mountains."

Ethan scowls.

"There are some of the finest hospitals in the country in that area. You know, if your Cêpan hadn't forced you to stay hidden on the island for as long as you did, he probably would have lived," Ethan says. "It's a shame he was so shortsighted that he couldn't see the inevitable future of Mogadorian progress."

"He thought the warmer air would help him."

"What he probably needed was a shot of antibiotics." Ethan shakes his head and crosses his arms. "I'm just glad you were able to get off of the island before you ended up going crazy and talking to the pigs. I still can't believe someone as powerful and smart as you was expected to raise those slop-covered animals."

I laugh a little. Over the last few weeks I've told Ethan basically everything I can remember about my life. All about the tiny little shack and the pigs I raised and how I trained myself to use my telekinesis all on my own. He and the other Mogs seemed really impressed by that part. Like I managed to become something great even when every card in the deck was stacked against me.

When I look at Miami on the map, my mind flashes with memories of the time I spent there before Ethan took me in. When I was just a punk-ass street rat wasting my powers on petty stuff like picking pockets, totally oblivious to how much authority I should have been wielding. There was a girl. Emma. My partner in crime who turned on me when she saw what I was capable of. Who was afraid of what I could do instead of respecting my abilities. I frown at the memory, and my stomach drops a little because it's been a while since I've thought of her. There had been a time when she was my only friend in the world, but she was just using me too, wasn't she? I was the one with the real talent. She was just riding on my coattails.

There's a knock on the door, and then a Mog enters. One of the vatborn messengers and servants in the compound. I straighten up in my chair. This is a reflex.

Even though I've been here a few weeks, I'm still getting used to seeing Mogs every day. More than that, I never know what they're going to ask me to do when they show up in the interrogation room that's been turned into my study or track me down in my bedroom. For all I know, they could be telling me that I've failed some test of theirs I didn't even know I was taking.

"You weren't responding to your radio," the Mog says to Ethan, clearly a little ticked off.

Ethan points to the little earpiece that's hanging out of his collar.

"Of course not," he says. "All of your superiors know that I never wear my earpiece when I'm with our guest." He motions to me. "It would be rude."

"Commander Deltoch requests your presence in the detention wing," the Mog says.

"I'll be there at once." Ethan nods.

"You *and* the Loric."

I tense up. What do they want from me in the detention wing?

"Is that how you would address an honored guest in this base?" Ethan asks. "How about 'sir'?"

The Mog seems a little apprehensive but nods his head to me.

"Sir," he says.

"Dismiss him," Ethan says to me.

"What?" I ask.

"You're going to have to get used to giving orders at some point."

I look at the Mog, who's got a full-on grimace now. I suddenly feel awkward. I hate it when Ethan does this. He's always trying to make everyone on the base treat me like their king or something. And while I'll be leading them one day in the future, I'm still unproven potential, and the last thing I want is anyone stirring up animosity against me.

"Five," Ethan says.

"You're dismissed," I say.

The Mog hesitates a moment. I assume his orders were to escort us to the other side of the building. I can almost see him trying to figure out who outranks whom in his head before Ethan clears his throat and, in a flash, the servant is gone.

"Conflicting orders, I'd imagine," Ethan says as if he could read my brain.

"Do you think I'll get him in trouble?"

Ethan's face goes serious.

"You can't worry about that. Don't forget who you are. When the Mogs take Earth, you'll be one of their officers. A leader. You may be new here, but you are the powerful Number Five. Show them mercy now, and they won't respect you when you're in charge."

"I need a chart to keep the ranks all straight in my head."

"Just always act like you're at the top of the food chain. Now come along," Ethan says, motioning towards the door. "Let's see what Commander Deltoch is up to with the prisoners this afternoon."

He doesn't give me time to react, only turns and heads out the door. I can't help but glance to the wall across from my desk, where a photo is taped up. It's a guy who looks like he's a few years older than me, with long, brown hair. He's built like an athlete—way fitter than I've ever been in my life. He looks smug. He's jogging in the photo and seems to be unaware that his picture is being taken. I haven't met him yet, but I know he's here on the base with me. Locked up. They've tried to torture him, but that doesn't really work. He's protected by magic, like I am. By a charm put on us when we were kids that keeps us from being hurt until our number is up.

He is Number Nine.

The Mogs want me to kill him. His is the blood that must be spilled for me to advance.

He is my proof of loyalty.

CHAPTER
TWO

FOR A LONG TIME, THE THING I WAS MOST afraid of was being left out. Alone on an island in the Caribbean. Left behind as the other Garde banded together without me. That wasn't exactly helpful when I was also afraid of getting too close to anyone for fear of them finding out my secret: that I'm not human. I had a really crappy life because of all this.

Until I met Ethan. Until the Mogs took me in. Now I have no worries of ever being left out. And I'll definitely never feel alone. It would be impossible to: there must be thousands of us living together on the West Virginia base.

The compound the Mogs have here is maybe the most incredible structure on Earth, even if few humans will ever see the inside of it. It's hidden in a hollowed-out mountain, and is so vast and full of trailing tunnels and caves that I doubt anyone has seen every corner of the place. I've spent a lot of my free time floating around the corridors and rocky hallways, and I think I've only seen a twentieth of it.

It's almost all Mogs here—the vatborn soldiers and servants and the trueborn higher-ups—but there are a handful of humans. Most aren't here by choice, though Ethan's an exception, as are the men and women in dark suits and military garb whom I pass in the halls on occasion.

And there's one other Loric. Nine.

I follow Ethan through the cavernous main hall, floating a few feet above him because flying is good practice and Ethan says it reminds the others that I'm powerful. I don't mind, really, because it's easier than walking. There are dozens, maybe even hundreds, of Mogs that we pass as we head towards the detention cells. They stop walking and step aside as I go by, staring at me. Some of them nod in respect, knowing that one day I'll be a powerful force in the Mog ranks. Others look at me with skepticism. I can feel their eyes on me as I fly over them.

The only really annoying thing about the base is the scalding-hot green stuff that flows throughout it and pools in the main chamber. It's some sort of energy source for the Mogs, Ethan said, but if you touch it, it'll eat through your skin like acid (or a least that's what I hear—I haven't been dumb enough to actually test that theory out). Whatever it is, it smells like sulfur and rotten coconuts. As we pass through the main hall, the scent is heavy in my nose, and I grimace.

"Why do you think we've been summoned?" I ask Ethan.

He shrugs.

"Maybe Commander Deltoch thinks it's time for you to take your place in the leadership."

As a commander, Deltoch is the highest-ranking Mog in charge of the base. He reports to a General Sutekh and sometimes our Beloved Leader directly. He's also become my de facto keeper—the person Ethan reports to and who I assume is on the other side of the one-way glass watching me in my study half the time. He's an aggressive, trueborn Mog—I've come to learn that's something to be proud of around here—and takes exquisite delight in telling me that I don't *look* anything like a soldier. He has never explicitly said that I'm maybe a little on the heavy side, but it's almost certainly what he's thinking.

I'm always a little on edge around Deltoch. I can't help but want to impress him every time I see him.

For my part, the detention area is the one place I'm not allowed to go on the base. I've only seen the first few cells. Ethan says it's because they don't want me to hurt Nine just yet. They're still trying to figure out a way to force him to spill everything he knows about the Garde—and besides, since his death will be so important, it must be ceremonious. I've wondered what it would be like to be imprisoned here, like Nine. To spend all day in a cold stone cell. It sounds terrible. But then, I don't have to worry about it. I chose to join the Mogs—to serve their cause in order to elevate myself. I'm sure the others here had the same chance. They just threw it all away. And for what? Do the imprisoned humans really think their own resistance to the Mogs means a damned thing in the long run? That they're anything other than a speck of dust in what will be the vast empire of the Mogadorians? Maybe I would have thought that once, but not after seeing their resources and strength with my own eyes.

We pass row after row of containment cells in the detention wing, the entrances barred and pulsing with some kind of blue energy field. I keep my eyes darting back and forth, trying to catch a glimpse of Nine, to no avail. Inside are the weak and unrepentant enemies of the Mogs. Most of them are humans who got a little too close to figuring out what was happening around them on Earth and refused to quit snooping , or who disobeyed orders. The traitors are being taught an important lesson about crossing their superiors—one they won't forget when they go back out into the world after they've served their time, which is what Ethan says happens to most of the ones who realize the error of their ways. A few are test subjects or people some-how related to the Loric cause—I hear there are even a few Greeters in captivity, those whose job it was to introduce the Loric to the human ways of life on Earth. Not all of them were as smart as Ethan was. It's hard to imagine that he might have been in one of these cells had he not foreseen the Mogs' inevitable victory.

Deltoch stands in the middle of the hallway. He's at least two heads taller than me and built like a giant wrestler shoved into an ominous black officer's uniform. His skin is pale, and his hair is gleaming jet-black and pulled into a tight ponytail. Dark tattoos peek out around his hairline, above eyes like big black marbles.

"So thrilled you could join us," he says flatly as I approach. He glances at Ethan and sneers slightly—despite Ethan's role as my recruiter and mentor, I don't think Deltoch has been a big fan of having a human roaming around his base with so much authority.

"Whatever our Beloved Leader requires of me," I say.

"Our afternoons are usually spent expanding upon Five's powers for the good of Mogadore," Ethan says, which I recognize as his way of asking why we've been ordered to come to this side of the compound.

Deltoch narrows his eyes a little. "I assume you must have been in the middle of something very important since it took you so much time to get here."

I start to stammer a response, but Ethan speaks on my behalf.

"He was just reading from the Great Book," he says, grinning. "What could be more important than our Beloved Leader's words?"

Deltoch smirks in a way that bares all of his gray, sharklike teeth. It's not exactly a happy expression.

"You're here because the all-wise Setrákus Ra is *anxious* for Five to prove himself loyal to the Mogadorians."

"We're looking forward to him taking his rightful place as a high-ranking member of the Leader's forces as well," Ethan says. "But these things take time, as I'm sure—"

"Five," Deltoch says, ignoring Ethan. He steps aside and points a long, thick finger at one of the cells. "Do you wish to see the power of the Garde?"

Ethan starts to protest, but I nod.

"Yes, sir."

I step up to the blue force field and stare. There's a prisoner inside, stretched out on a dirty slab of rock serving as a bed. The guy is shirtless, his muscles glinting under a sheen of sweat. Long, dark hair is spread out around his head. His eyes are closed, and his lips move slightly, as if he's meditating or saying some sort of prayer.

Number Nine.

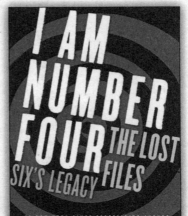

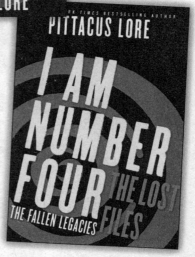

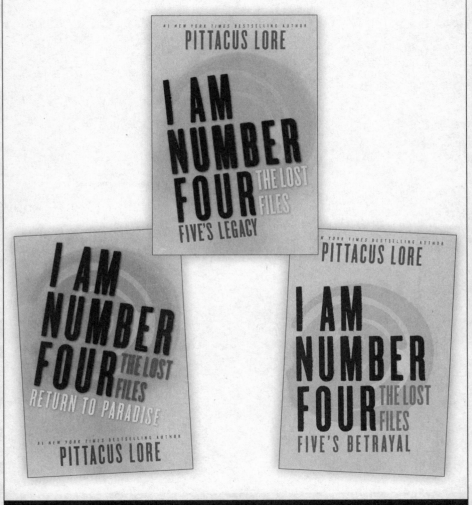